CW00430064

Praise for Sarah Kavanagh's first novel,
Wired to the Moon:

'Brilliant . . . I love this book – read it'

John Hurt

'This debut novel is packed with pace and sympathetic
characters that reach out and pull you into the story . . .
enjoyable read'

Irish *Tatler*

'Genuinely a good thing – a fine, human-sized story
that grows deliciously in the reader's mind, luring
them onto a well-crafted, but not too neat conclusion
. . . A good story well told'

Birmingham Post

Also by Sarah Kavanagh

Wired to the Moon

Fear of Custard

Sarah Kavanagh

FLAME
Hodder & Stoughton

Copyright © 2000 by Sarah Kavanagh

The right of Sarah Kavanagh to be indentified as the
Author of the Work has been asserted by her in accordance
with the Copyright, Designs and Patents Act 1988.

First published in Great Britain in 2000
by Hodder and Stoughton
First published in paperback in 2000
by Hodder and Stoughton
A division of Hodder Headline

A Flame Paperback

10 9 8 7 6 5 4 3 2 1

All rights reserved. No part of the publication may be
reproduced, stored in a retrieval system, or transmitted,
in any form or by any means without the prior written
permission of the publisher, nor be otherwise circulated in
any form of binding or cover other than that in which it is
published and without a similar condition being imposed
on the subsequent purchaser.

All characters in this publication are fictitious
and any resemblance to real persons, living or
dead, is purely coincidental.

A CIP catalogue record for this title
is available from the British Library.

ISBN 0 340 71264 3

Printed and bound in Great Britain by
Mackays of Chatham plc, Chatham, Kent

Hodder and Stoughton
A division of Hodder Headline
338 Euston Road
London NW1 3BH

For Mum, Dad and all the old pros

ACKNOWLEDGEMENTS

Lyrics from 'BROWN EYED GIRL' (MORRISON) © 1967
by kind permission of WEB IV MUSIC/UNIVERSAL MUSIC PUBL. LTD

IF YOU WERE MINE
by Johnny Mercer and Matt Malneck
© Copyright 1935 by Bourne Co.
Copyright Renewed
All Rights Reserved International Copyright Secured

Chapter One

Dora was once a magician's assistant in a blue, ostrich-feather shawl. When she stepped onto the stage, her spangled bikini sent pinpoints of light shivering across the astonished faces in the audience. Now she was in a quilted dressing gown with a pattern of purple, sixties daisies. A pair of red slipper-socks had tumbled down her tiny legs and were sitting like two coil pots over her ankles. She stood in the refectory and leaned through the serving hatch, feeling the cool steel beneath her fingertips. 'Hello?' Nothing. Just the faint hum of the water heater. They could be playing a trick on her. Standing there like statues in their checked uniforms and their hairnets, knowing she couldn't see them. She studied the raised numerals on her wristwatch. Five-forty-five in the morning, much too early for breakfast. Then she heard it again. A series of clicks and squeaks like somebody knitting with giant needles and very tight wool. It was coming from the other end of the corridor.

As she got closer, she could make out footsteps scurrying over the linoleum and rapid breathing. 'Yes!' That was Darren's voice. Big, tall Darren. Clack! Clack! Clack! Sword-fighting? Who with? Dora leaned against the handrail. One of her hairclips had come adrift and was dangling against her face. She opened it, put it in her mouth, then twisted the rogue lock of hair into a coil the size of a polo mint. Snap! She fastened it to her scalp.

The footsteps came to a halt and for a moment it was silent. 'Hello Dora,' said Nurse Maizel. A familiar, Jamaican voice with a crackle in it like an old record. 'Do you want me to bring you a cup of tea, darling?' Dora heard Maizel approaching and felt a warm hand on her arm. 'Come on. It's early still.' Before rounding the corner with Maizel, Dora glanced back over her shoulder, wishing she still had her sight.

At the other end of the corridor, Darren Marks and Alison Mahoney breathed a sigh of relief. They couldn't go on, because Maizel was the referee. Zimmer hockey was Darren's invention. A great way to brighten up the dead hours before the day shift arrived. Goals were constructed by taping plastic bags around the arched backs of two frames. These were then placed twenty feet apart, facing each other along a corridor. Using an upturned walking stick and a ball of tin foil, each player tried to score as many goals as possible in half an hour. A mini-league existed among the nurses and care assistants. Sometimes, they came in when they were off duty to fight for the FA cup (so called because there was no prize).

When Maizel returned, Darren and Alison stood head to head as the home-made puck was placed between them. He towered over her like a praying mantis waiting to pounce. The score stood at five all, so there was everything to play for. It was so quiet that the rattling of a Strepsil against his teeth sounded like gunfire. Alison twirled her dark hair and pinned it up, shoving the last few strands behind her ears. On the word 'go', Darren darted forward. Alison swerved to the left, hitting the puck with sharp jabs, sending it skittering over the chequerboard flooring. She drew her stick back and was just about to go for a goal when Darren put his hand on her shoulder. One of the lights was flashing on the alarm panel.

'Bugger!' Maizel straightened up and clasped the small of her back. 'What now?'

Darren looked at the number next to the light. 'It's Ben.'

'I'll go!' Alison propped her stick against the wall and

marched towards the staircase. She wasn't allowed to run. Instead, she shot along the top corridor like an Olympic speed walker, her heart thumping behind her white plastic name badge. All sorts of images were going through her head. Ben never used his emergency button. The others were at it all the time, calling her in to plump up their pillows or take them to the toilet, but never him. She flung his door open without knocking. Ben was sitting up in bed with a newspaper on his lap and the reading light on beside him. He clapped his hand to his chest. 'Oh, God! Is it your heart?' She rushed forward to take his wrist.

'I'm fine. You frightened the bloody life out of me.'

Alison leaned over and cancelled the call button, then sat on the side of his bed breathing in the scent of his pipe tobacco. 'So?' she tried to sound businesslike. 'What's the emergency?'

'I heard Cowpat coming. The exhaust is hanging off her car.'

'Oh, blimey!' Alison did run this time, straining the buttons on her pale blue uniform. The walk from the staff car park took two minutes at most. 'Pat!' she screeched over the banister. Right away, she could hear the tape being ripped from the metal frames and the walking sticks clattering together. As she reached the hallway, the door buzzer sounded and in came Pat. 'Don't run, Alison,' she said. Pat was an hour early. Hoping to catch them at something they shouldn't be doing. As she hung up her coat, Eddie the cat shredded the silver ball to tinsel with his back paws.

Alison found Darren in the storeroom, finishing the weekly itinerary. He was leaning over the work surface holding a pair of disposable incontinence briefs against the side of an unopened box. In profile, he looked less attractive. His centre parting accentuated his long nose and small chin. He was so tall that his legs stretched nearly all the way back to the door. 'How many are in this one?' he asked. 'I can't work it out.'

'A hundred,' she said, pointing to some green lettering on the box.

'There's never a hundred in that. They're massive, these, like crash helmets for your arse. Look.' He opened out the one he was holding and held it against the top of his trousers.

'It's the air,' she said absent-mindedly. 'They're all, you know, vacuum-packed. You break the seal and they ping up.'

'Brilliant!' Darren lunged forward and tore at the cardboard zipper that ran along the top of the box.

'Don't, Darren! We haven't finished this box yet. Just put one hundred down on the list, plus what's left . . .'

'Oh, go on!' he groaned, wrestling with the heat-sealed plastic packaging inside. 'It's like those lifeboats. I always wanted one of them.'

'Darren!' she squeaked, checking the corridor behind them. 'Pat will kill you. They're supposed to be sterile.'

'No they're not. Do you keep your knickers sterile?' He grinned into the box, suspecting that she did. Using his teeth, he made a hole in the plastic and ripped it apart. He jumped back, bracing himself against the door. The briefs rose slowly like a soufflé from the top of the box. A short, unspectacular parade. Darren put his hands on his hips. 'Bum!' he said after much consideration. He was nineteen. His tunic made him look square and sturdy on top. Only his arms belied his true shape. They twisted down from the starched sleeves like roots from the base of a plant pot. Though she was barely four years older than him, he gave Alison the same guilty look a child gives to its mother. 'Sorry!' The reinflating knickers toppled onto the work surface.

Alison gathered them up, using big theatrical gestures. 'Give us a hand.' She jammed them back in the box which was filling up like a magic cooking pot. 'They've got a mind of their own.'

Darren pretended that the knickers were alive by trying to stun them with a stainless steel bedpan. 'Take that, you vermin!' he shouted, crashing the pan down on one and adding a little squeaky noise from the knickers. 'Oh, no!' He held one of the pads up to his windpipe, as if it was throttling him. 'Help!'

Alison was paralysed with laughter. They often got like that at the end of the night shift. Darren writhed beside her. The incontinence pants over his head made him look like a giant insect with huge eye sockets.

'What do you think you're doing?' Pat was standing at the door, pink with rage. 'Get that thing off your head, Darren! Alison, I expect more from you.'

'We were counting stock.' Alison scrambled to her feet, her face burning. 'Sorry, Pat. I'm really sorry.' Before exiting, Pat cast a brief glance around the storeroom, taking everything in. The overflowing box, the pads on the floor, Darren, still grinning, and Alison looking horrified. She would have said more, but it was too early for tears.

After she left, Alison spotted a crumpled ball of Sellotape from Zimmer hockey hanging from Darren's arm. She pulled it off sharply.

'Ouch!'

'She suspects something.'

'Cowpat? Nah.' He started to throw the knickers into the half-empty box on the floor. 'Though Bettina keeps telling her we've got mice in the skirting boards. Says she can hear tapping at night.' He turned and let out one of his breathy laughs. 'Mice hockey, geddit?'

Pat unlocked her office and flicked the electric bar fire on with her foot. It was a new room, part of the extension, and had three outside walls. At times it was bliss to be in there, away from the stifling heat of the main building, but it was six-thirty and the chill seeped into her skin as she took off her coat and hung it on the rack. She wished she was still in bed, or sitting in the staff-room, warming her hands on a cup of tea, but she knew very well that as soon as she went in, all the natural conversation would stop and people would busy themselves and she would be left alone. That was the trouble with her job. Someone had to take control. Maytime House was no ordinary residential home. All the occupants were theatricals, and theatricals never retire without a struggle. They were used to a kind of independence which is rare, even by modern standards. A lifetime of thumbing their noses at the Establishment. Outsiders thought it must be great fun dealing with a house full of colourful characters, but it played havoc with the order of things. Pat had seen it happen time and time again. New nurses and care assistants would arrive, eager to learn, but within weeks they would be larking about with the piano or playing poker with the residents in their lunch hours. Somebody had to make sure that the sheets were changed. Being popular with the residents was one thing, but it didn't keep the books balanced.

Maizel bustled in carrying the paperwork from the night shift. 'Good God, woman. Don't you sleep?' she said, rubbing the chill from her arms.

'Lots to do,' said Pat. 'Busy night?' Maizel was Pat's night-time counterpart. They were opposite sides of a coin. Pat was forty-two and single. Her skin was pink. Her short hair was so fine and pale that in certain lights her whole scalp was visible. She wore big, pink-framed glasses and behind them her pale grey eyes looked like afterthoughts. Maizel was fifty-four with a husband who had just retired, three children and two grand-children. She was a large, elegant black woman. Her thick, greying hair was worn in a sixties-style chignon; her glasses were rimless with gold filigree arms. Maizel had been nursing for thirty-two years, eight of them at Maytime. She knew that Pat respected her as a colleague, but try as she might, she found it impossible to steer the conversation away from administration. As they spoke, Eddie the cat strolled in and sat on a pile of box files in a corner.

The caterers arrived and set up for breakfast. The dispensary was opened and the tablets were lined up in little ice-cube trays with snap-on lids. The day shift came, shaking umbrellas and wafting the scent of toothpaste. Alison changed into her leggings and a T-shirt. She retrieved her white anti-pollution mask from her duffel bag and headed for the front door. Outside it was getting light, but rain was falling, swishing under car tyres. She decided to wait for a few more minutes and have a slice of toast. The kitchen was warming up already, and from around the building, hungry residents were hovering outside the refectory door.

It hurt Alison to see them like that. She thought it one of the worst things about being in a home. That waiting for food and cups of tea instead of popping to the kitchen to get one whenever they wanted. She had learned over the years that theatre people had completely different body clocks to anyone else. All their working lives they had enjoyed late breakfasts, light lunches and a large, warm meal at night after the second show. At Maytime, they had breakfast at seven-thirty, a cooked lunch at one, then a light snack at five-thirty. That was it until the following day, save for a milky drink before bed. There was no alternative if the home wanted to keep within its budget. They couldn't have caterers on call twenty-four hours a day. As a result, every resident was a hoarder of sweets and snacks. Some even kept their lunch, preferring to eat it cold, spooning it out of plastic containers six hours later. One old man lined his jacket pockets with shopping bags and piled food in. Meat, potatoes, even gravy. They lost a good laundry service as a result. Alison was forever finding things tucked away in wardrobes and sink cupboards. Midnight feasts were traditional. Sometimes as many as six residents could be found in one small room, passing around tooth-glasses of Martini and large bags of nuts and raisins. When she was on nights, Alison could hear them giggling. It made her feel like the spoilsport female bandleader in *Some Like it Hot*, patrolling the railway carriage, slugging on a bottle of ulcer medicine while all the musicians are squished into Jack Lemmon's top bunk mixing Manhattans in a hot-water bottle. She usually turned a blind eye, unless someone lit a cigarette and set off the smoke alarms.

As Alison sipped an opaque-glass mug of tea, the doors opened. First in were the 'Overtures and Beginners', as Ben called them. Retired showgirls who were never seen without their make-up or the jewellery they wore like medals. Chubby and bottle-blonde, they waved cheerily to the staff, brandishing the thermos flasks they brought in to be washed. Other residents followed them with frames and walking sticks. Some stayed in dressing gowns. 'Whistling' Harry Jackson wore a silk smoking jacket and a brown Derby hat. Ben took up the rear and slipped into his usual seat by the window. The front garden was covered by a slippery mulch of yellow and brown leaves, and for a while he sat and watched a late rose bobbing on the breeze like a cotton wool ball. The warm smell of toast and the gurgle of the tea urn drew him back from the brink of sadness and he smiled over at Alison, knowing that she would soon be flinging herself into the cold outdoors. She wove her way towards him, saying her good mornings.

'I hope you've got more than that to wear,' he said.

Alison pulled her cherry-red cardigan down smartly, loosening two of the fastenings. 'I'll be fine, thanks,' she said. 'I have a hat, but it's really embarrassing.' In spite of his age, Ben Castle was the best-looking man Alison had ever met. He was tall but not bony. His muscle tone had remained and he walked upright and elegant. His hair was silver and as fine as silk. His jaw was square, and around his neck he always wore a cravat, so there was no sign of the gizzard of crêpey skin which the other men displayed. His eyes were a vivid blue. If age had faded them, goodness knows what they must have looked like when he was younger. His devastating looks were visible in a large, sepia photograph in the 'hall of fame' in the corridor. It was pure Hollywood: a little like Douglas Fairbanks Jr. with a pencil-thin moustache and his black hair slicked back. He had been a bandleader, but Alison imagined him as a swashbuckler, swinging from the rigging of a pirate ship to fight for her honour.

'Well, mind how you go,' he said.

8

'I always do!' She backed away from him into the table behind her, swung around to steady herself and caught a resident called Lillian on the back of the head with her bag. There was much apologising and mopping up of tea.

'Knocking you about again, is she, Lillian?' said Ben, and though Alison knew he was kidding, she wanted to kneel by the side of his chair and beg for his forgiveness. She tried to think of something witty to say, but as usual she was flummoxed, so she made her way out of the refectory without looking back. It was all Ben's fault. He had an effect on her like no other person. A feeling so strong that she was scared it would show; that a great big crimson cartoon heart would come breaking out of her clothing.

The rain stopped, and as the chairs scraped away from the tables, Alison closed the front door behind her. Ben watched her unchain her bicycle. There was a hole in her tights, just above the line of her shoes. He had noticed it when she came to his room. A perfect circle the size of an old halfpenny revealing the soft, white knot of her ankle-bone. It had moved him. He wanted to see it once more so he went over to the window. Alison put her chain in her bag and pulled out a black fake-fur hat with earflaps. She unfastened her hairclip and Ben watched her limp, dark hair flop down over her shoulders, wavy where it had been twisted around itself. She put the hat on, leaving the flaps to hang like spaniels' ears, and lifted her face mask. Before she climbed on, she pulled a Walkman from her cardigan pocket. Then she turned and Ben searched for the hole in her tights. It had been turned into a half-moon by the hem of her trousers. He didn't like those tight trousers that women wore these days. It made them look like frogmen. As she rode to the gate, she glanced over at the window and her eyes smiled at him. He smiled back and remembered summer days when women wore skirts even to cycle, and let the wind lift and twirl their hair behind them.

Chapter Two

Alison pushed through the amber-lit streets of north London. The traffic was already building, crunching her up against the doors of parked cars. 'For my next trick,' she murmured into her face mask. That's what she should have said earlier. She always thought of an appropriate line on the way home. She cut onto the pavement to avoid a milk float, standing on the pedals over the kerb. As she reached Caledonian Road, Peggy Lee sang 'Fever' through her earphones. It made her feel better, like she was riding home in triumph after a night of love.

The front steps of the flat were rubberised. They shone like liquorice in the glare of the security lantern. She lifted her bike up. The spinning pedals tripped her as she climbed, adding a new bruise to those already yellowing on her shins. The paint in the hall was striped with black marks from her handlebars, but it was the kind of apartment that could take any amount of abuse without looking different. A Bart Simpson alarm clock was saying: 'Yo! Dudes. Get up. Get outa bed!' in adenoidal tones behind her flatmate's door. She knocked. 'Cup of tea, Mel?'

'Thanks.'

Alison put the kettle on and wandered into the lounge to rewind the videotape. The remote control was on the coffee table in front of the sofa. Alison picked it up and flopped down. Instead of the soft, dusty cushions, she landed on a pair of legs.

Jumping up, she saw a skinny Japanese guy with shoulder-length hair, wearing only a pair of khaki fatigue pants.

He held out a hand. 'I'm Daichi,' he said. Alison was used to waifs and strays. Over the years, many had emerged from Mel's room and sat sullenly eating toast, watching the football. Some had stuck around for a few months. A couple had been shooed out of the door before they could tie the laces on their trainers. Alison took his hand. It was slender and clammy from sleep. His fingernails were tiny ovals, jagged at the base. Girl's hands, she thought. If there was one thing she couldn't bear, it was men with girl's hands. Ben's hands were big and square.

Mel shuffled in wearing an oversized T-shirt. Her hair was sticking out in all directions. She and Alison had been best friends since they were eleven years old and stood shoulder to shoulder in assembly . . . 'Morning has broken, stick it together' . . . 'Hi, Mel!' Daichi had now found his glasses and was pulling a jumper over his head.

'Oh. I forgot you were here.' She pulled the shirt down over her knees and fled back to her bedroom. Daichi, it turned out, worked for a company which supplied sound systems to clubs. As Mel spent every minute of her spare time in clubs, either helping the DJ or watching him, she and Daichi had got to know each other. 'She's really beautiful,' he said as his mind caressed an image of Mel in a flashing strobe. Her dense, dark curls spiralling over her face, her milk-coffee skin and the freckles around her nose.

'You should be telling her that,' smiled Alison.

Daichi pulled a face. 'You are beautiful too.'

'Nice try,' she punched his arm playfully. At least he was sensitive. She wasn't beautiful. Ben had called her 'pretty girl' once. 'Come over here, pretty girl,' he had said, but she suspected he was just being nice. In part, he was right. At five feet one and a half, she was and always would be a girl. Though she was twenty-three, womanliness seemed an impossible dream. She was like one of those tiny Eastern European gymnasts. Perky and springy, occupying the same childish bodies all the way to retirement. She had tried a Wonderbra once, but it just stood out from her chest like two cupped palms. Mel was five feet ten. She worked at a trendy shop in Covent Garden. They let her wear the stock for free because she looked so good in it. Alison had only been in there once. She had tried on a pair of trousers, and they'd had hysterics when she emerged from the fitting room with the ends of the legs flapping out in front of her like clown's shoes.

She and Daichi sat silently and sipped tea. The lounge was large with overlapping bits of different carpets and crumpled, batik throws over the soft furnishings. The walls were plastered with rave posters, and in the corner by the television was a life-sized cardboard cut-out of Captain Kirk, donated by one of Mel's ex-boyfriends. 'Nice flat,' Daichi said. 'It's funky.' His accent sounded more American than Japanese.

'It's falling apart, but we get it cheap, so we're not complaining.' She explained that it belonged to one of Mel's uncles who was back in Barbados. '. . . So, what were you two doing last night?'

'Some DJs were doing a set at an internet café. Mel saved my life.'

'No I didn't,' said Mel from the doorway. 'He only forgot his keys.' She made a geeky face at Alison. 'Budge up, you two.'

Alison fingered the remote control. 'We'd better start,' she said. 'Or you'll be late for work.'

'Can't we watch it later, Ali?'

'I want to watch it now.'

'Well, you watch it now, and I'll watch it tonight.'

'Oh, Mel! It's *EastEnders*.'

'Duh!' Mel was playing up for Daichi. He wouldn't understand. It wasn't just the soap, it was about their friendship. They had been there together, right from the beginning. It was the thing they had talked about at school the following morning. No matter how busy their lives were or how little time they spent in the flat, they came together for *EastEnders*. When Mel went on holiday, Alison taped all the episodes and they watched them as they always did, hunched up on the sofa with cups of tea, shouting at the characters and anticipating the drumbeats that marked the end credits. It was no fun on your own. Mel pretended to be engrossed. She couldn't bear to tell Alison she had watched it the night before while putting her make-up on. They had so little in common these days.

When *EastEnders* was over, Mel went off to work with Daichi hot on her heels and Alison got into her nightdress. As she changed, she was watched by a hundred eyes, gazing heavy-lidded from her walls and wardrobe doors. Her friendly collection of movie stars. Cary Grant, Katharine Hepburn, Bette Davis. She couldn't believe her luck when she walked into Maytime for her interview and realised that she would be dealing with a cadet group, the ones who never made it to Hollywood. They were stars, though, in Alison's opinion. She put her nightdress on over her bra and pants, then pulled them out with a flourish like a magician. She didn't want to shock Jimmy Stewart. He was a sensitive type.

She dreamed about them most nights, her movie stars. Not real dreams, but the ones you make up before you drift off, when you are warm and comfortable. Thoughts you try to carry with you into sleep. She dreamed about becoming their friend, going to their parties and swimming in their pools. 'Have you met Alison?' they would say before drawing on their shiny, white cigarettes. In her dreams, she put them together and made them talk to each other and fall in love. When she grew tired of them, she dreamed about the characters in *EastEnders*, pushing the storylines along, sorting out their problems, then retreating into the shadows to watch them being happy. They could have done with someone like her on *EastEnders*.

The phone rang. Alison carried it into her bedroom. It was her mother calling from Ireland. 'Hi, Mum . . . I'm fine . . . How's the house coming along? . . .' Her mother's voice sounded thin and reedy. It was the phone at Granny's cottage.

A black Bakelite pyramid, like the ones in old Scotland Yard films. Her mother was wearing big earrings. They were clacking against the receiver. Alison climbed into bed and threw the cushions on the floor as the voice soothed her. 'Look, I can't, Mum. I told you!' Christmas had reared its ugly head again. She couldn't go over to Ireland. 'I wish I could, Mum, but people at work have children and they get priority.' She was feeling sleepy. Alternating between day and night shifts had given her a talent for drifting off whenever her head hit the pillow. When she replaced the receiver, her mother's last sentence was dragged down with her into the land of nod.

'Did you check on Custard, darling?'

Chapter Three

The story of Maytime began deep in the English aristocracy. The Honourable Isabel Knight was the youngest and prettiest of four daughters. The family name, by rights, should have been Knight-Porter, but Isabel's father thought it to have lower-class connotations. Little Isabel had a dreary childhood. She had few friends and was taught at home by governesses. Her greatest pleasure came at Christmas, when the family was forced to entertain her uncle Peter. Peter Knight-Porter was a patron of the arts. A stage-door Johnny type. Every year, he would bring a different companion to the festivities. These poor girls would arrive with their spangled dresses, expecting a warm welcome. By the second day, Isabel would find them in tears, looking out of a bedroom window, dreading the thought of going downstairs. To Isabel, this was paradise. The tear-stained gaiety girls loved to do up her hair and rouge her cheeks and teach her a song and dance. They praised her and cuddled her and feasted with her by the nursery fire. When they left she wept and wept. She begged them all to take her with them. She promised each of them that she would practise every day and join a juvenile troupe and be a big, big star.

Of course, Isabel's parents were against most forms of entertainment. They sent her to finishing school, then to Italy, but each time young Isabel returned with a wider repertoire.

They introduced her to eligible men with square chins and a knowledge of opera, but to no avail. Isabel sneaked away at night and visited variety theatres with the staff. She entertained the cook's children and the coalman and the chimney sweep, who applauded loudly and told her that she should be on stage. One day, her father caught wind of her Florrie Forde impersonation and called her upstairs. He told her that unless she stopped all such nonsense and carried herself with a little more decorum, she would be cut off without a penny.

So, Isabel packed a trunk. She filled it with dresses and shoes and her grandmother's emerald necklace and waved goodbye to a life of privilege. She rented a dingy room in Soho, sold the necklace and walked into the office of the biggest impresario in London. Thanks to her grandmother and the depressed state of the theatre, Isabel managed to buy herself into the celebrated bill known as *Tally Ho!*. A precursor of *Hellzapoppin'* and *The Crazy Gang*, it featured a mixture of top-class comedians, magicians, soubrettes and novelty acts loosely joined together by a plot. As this plot revolved around a hunting party at a stately home and a group of wandering circus performers, Isabel fitted in rather nicely as the daughter of the house. Until the first rehearsal, nobody knew what to expect of their new lady benefactor. They had their suspicions. They surmised that she would be a shaky but pleasant enough soprano, who could be covered by a good arrangement. She was lovely to look at, so they weren't worried. By the end of the week, however, they were musty with their own perspiration. Several times they tried to dissuade her from taking such a bold leap, but her enthusiasm knocked them back. The posters went up introducing Miss Isabel Day (a name adopted to confirm her rebellion), and the first night arrived.

After the cast had assembled on stage for the hunting party and a group of boy jugglers called Binnie's Babes had done a stunning routine dressed as footmen, on came Isabel. She was discovered in a mock garden pergola, surrounded by painted, pink lavatera. She was dressed, inexplicably, in a Marie-Antoin-ette-style gown with a gardenia in her hair. The pit orchestra started the introduction to 'I Dreamt That I Dwelt In Marble Halls', the impresario and the director buried their heads and Isabel opened her mouth, starting the performance that would launch her to stardom.

Isabel was the worst singer in the world. She couldn't hit a note to save her life, and no matter how loud the orchestra played, she sang over them. She was clumsy, too. She dropped her fan and knocked over part of the pergola while hitting top notes which made the light fittings in the auditorium vibrate. Blinded by limelight, she was unable to see the horror on the faces of the audience. She was having the time of her life. They started to laugh. Isabel was so bad, she was absolutely marvel-lous. They nudged each other hoping that her next climax would be even more tuneless. She didn't let them down. They cheered when she assaulted the final note of the song, and she left the stage in seventh heaven as a bewildered comedian, who played the butler, called her to prepare for the hunt.

Later, as she sat in her dressing room, people came round to congratulate her on such a hilarious performance. The truth dawned on her. Like Uncle Peter's showgirls, she felt out of place and wished more than anything that she could go home. But then, when she completed her second number and took her bow, she received the loudest cheer of the evening. Her fellow performers let her take the final curtain call alone. After the hubbub had died down, the impresario sat with her until the small hours of the morning, convincing her that she had far more going for her than just some pretty soprano. She was a natural comic. He claimed that he could make her a big star, as long as she kept two promises. The first was that she mustn't reveal that she wasn't playing for laughs, and the second that she must never take a singing lesson.

As the years went by, Isabel's popularity grew and she was able to indulge her love of lavish costumes and scenery. Her repertoire stretched from operetta to hot jazz (her interpretation of 'I Got Rhythm' became a classic). She travelled the world, enrapturing audiences wherever she went. She was particularly popular with the upper classes, who had endured many a front-room soprano. People came to see her again and again, sitting on the edge of their seats, waiting for her voice to reach the kind of sharpness that shattered glass. (Ivor Novello was reputed to have coughed an asparagus tip into the lap of a duchess during Isabel's torturous rendition of 'We'll Gather Lilacs'.) Once again, she was welcomed into the hunting and shooting set. Her wealth was fast outstripping that of her own family. She had many successful seasons in revue, but preferred the hurly-burly of the number-one variety circuit.

While touring in an offbeat production of *Maytime*, the musical made famous by Jeanette MacDonald and Nelson Eddy, she met her very own stage-door Johnny. Ernest Smoult was a pudgy man with an explosive laugh, but he treated her like a queen. The way her uncle Peter should have treated his show-girls. She loved him for it. Ernest and Isabel married and moved into a large property in north London. They were not blessed with children, but Isabel ensured that the house was always a hive of activity. Parties began after the shows and went on until dawn. Champagne was delivered in crates and a small stage was erected in the drawing room so that they could 'go into their acts' whenever the mood struck them. Luckily, Ernest was both extremely wealthy and incurably stage-struck, so he was de-lighted to welcome Isabel's friends for long weekends. Some of these weekends were so long that they stretched into months.

People who worked in variety seldom had a permanent address, so Maytime House also became their post office, with letters collecting in alphabetised pigeon-holes in the front hall. Acrobats flick-flacked down the mirrored corridors, while dancers pliéd at the newly installed handrails. As Isabel's career wound down, she became more and more involved in the lives of her guests. She helped them with their acts, and Ernest reconciled them with the taxman. They spent their afternoons happily swapping stories and remembering the old times. Isabel was flattered, entertained and mollycoddled, easing through the years when her career finally faded. (As she grew older and her voice mellowed, she started to hit the correct note with increasing regularity. She even developed a basic sense of rhythm. Although this sent her into retirement, it brought her great happiness in her old age.)

After Ernest died, Isabel and her 'dear chums' continued to work for the welfare of impoverished 'turns'. She founded a charity called The Smoult Foundation, which fought to improve the pay and conditions for performers. After her death, Isabel's fortune ensured that Maytime House was to be home to generations of money-foolish troupers who needed a place to stay.

Variety started to dissolve in the fifties, unable to fight against both the big and the small screen. Some acts became pioneers of British television; some returned to the circus and many moved to the less elegant surroundings of the Working Men's Clubs. Burlesque was alive and high-kicking for a little longer than the class acts, but it too lost some of its shine. By the time Alison came to work at Maytime, there were few who could remember Isabel's act. The older residents saw Maytime as a refuge, somewhere they could rub shoulders with people who understood them and feel safe in the knowledge that they had a home for life. The younger residents had fallen on hard times. To them, Maytime was a boarding house. A place to rest until their agents got in touch.

The Smoult Foundation was now run by an agent named George Jakobi, who used to be a cool breeze in the Delfont Organisation in the sixties. He was Maytime's guardian angel. He organised fund-raising, ran the newsletter and oversaw the list of claimants. He was a busy man. Several leading TV personalities and club comics were on his books, but he still took time out whenever he could to pay a visit. Alison had seen him in the bar many times, sitting with the residents, telling stories about the days when he used to be the tea boy for *Sunday Night at the London Palladium*. George was an overgrown Teddy boy. His greying hair was swept back into a lacquered duck's arse and his fingers were ablaze with gold rings. Darren said he dressed 'all Costa Del Sol'. Pastel polo shirts, grey slacks, silk socks and white patent shoes. He drove a silver Rolls-Royce with personalised number plates (GJIII – giving the impression that he had two others). Very flash, but a nice man nonetheless.

The home held sixteen residents at a time, six of whom could be given nursing care. It was a female environment. The walls were all pinks and marigold yellows with dado rails. The furniture was worn chintz and high-backed armchairs with matching footstools. The bookshelf was filled with romances and the air was thick with the smell of pot-pourri. (The potpourri was a bit of a mixed blessing. One of the care assistants had a sister who ran a gift shop in Lowestoft. This sack of peach-coloured wood shavings had been hanging around the back of the shop unsold for some time and was sent down by parcel post as a gift, so that the smell of disinfectant could be banished from the building. What replaced it was the scent of cheap talcum.)

Although the house was large even by Victorian standards, an extension was added in the seventies. However well they hid the join, Maytime still looked like two houses stuck together. The original part stood high and imposing. The large entrance hall had double doors and a tiled floor. Rising through it was a Gothic staircase which had been painted white to brighten the atmosphere. The mushroom-coloured walls were covered by old variety bills and framed prints of Marie Lloyd and Dan Leno. These continued along the corridor and into the refectory with its long pine tables and large bay windows. All the rooms in the main building had ornate, high ceilings. Some had been partitioned into smaller spaces, making them taller than they were broad. The television room was one, like a big lift with chairs in it, all facing away from the door. Alison was surprised at how few of the residents watched the television. The Overtures and Beginners were keen on the soaps, but they were looked down on by the others who preferred to sit with books and newspapers or to listen to the radio in their rooms. Alison wondered if it was political — deliberately snubbing the industry that killed their profession.

The old conservatory that once ran the full length of the house was stacked against the high wall at the back of the garden, rotting slowly away, its glass panes covered by a film of green. The replacement was less attractive: brick-built and double-glazed with a clear, corrugated roof that trapped the blackened leaves blown over it in the autumn. It was chilly in the winter. Just the occasional resident could be found there, sitting among the potted plants, watching the progress of the garden.

In the summer, the temperature soared and the room filled. The plants awoke from their slumber and became bright and succulent. The jasmines that climbed the far wall exploded with white flowers, drowning the room in a heady scent. Into this hothouse came the broken blossoms. The Overtures and Beginners gathered there in their djellabas and their pastel, velour tracksuits. They chose the comfiest chairs, balancing thin, moulded-tin ashtrays on the arms and sat forward, striking well-practised model's poses (ankles crossed, backs straight, chins lifted). No matter how their conversations started — the weather, a book from the library, a story in the newspaper — they always turned, like a parlour game, in three or four sentences, to their one and only topic: men.

Names of past lovers were turned over on their tongues as if they were tasting their last remnants. Some names were spat out, and then palates were briefly cleansed by the mention of a movie star (usually a young Marlon Brando) before moving on. In the white window light they sat, their heavy make-up hardening their faces. They were like the seaside landladies that cropped up in their stories with their brick-red hair and lime-green blouses, gazing out at a rain-lashed pier, waiting in vain for the return of an ageing matinée idol.

Maytime was woefully short of eligible men. They had all taken a crack at Ben, but without success. 'Whistling' Harry Jackson complemented them and linked arms with them when they strolled into town, but his response to their request for intimacy was: 'I would if I could, but I can't.' The only other men were big Ernie who did odd jobs, and Simon the hairdresser, who was, to quote Harry: 'as queer as a two-bob watch'. That left Darren. He was just a boy, really, but a good-looking one from most angles. Wonderful for target practice. He took their advances in good humour and returned them sometimes with touches and kisses to their powdered cheeks. Alison thought she was the only one who saw the desire in their eyes just before they laughed it off.

On the other side of the building, the nursing wing jutted out in an L-shape. It took up the lion's share of the original lawn. As well as six bedrooms, the wing contained a specially adapted bathroom and Pat's office. The walls and partitions were thinner than in the rest of the building, and the corridors shone with fluorescent light. The two sides of the building met in the large central lounge with Isabel's stage still at one end. The curtains were tied back, revealing a black upright piano and a set of windows overlooking the front driveway. At the other end of the room, next to the door which opened into the conservatory, a small bar stood with an ice bucket on either end and a large signed photograph of W. C. Fields peering out between the upside-down spirit bottles on the back wall. The photograph was signed 'To Isabel', and was placed at such an angle that he was looking directly at her, or rather, at her portrait. The portrait was enormous, dominating the wall above the fireplace. It was hard to imagine that such a beauty could produce a bum note. She was semi-reclining on a set of pink silk cushions, wearing one of those sleek, satin dresses straight out of Hollywood in the thirties. Beneath her, the log-burning grate had been converted into a coal-effect gas fire. On quiet winter afternoons, it fluttered away like a captive moth, adding a glow to the rouged cheeks of variety's lady benefactor.

Chapter Four

When Alison arrived, tucking her bicycle lights into her bag, the bar was full. It was approaching closing time, which was only two hours after opening time, as Shirley, the barmaid, was a voluntary worker. A round, glum-faced woman, she was herself a retired turn. Known as Shirley-whirly, she had done a hoop act for many years at seaside resorts. With her husband, Juan, accompanying her, she had twirled dozens of silver hula hoops around her body and sent them boomeranging back to her from all over the stage. Now, she stood with her elbows on the bar top, arguing with one of the residents about the introduction music used by Billy Cotton. Ben was sitting at his usual table with his son, Kenneth. Alison went over to them and Ben stood up and motioned towards the chair next to him. 'Alison, dear,' he said. 'Can Kenneth get you a little something?' She sat and wriggled out of her jacket, spreading it over the back of the chair. 'Diet Coke, please. I'm on in half an hour.' As Kenneth stood awkwardly, Ben sat again. 'Are you sure?' he asked, tapping her hand.

'I'm not very good with alcohol.' Alison giggled and shivered at the tickle of his fingers on her knuckles.

'Then you must try harder,' he smiled. As Kenneth stumbled, catching his foot on the table, Ben called after him. 'And tell Shirley it was *Somebody Stole My Gal.*' Kenneth screwed up his face.

'She'll know what I mean.' Ben watched his son as he sidled up to the bar and waited with his hands clasped in front of him for Shirley to finish her conversation. 'What am I going to do with him?' Ben said to the air. Then he turned to Alison. 'He was born middle-aged.' Poor Kenneth was a bit of a trial. He was a broad man of forty-five with round shoulders and ginger hair that went in the wrong direction, sticking out from his scalp in waves. He had none of his father's elegant bearing or witty conversation. He was a good son, though, making the journey from his florist's in Lewisham three evenings a week. He drove a little white van. Alison had seen it in the car park from time to time. 'Forget Me Not' was written over the sides, with a picture of a blue flower with a knot in the stem.

Kenneth returned to the table clutching a circular tray with their drinks. Alison noticed a packet of photographs in the pocket of his brown tweed jacket. 'Been on holiday?' she asked. 'Oh, you must show Alison your masterpieces,' said Ben. Kenneth fished the envelope from his pocket and put on the bifocal glasses that dangled on his chest. Alison could feel the heat of his excitement as he handed them over to her. They showed a series of podium arrangements for a wedding. They were very pretty, with ivies and lilies amongst the standard flowers. One photograph was stuck to the back of another, and Alison prized them apart with her fingernail. It showed a large woman in a blue jumper, holding the bridal bouquet in front of her and grinning at the camera. Kenneth snatched the photograph from her. 'Who's that?' asked Alison as the round, cheerful face was ripped from her vision. 'Just a woman who works in the shop.' He tucked the photograph into his pocket and steered Alison towards the next few in the pile. They were of the wedding itself. Kenneth had been invited. Quite an honour for a florist, but then he was friendly with the bride's family, having done the flowers for her father's funeral two years before. Kenneth explained with affection that the bride's late father had been a keen gardener, and Kenneth had been set the task of spelling out the word 'Dad', using some of the flowers from their own garden. Alison sipped her drink and listened as Ben gazed over at another table. He had heard the story before and made no attempt to hide it.

Ben was not the only one looking at the table next to the bar. Two of the residents had some very odd-looking visitors. They had arrived in a fancy car which caused a scrum of staff members around the front windows. One was tall and slim with short, bleached-blond hair. His companion was heavy and dark with wraparound sunglasses and an immaculate black suit. They both carried briefcases. They had come to see two of the female residents. Plum and Blossom were ex-glamour girls and stalwarts of the Overtures and Beginners. They were not yet seventy. Plum was the taller and more elegant of the two. She wore a two-piece suit and a round-necked lambswool sweater. The jacket buttons didn't do up because she always wore them a little small. That way, she could draw attention to a bosom which had been the toast of Soho for many years. She kept the faith by wearing old-fashioned pointy brassieres and swayingly high-heeled shoes with pencil-sharp toes. Her hair was black and her lipstick a pillar-box red which stamped her signature on at least one cigarette in every ashtray. She was truly sexy after a blowsy, Elsie Tanner fashion. Blossom was a graduate of the 'fluffy bunny' school of glamour. All frills and flounces and plunging necklines, jumpers with studs and satin appliqué were draped around her soft, rounded body. Her hair was a mass of honey-blonde curls and her face a blaze of colour. Iridescent pastel eyeshadow made rainbows of her eyelids, and her lips and nails were pearlised pinks and corals. A set of dentures had done nothing to dim the dimpled smile that radiated from her early publicity shots.

She and Plum had not met before they came to Maytime, but as they had so much in common, they quickly formed a partnership. Plum was the one in command. She decided where they were going and what they thought about it when they got there. At first, Alison had hated Plum for being so bossy, and pitied Blossom as she wobbled behind her in gold mules, but soon she learned that there was a balance to their relationship. Listening in to their hothouse conversations, she realised that Blossom had been at her happiest when she was with dominant men. She liked to be looked after. Without Plum she was listless and unsure of herself. She sat and fidgeted and gazed out of the window. Left to her own devices, it was possible that she would sell herself for a bag of beans.

Their guests seemed enchanted with them. They were leaning forward in their chairs, leafing through a couple of large brown envelopes. Everybody at Maytime had a collection of brown envelopes. They contained ancient band parts, publicity photographs or reviews. As soon as they were produced from a battered Harrods tote bag which Plum kept under her chair, every eye in the place was upon them. Brown envelopes in the bar meant one thing and one thing only. Work. These men looked and smelt of money. They opened their briefcases and pulled out a couple of documents. Shirley nearly cut herself in half leaning over the bar to try to see what they were.

Kenneth sneaked away, nodding goodbyes to his father and Alison. She wondered if he took after his mother. Surely she must have been as graceful as a swan to have attracted Ben's attention. Alison knew very little about his late wife, except that her name had been Vera and that their marriage had been a long one. Ben was a private man. Alison liked to think that because he had never opened up to her, never told her how he felt or how he loved. She longed to scratch the surface of him. Her imagination ran wild, diving time and time again into his movie-star photograph, imagining the smell of his hair oil, the sound of his voice back then, the feel of his dark suit fabric.

By the time Alison had changed into her uniform, residents had started to appear with small bags of props and sheets of music. Three of them moved the piano to the centre of the stage. 'Just a little impromptu concert,' they said, beckoning Ben over to accompany them. Whistling Harry was there with his hats and his fingers flexed, ready to launch into 'In A Monastery Garden'. It was obvious that this was all for the benefit of the visitors. Plum and Blossom glowered over at the stage and pulled the young men back to them with squeezes to their knees. Alison went to prepare their milky drinks.

When she brought them through, the guests had gone and the piano was all that remained on the stage. Plum and Blossom were still at their table, looking like the cats who got the cream. Other residents were sitting with them now, trying to find out what they had been up to, but the documents and the brown envelopes were back in the tote bag and the mystery remained. Alison was as intrigued as everyone else, and delighted to see how charming the others were being to them.

Plum and Blossom were at the bottom of the league at Maytime. They had never topped a bill or created an act which defied the laws of gravity. They were sixtysomething interpretative dancers who appeared in nude tableau shows and all-girl revues. Their photographs hung with the others in the hall of fame; glamour shots, lit in the Hollywood style. Blossom, bleached blonde, sat on a stool with one leg hugged to her chest. She was wearing a net 'nude' suit trimmed with feathers, and smiled at the camera with her heart-shaped mouth. Plum, billed as 'Miss Victoria Plum' was naked behind the fans she posed with, dark and sultry like Jane Russell. Alison would have killed for the bodies they once had. They were still beautiful, but this was north London and not Hollywood, where all the glamour queens move to a neverland of plastic surgery and silicone. Their faces were lined and their hair badly dyed. Their spangles were wearing a little thin, but when they talked about the old days, they lit up. Alison had a soft spot for both of them. They were always cheery and kind, and just because they couldn't solve the conundrums on *Countdown*, they were looked upon as mere decoration.

Maytime's residents were once the brightest, most envied young things in the country. Alison loved to gaze at their photographs down the corridors. Dashing men in top hats, contortionists bent double, magicians in capes with doves on their fingertips. In their rooms were pictures of Round Table dinners: everyone in evening dress; silver service; women with hair like topiary. The men who sat with them were Brylcreemed and portly, oozing money. Sometimes there was a famous face or two: Sophie Tucker, Tommy Trinder. All those long-gone but not forgotten parties at the Water Rats or the Masonic Halls. All that remained were the photographs in their yellowed presentation folders with the gold-embossed name of a Soho photographer on the front. All those beautiful, smiling faces, and this was where they gathered now – those who didn't marry the man with the big cigar. Once, they had money and clothes and gin and tonic and champagne. They had men and roses and hangovers in rented accommodation. They had the time of their lives. They lived for the moment, and even though the moment had long passed, they had few regrets. They saw their work as a privilege, something they would have done without pay. It saved them from mediocrity, at a time when mediocrity was widespread.

Chapter Five

———◆———

There was an envelope with an Irish stamp on it waiting for
Alison. She had heard the *kerflap* of it coming through the
front door, but had managed to drift off again. There was
something most weeks. Never a letter – Alison's mother
didn't see the point because they talked on the phone (or
rather, she talked and Alison listened). She was fond of
sending *Peanuts* cartoons, though, neatly snipped from the
newspaper, or humorous postcards. This envelope was too fat
for that. Inside, Alison found a brochure for ferry crossings
with the new year prices highlighted in yellow. The postcard
that accompanied it showed a fifties photograph of a couple
on a bench. They had comic expressions on their faces, and
the caption that ran along the bottom of the card suggested
that one of them had farted. 'Typical,' said Alison, turning it
over quickly, then slowly back again. The message on the
back said:

> Hey Kiddo,
> I thought I would send you these in case you changed
> your mind about driving. It could save you a few
> pounds, and would do Custard a power of good. Also,
> you could bring over Auntie Mary's sewing machine.
> Granny says she has found a man who can fix it. So

sorry you can't come for Xmas, but we will make up for
it.
Lots of love,
Mummy, Granny and B.

She had started in her usual big, loopy handwriting, but had run
out of space. The last couple of sentences clung to the edges of
the card, forming a box around the rest.

'Hey kiddo,' said Alison. 'Who does she think she is?' She
threw the ferry brochure into the paper recycling bag. Her
mother knew damn well that she would be flying. If she was any
kind of mother, she would send her over the air fare – seeing as
she was the one who had moved away. Christmas trips to Ireland
meant no money for summer holidays. It still puzzled her why
her mother had moved back so suddenly. She had friends in
England, and Granny could have come over. When they were
living in Croydon, she spent all her time saying how lucky Alison
was to have so much to do. It certainly wasn't the bright lights,
then. It wasn't the bereavement, either. Alison's father had been
dead for years when she left. It must have been something else.
Alison had a theory, but she didn't mention it. Somewhere in the
back of her mind was the belief that her mother had moved to
Ireland to get away from her.

Alison's parents were called Colm and Angie. They met at
college on the west coast of Ireland, and their song was 'Brown
Eyed Girl' by Van 'the Man' Morrison. Colm was a big man
with sandy hair and a deep voice. When she was really little,
Alison used to lie on his tummy like Mowgli in the *Jungle Book*
cartoon, floating down the river on good old Baloo the Bear.
When he laughed, she could hear it buzzing the whole length of
her body. 'Shall we sell her to the gypsies?' he asked Angie. 'Shall
we? We'd get a good price. They pay a lot for naughty little girls.'
Alison wriggled in his arms and yelled 'No!' Nothing would take
her away from them.

She was a child and her parents were parents. She went to

school and they went to work. Her mum cooked dinner and she and her dad flicked peas across the table at each other. They ordered her to tidy her room and she complained. They took her to hospital when she got a Pop-A-Point pencil lead stuck up her nose and held her hand when the nurse arrived with the big tweezers. Then one day, when Alison was eleven, they got a new car. They called it Custard, and it was the best car in the whole world.

Well, he was supposed to get a new car, but this was too good to be true. A reconditioned Triumph Herald, just like the one he used to drive when he was a student. He came into the lounge that afternoon, praying that Angie would remember the great times they used to have in the other Triumph – the one he had bought from a college dinner lady for twenty pounds. The car that gave them their golden summer, tearing down the country lanes with their friends all squashed in the back, singing along to Van the Man and feeling the wind in their hair. Wind provided by Colm, who had always fancied a convertible. He had blowtorched the roof off one night and left it on the front lawn, looking like a car that had sunk in a swamp.

He led Angie out of the front door, hoping she would only remember the sunshine and the good times, and not the winter when they missed the roof and had to wear layers of clothing. At least this car was complete. Angie stood still, just looking at it. Colm stared at her, trying to read her thoughts, but they were way beneath the surface. Alison ran to it and stood with her mouth open. She stroked the gleaming yellow paint and looked it straight in its glass eyes. It smiled back. When she turned to her parents, they had their arms around each other. Her mum's brown hair was tucked over her dad's shoulder. His chubby cheek was pressed into her forehead. Alison galloped towards them. 'It's brilliant!' she yelled, spinning and jumping. 'It's fantastic!'

The neighbours came out and stood with their arms folded in front of them, looking at the yellow car that shone so brightly.

Custard made everybody smile, every day like summer, and all trips like trips to the seaside. They went for a spin, singing along with the tape, waving at all the people on the pavements as if they were astronauts just back from the moon. *Hey, where did we go? The days when the rains came?*

There must have been lots of rainy days, but Alison could only remember one. Every second was burnt into her brain with a branding iron. Colm's hair was wet before they started off. It had formed little fork-prongs over the collar of his anorak. She remembered tracing the streams of water down the glass with her stubby, thirteen-year-old fingertips as the seat belt strained against her waist; the hush of the shower that drowned the last words he ever spoke, then later, the raindrops on the windscreen which turned to sapphires in the lights from the ambulance.

In the months that followed his death, it was Angie who forgot to tidy her room. She sat for hours sometimes, just looking in the mirror. Alison never saw her cry, apart from on the day of the accident when she had sat on the kitchen floor for two hours holding a piece of dried mud that had fallen off the bottom of his shoe. By the time she had stopped screaming it was dark, and her tears had turned the pattern formed by the sole into brown liquid. This was the most frightening thing Alison had seen, and yet it was comforting. From then on, all histrionics were banished to the bedroom, and that was what really hurt. Alison could hear it through the wall; the low moaning, the clap of her palms against the wardrobe doors. She imagined Angie spinning out of control like the Tasmanian Devil, but as soon as she knocked and stepped in, Angie said, 'I'm fine, darling,' and Alison had to go on aching for someone to put her arms around.

Angie went into negotiation with God. At mealtimes, she announced the latest deal as if she were a trade union representative. She sat there, pushing her food around, telling Alison what she would do just to see him again. She would give her arms, her legs, her sight, her hearing – even her life, if it meant she could be with him for a few more days. Alison woke up at night sometimes, sure that she heard Angie's voice through the wall saying: 'My daughter. I would even give my daughter.'

Her daughter was a teenager. Thirteen. In Croydon that meant hanging around empty shopping centres at night with boys who smoked and carried large bottles of cider; feeling passionate about pop stars and thinking Martini and lemonade would always taste wonderful. 'Go out and enjoy yourself,' said Angie. 'You're only young once.' Alison liked it at home. She liked cooking the dinner and keeping the house clean. At night she sat with Angie watching *EastEnders*, believing sometimes that Colm had just popped out. All the while, Custard sat unused and sticky with sap from the trees at the side of the road. They preferred to take the bus.

A year later, when Alison was getting used to being the grown-up, Angie awoke and the world was a familiar shape again. She looked in the mirror and smiled, and from that moment, she was the one acting like a teenager. She got a new job in an office. She started to drive again, nervously at first, but soon she was flashing around in Custard with her sunglasses on and 'Now That's What I Call Music' blaring out. She bought trendy clothes and flirted with men in other cars, even when Alison was sitting next to her. 'She's not my daughter,' she'd say. 'She's my best friend.' Alison was keen to point out that a best friend wouldn't go out to Sinatra's nightclub with a load of divorcees and leave her sitting at home, waiting, worrying that she might drive away for good.

Alison took refuge at Mel's house. Everybody went to Mel's house. Being half Bajan and half Irish, Mel's family circle was the size of a roller-coaster loop. Groups of women sat around the kitchen table drinking tea, while the washing machine churned with football kits and leotards. In the lounge, kids bounced and somersaulted on the sofa while Mel's dad, Derek, sat at his desk, oblivious. He smiled when Alison came into the room and said, 'How are you doing?' in his deep, soothing voice, not unlike Baloo the Bear. Alison sat with him and was safe.

When Alison was studying for her mock GCSEs, Angie went out in her lunch hour to get a sandwich and found herself in the travel agent's, snapping up a last-minute bargain to Crete. A three-star hotel with a pool and a tennis court and nightly entertainment. Just the ticket for a couple of girls on the razzle. Angie and Alison went paragliding, took lambada lessons and danced at the hotel disco in the evenings. It was fun, but after a few days, Angie seemed to tire of her. She started flirting with the waiters at mealtimes, making rude jokes about their pepper grinders. Alison feigned a stomach bug and stayed in their twin room, reading schoolbooks. Even then, she could hear Angie's laughter from the pool below. She wished that Colm would just fly over like Superman and scoop them up, one under each arm, and take them home.

There was a couple with a daughter of Alison's age. Every time she saw them, Angie said: 'Ali, why don't you go over and talk to that girl? Go on, I'm sure you must be fed up with your old mum all the time.' Gina was thin and lanky and her mousy hair was so long she could sit on it. She wore long, strappy sundresses and big heavy sandals. Her hair was either worn loose (making her head look the size of a marble) or in two huge plaits. She was quiet and terribly posh and said 'actually'. She didn't know what the number one was and her pin-up was a show-jumper. Her father looked like a nutty professor. Her mother was an older, pear-shaped carbon copy of Gina in a tie-dye wrap-around skirt. They were delighted that their daughter had found a 'little friend' and invited Alison to join them as they explored the island.

Their one attempt to invite Angie along was a disaster. Halfway up to a ruined temple, her sling-backs bit so hard into her ankles that she had to retire to a café and wait for them. 'Such a shame,' said Gina's parents as Angie's magenta blouse faded to a dot behind them. Alison knew what they were really thinking.

When they returned to the café, Angie was nowhere to be seen. They sat down at a table on the cobbled forecourt and ordered mineral waters. Alison wanted Coca-Cola, but had lost the will to be argumentative. Gina and her mother went to work pointing out the poor uses of grammar in the pamphlet they'd picked up at the temple. Alison looked for the bright flag of her mother along the side streets. The next thing she knew, she was being hissed at from the door of the café. It was Gina's father. He had gone inside to find the Gents and now he was crouched over, bracing his arms against the door frame as if awaiting a charge from behind. She slipped away from the table and made her way to him. 'Sorry, Alison,' he said. 'I thought you would be the one to deal with this.'

Angie was in the back, playing cards with two elderly men with moustaches, captains of small boats that took holiday-makers from beach to beach. She was wearing one of their blue hats. It had slipped down over one ear. 'I'll see you,' she said, drunkenly sticking two fingers towards her eyes by means of translation. The men laid their cards on the table. 'Mum?' Alison tugged at her sleeve.

Gina's dad had put the others in the picture. Alison could see their pinched expressions as they approached. 'I'm all right, darling,' said Angie, her hands pulling on Alison's arm. 'They were lovely fellas, those two.' Alison guided her to a seat. 'How was your walk?' she asked, accidentally clipping the table with her foot, sending it rocking on the cobbles. Everyone dived forward as the glasses of mineral water toppled. 'Oops!' laughed Angie, as a green bottle rang over the stones. Alison got up and walked away.

By the time Angie caught up with her, she was halfway up to the monument again. 'Darling,' she said, her voice ragged from climbing. 'Darling, please.' Alison turned around, her arms folded. 'I'm sorry. I embarrassed you in front of your friends, didn't I?'

'They're not my friends. I hate them.'

'Phew!' Angie grinned at her. 'They're awful, aren't they?'

'At least they're sober.' Alison kicked a stone and watched it cartwheel down the hill.

Angie took her arm. 'I'm doing my best,' she said. 'I'll try to be better. I will. Just let me do one more thing, though.'

'What?'

Angie pointed at the figure of Gina's dad pacing around the car park. 'When we get back to the hotel, would you mind awfully if I pushed him into the pool?'

Alison sniffed and looked down at him for a moment. 'OK,' she said, trying not to smile.

Angie did try to be better. When they got home, they redecorated the house and sat together in their gleaming lounge, watching soap operas. 'Do you think Dad would like it?' asked Alison, surveying the yellow wallpaper.

'Probably wouldn't notice,' joked Angie. 'You know how men are.'

Alison didn't, of course. 'You should be out,' said Angie. 'With your friends.' Alison felt obliged to nod. 'It'll take you out of yourself, darling.' So Alison joined Mel's dance group and the youth club. It was fun for a year or so, but then boys started to suck her friends away one by one, leaving her alone on the dance-floor or standing in the kitchen with the grown-ups. A few did ask her out, and she went with them to the cinema or to Pizza Hut so as not to feel left out, but it was never quite right. They seemed nervous, almost grumpy at times, staring blankly at the screen, picking wax from the candle on the table as she ate. When they said goodnight, Alison braced herself as their wet, spot-rimmed mouths came towards her. She closed her eyes and tried not to panic, keeping her teeth clamped together. Eventually, they backed away with a clammy squeeze of her hand. They didn't return for seconds.

It was because of her father's death. Everybody knew about it. It had been in the papers, even the national ones. His name was mentioned on *Newsroom South-East*. The boys who dared to approach her felt they had to watch what they said, like she was a piece of badly glued china that would fall apart on the spot. Alison was happy to be single. She could never see herself in one of those slobbery clinches on staircases, with people kicking you on their way up to the toilet. Her dream kisses were from old movie stars. Men who looked forty when they were twenty, and wore suits and smoked pipes. Men like Ben.

Chapter Six

Two days after the visit from the men in the foreign car, Alison arrived at work to find Darren holding court in the staffroom. He had witnessed another strange event concerning Plum and Blossom. The doorbell had rung at ten-thirty that morning. On the chilly step stood a very elderly man dressed from head to toe in black. His face was pasty and fleshy with huge white eyebrows. He raised his hat and entered, removed an astrakhan-collared coat and folded it over his arm. Age had bent and shrunk him, and a dewdrop hung from his nose. He pulled a handkerchief from his pocket and dabbed it away. Darren hung his coat up and was just about to enquire after what he wanted, when the old man was yoo-hooed from the top of the staircase by Blossom in her purple shellsuit. 'Scatty, dear. We're ready for you up here.'

Scatty made very slow progress up the staircase, egged on by Blossom, who was in a state of great excitement, jumping and clapping her hands. A care assistant came down on the other side carrying a pile of towels. 'Sandra, dear,' Blossom called to her. 'Would you be so kind as to bring us a pot of coffee? Mr Samuels has had a long journey.'

'You lay down and I'll dance for you,' tutted Sandra, leaning against the wall as Scatty lurched by. Coffee wasn't for half an hour yet, and it was always served downstairs. Darren volunteered and dashed off to the kitchen as Scatty finally reached the first floor and was wrapped in the perfumed arms of an old friend. The kitchen staff scolded Darren as he removed three cups and saucers from the trolley then opened cupboards, banging their shins until he found a pot. He had to hurry, as he had left Harry Jackson in the bath. He crashed up the stairs with the coffee and knocked with his heel on the door of Blossom's room. It was one of the largest in the building and was crammed with lace cushions and cuddly toys as well as a paper-strewn desk, at which she was attempting to write her memoirs. Plum had brought in a spare chair from her room and the three of them were seated around a coffee table, leafing through documents. Scatty looked confused, gazing through the thick lenses of his glasses at the paperwork. As Darren approached them, they put the papers face down on the table and smiled up at him. Normally, they would be bursting to tell him every last bit of gossip, so their stony silence threw him. He stood at the door grinning as they said thank you again, then backed out into the corridor.

As Darren approached the bathroom, he could hear Harry singing away to himself. He knocked and opened the door a crack. Harry was red in the face. 'By gum, lad, you took your time.' Harry Jackson was a gnome-like little man with rosy cheeks and teeth that looked two sizes too big for him. In spite of his size, he had been quite a ladies' man. He still enjoyed the attention of the females, always volunteering to stagger down to the corner shop for them to buy a few packs of Rothmans. 'One at a time, please, ladies, one at a time. I can't satisfy you all at once,' he said as they came towards him with their handbags looped over their arms. Darren helped him out of the bath and handed him a towel. As Harry had been at the front of the line trying to entertain the mystery guests, he was all ears as Darren detailed the meeting upstairs. 'Scatty Samuels,' said Harry in amazement. 'He must be as old as God.'

'You're not kidding. Who is he?'

'He's an agent, that's who. Well. That proves it. They've got a gig, them two. I bloody knew it!' Harry reached up and retrieved his hat from the back of the door. With his dressing gown barely around him, he padded down to his room, mumbling, 'Get us me clothes, lad. I need to get to the bottom of this.' With Darren's help, Harry dressed in record time and was soon heading for the lounge. 'Do you know this Samuels, then?' Darren called after him.

'Not personally. But I know a man who does.'

Ben was sitting by the window, reading *The Stage*. Harry tweaked the top of the paper and sat down opposite him. 'Samuels?' said Ben. 'Good God!' Leonard 'Scatty' Samuels was once an oboe player with a popular Jewish jazz band, but had given it up to run a small agency specialising in glamour acts and dinner entertainment. Ben imagined that he had been either Plum's or Blossom's agent in the fifties. Harry was instructing Ben to 'cut him off at the pass' when Pat appeared and called Darren over. She laid into him for wasting time. 'I gave you three things to do this morning. How many, precisely, have you done?'

Darren did a very good impression of Pat, and the others in the staffroom were laughing as he recounted this part of the story. Darren never did find out what was going on. Pat had followed him around all afternoon, and by the time she eased off, Shazia had come on duty, and Darren would much rather spend time with her. She was standing by the open window as he told his story, leaning out every few seconds to exhale her cigarette smoke. Her sleek black hair was cut into a long bob (she did it herself with meat scissors), and pinned back on either side of her forehead with two blue plastic clips shaped like love hearts. She had a gap between her front teeth, but the rest of her face was so beautiful she looked sexy, rather than goofy. 'Maybe they're going back to stripping,' she said drily. 'Be a laugh, wouldn't it?' Shazia was the newest member of staff. Her father was a doctor at a local practice and she was working at Maytime for her 'year off before going to university. Knowing her father, the staff were all expecting a quiet, devout little thing in a sari, not a cheeky 'wide girl' in short skirts with silver eyeshadow and a tattoo on her ankle. Pat couldn't believe her misfortune. The residents loved Shazia. She was welcomed aboard with loud cheers, and pretty soon the old ladies were matchmaking. She and D'arren were regularly thrown together by bogus emergency calls and sent on wild-goose chases.

As if they needed any encouragement.

Later, as the lights were going out all over the building, Alison checked in on Ben. She had set up a nebuliser in his room for his asthma. His radio was on, playing classical music, so she entered silently. He was lying back on the pillow with his eyes shut. His mouth was set into an expression of quiet happiness. In the soft light his silver hair shone. He looked young, with the lines pulled away from his face. His cheekbones were strong and the collar of his silk smoking jacket was rich against his skin. He was, once again, the man in the black and white photograph. She wanted to pull back the bedcovers and climb in next to him. She had changed the sheets that morning and knew how fresh they would smell. She was so small she could just tuck herself in under his arm without either of them being uncomfortable. It would be the warmest, loveliest place in the world, with his heart beating under her ear and his arm curled around her. She stared and stared but he didn't move. She was suddenly afraid that if she touched his hand it would be cold. The music twirled her insides around.

An image came to her of Cary Grant sitting high on a tree branch. It was an old movie she had seen. Cary dies when his car crashes into this tree, and while his dead body lies with its head pressing against the steering wheel, his spirit sits up above, playfully dangling his legs like a child ready to set out on a great adventure. Then his wife dies, and the two of them are up on the branch. Ben's wife was already up on a branch somewhere, waiting for him. Alison wanted to poke her down with a stick. She took an involuntary gulp of air and Ben's eyes popped open. He turned to her.

'Alison. I didn't hear you.' He focused on her swimming eyes. 'Are you all right, love? You look like you're about to burst into tears.'

'Fine. It was just . . . well, you know when you start a sneeze but don't actually sneeze.' She raised her fingers to her nose. The blood was rushing from the centre of her body to the surface, blushing down her neck.

'Ah.' He lay back again and nodded. 'I thought maybe it was the music.' Another sublime orchestral passage flooded the room, making his eyelids flutter. She had never seen anyone listen to music the way Ben did. He came from a time when it did not invade every corner of life. When it was there, it held your attention so completely that nothing else existed. She stood for a moment and listened to the violins which seemed to be looping in and out of each other's plane trails, making a squiggly pattern. 'It's lovely,' she said, bending down to unplug the nebuliser. 'Imagine writing something like that.'

'I only wish I had.' Suddenly he looked sad and old again. 'I listen to that and I think, what do I have to show for myself?' Alison sat on the side of his bed.

'Oh, come off it, Ben. They were playing your records the other day and Harry and Blossom started dancing. You can't dance to classical. Not unless it's a waltz or something.' She trailed off.

Ben took her hand. 'You are sweet,' he said.

The radio fell silent, then the announcer told them that they had been listening to Delius. Alison knew that in spite of what she had said, Ben would give a million quid to have written something like that. His arrangements had been popular for many years. Some of them were still used by bands who played at ballroom-dancing competitions. They were simple and competent, but not great. Before she said goodnight, Alison asked about Scatty Samuels. Ben shrugged. 'Couldn't get a word out of him. He looked like he'd had a fright, poor old thing. I certainly wouldn't relish a couple of hours alone with those two. They'd bruise your face talking to you.'

'I suppose if it was work, they would have to be careful.' Maytime was a charity, after all.

'Oh well, I'm sure we'll find out in good time,' he said, settling himself under the blankets. 'I can't imagine the girls keeping anything secret for long.'

Alison walked back along the corridor with the nebuliser under her arm. People fell in love to your music. That's what she should have told him. Couples in ballrooms, people like me who never know the right things to say, could just hold their arms out and wait for you to do the rest. Ben and his music were probably responsible for babies who now had children of their own. Alison was going to tell him, but the light was off in his room.

Most residents had a radio and chose to drift away with Radio Four. To her young ears they were loud, coming like ghosts through a castle wall. 'Sailing By'. The ghosts were waltzing through the cobweb-covered ballroom of the *Titanic*. Women in picture hats and men in evening dress, the fabric tattered and rotted by the salt water. Then the shipping forecast. 'Dover. White. Portland . . .' Maytime was drifting on the moonlit waters and Alison grabbed the handrail, almost feeling the floor tip and roll beneath her. Feeling lost, while all around her they were lulled by the familiar. The safe. The British.

Chapter Seven

The hairdressers came to Maytime every Tuesday afternoon. A mother and son team from Finchley, Joy and Simon were a double act. Their arrival always caused great excitement among the younger residents. They fought each other for appointments, often resorting to bribery. Maytime was not very well equipped: the one hairdressing sink was badly installed and too uncomfortable for arthritic necks, so they were forced to use one of the ground-floor bathrooms with their plastic shower-heads. This resulted in the thorough drenching of both the hairdresser and the client. While Simon got stuck into the Golden Girls, as he called them, his mother 'tidied up' the bedridden and less mobile residents in the nursing wing. At the end of the afternoon, they came together and the small room was thick with old-fashioned hairspray that caught in the throat.

Alison was walking up the corridor with Shazia. They heard raised voices and discovered Plum in animated conversation with Lena Chase, a new resident, formerly with a 'Lilliputian' company. They were standing so close to each other that Plum's generous bosom was like a shelf over Lena's head. 'Two packets!' demanded Lena's shrill voice again and again, until Plum finally gave in. 'Two packets it is. I'll get them tomorrow morning.' Lena stretched out her tiny hand and she and Plum shook on the deal. As Lena made her way back to her room with her hair still in an untidy bob, Plum breezed into the 'salon' and kissed Simon on the cheek. 'Outrageous!' said Alison. 'Look at her.'

Simon was wrapping a salon cape around Plum's shoulders. He turned to see Shazia standing with her hands on her hips. 'Right!' she said. 'What's going on?' Plum had removed her hairclips and was running a wide-toothed comb through her dark shoulder-length curls. Her parting glowed white, cutting a skunk-like line down the centre of her scalp.

'I'm having my roots done, dear.'

'I saw your little racket out there. You know Lena isn't allowed to smoke, with her chest. Are you trying to kill her?' This made Simon squeal. Plum was unfazed.

'Lena may be small but she's not a child. She can do what she likes as far as I'm concerned. I don't know what you're getting so aerated about, Shazia. I see you puffing away on the fire escape. Now, run along. Simon has work to do.' Plum flicked her hair back and picked up a battered copy of *Marie Claire*.

Shazia stood defiantly, pushing Simon out of the way as he approached with a bowl of freshly mixed dye and a brush. 'Not so fast,' she said. 'Not until you tell me what you and Blossom are up to with that old man. He was here again this morning.'

Plum just tapped the side of her nose with her finger. 'You'll find out in good time,' she said.

Simon's mother Joy came in with a bag of rollers and a hairdrier in her hand. She asked Shazia and Alison to look out for Blossom and send her in.

Blossom was waiting in the lounge with a cigarette in one hand and a half-empty bottle of honey-blonde rinse in the other. Shazia approached her. 'Plum was just telling Simon about your new job. It sounds very exciting.' A half-inch of ash fell from the end of Blossom's cigarette, landing in her lap. She didn't move. 'She told you about Germany?' The girls nodded. Alison could feel the flush of deceit creeping up her neck. Blossom was easily fooled. 'Well I never!' She stubbed out her cigarette and took Shazia by the arm. Together, they walked back towards the

salon. Alison dawdled in the storeroom, stacking the clean sheets
and pillowcases until she saw Shazia striding triumphantly
towards her.

Plum and Blossom were to star in a commercial for mobile
phones. It was to be filmed in Germany and shown all
over northern Europe – not in Britain, unfortunately. The
two men who came to visit were the producer and the director, and Scatty had worked things out with Pat so that Plum
and Blossom could keep some of their wages as 'pocket
money' and still carry on living at Maytime. Shazia didn't
find out how a producer from Germany came to hire two batty
old strippers from London. She was just about to ask when
Plum overhead and came storming out into the corridor,
dripping dye all over the floor.

Shazia and Alison started to change the sheets in Mr
Appanowicz's room. 'I hope you admitted it was your fault,'
said Alison. 'Plum will make life hell for Blossom.'

'Why are they keeping it secret, anyway? They're leaving next
Monday.'

'I don't know,' said Alison. 'It gives them one up on the
others, I suppose. You know what they're like here. All dying to
get back into the limelight.' Renko Appanowicz shuffled in and
the two of them helped him back into his bed. He stayed in it for
most of the day now, drifting in and out of sleep. Shazia leaned
over his one good ear. 'Can I bring you something, Renko? How
about a cup of tea?' He nodded, then stretched out his arm and
tugged gently on her hair.

'Sha-zee-ah!' said a cracked little voice from the corner of the
room. 'You spoil this old man!' Shazia looked behind her. It was
Mother, his last remaining puppet, a three-feet-tall automaton
whose workings were as tired as those of her creator. The paint
on her face had chipped away in patches, revealing the dull grey
metal beneath. The fabric of her shawl had faded to the colour of
processed peas, but she still had her voice. Once, Renko had to
work hard to throw it and make it sound old, but now it came

naturally. It was over twenty years since Renko and Friends last trod the boards. Max, the schoolboy in blue knee-breeches was in a music-hall museum now, mute and motionless. For decades he had skipped across the stage and chatted with Renko the park-keeper and Anya the nursemaid with the pram and baby Zuzu, who threw things at him and Mother, who took him home as the sun went down.

Both Maytime and variety in general had been home to many refugees. People like Mr Appanowicz, who left Eastern Europe when it was peaceful and golden, promising to return the following spring. They were waved off by their mothers and fathers, sweethearts and friends, faces which still clung somewhere to a wall in the back of their minds. Faces unaware that that one goodbye would have to last them for ever. War and the Iron Curtain turned Renko into a reluctant gypsy who never married, and whose children were made of tin. He talked to them in his own language, treasuring the feel of it, but when he found himself sharing a bill with another Polish act, he would blush and stammer. The thought that he could express himself fully to these people made him nervous. There was too much to say and nowhere to begin. Instead, he chose a life of small talk and the companionship of his fellow artists. Although most of them were gone now, Mother would be there until the end to talk to him in the small hours and remind him of the children who had watched; the way they laughed and pointed and believed in them and made them real.

After Alison had checked on the older residents, she knocked on the door of Pat's office. There was a faint clatter inside. The office always smelt of cherry drops. It fitted the pinkness of Pat's skin. She was sitting behind her desk, straight-backed with a file open in front of her. 'Hello Alison,' she said. 'Take a seat.' She gestured to a chair and Alison perched on the edge of it. In front of her was a magnetic desk tidy from which a sculpted tower of paper clips rose. A couple of clips lay on the sticky desktop beside it. Pat had been caught playing with them. No wonder she was looking so serious. 'I've had a complaint,' she said.

Alison's heart plummeted. 'About me?'

'No, not about you. Of course not. Anyway, complaint is probably too strong a word. It's about Shazia and Darren. I was wondering if you could have a little word with them.'

'What about?'

Pat raised an eyebrow. 'What do you think? Look, they can do what they like on their own time. What worries me is how their work is being affected by all this. They're never in the right place, always messing around. My responsibility is to the management and the residents. What if Shazia's father hears about this?'

'What do you want me to do?'

'Just keep an eye on them. You'd be doing me a great favour.'

Alison left the office and pressed her back against the wall. Why didn't she say something in there instead of standing with her mouth open? It was a horrible, thankless job dressed up as a favour – like being made blackboard monitor at school. A position that was always given to the goody-goody. Poor Pat hadn't a clue. Alison wanted to be bad and rebellious, but whenever she tried, she found that she just couldn't go through with it. She wished she was like Shazia, who encouraged Lillian the foot juggler to perform with the coffee table, or Darren, the creator of Zimmer hockey who ran a side bet on who would be the next to die (odds-on favourite: Beryl of Beryl's budgerigars). Alison was surrounded by rebels. Overgrown teenagers, and it made her feel old.

The refectory was filling for the evening snack. Ben came in from his stroll, smelling of wet leaves. Plum and Blossom were on the front step, waving goodbye to the hairdressers. They were backcombed and sculpted, like two sticks of candy floss. They turned their noses up at Alison and all her indignation melted away. She felt awful that they were cross with her. She wanted to run to them and tell them that she had had nothing to do with today's little deception. It was all Shazia's fault. Shazia was a bad girl who didn't love them and thought they were ridiculous. Not her. Not Alison, who was so good they had made her blackboard monitor.

Chapter Eight

Mel leaned back on the battered office chair in her bedroom and accidentally pulled out the jack on her earphones. The bass line she was working on shot out through her computer speakers, waking Alison with a start. It was switched off, and for a moment, Alison couldn't work out if she had dreamed it. Her heart was clattering away, though, too wildly for a dream. She didn't venture into Mel's room that often. It made her nervous. For a start, there was the extension lead, jammed with so many plugs and adaptors, she feared it might give up one day, leaving Mel fused to her Midi Keyboard with smoke coming out of her head. Also, there was the dust. It was bonded to every millimetre of the tower block of stacked black boxes, clumping dark and greasy around the various knobs and buttons. Sound Module, Drum Machine, Mixer, Effects Unit. Alison knew all of them because the boxes they came in were pushed into the cupboard under the stairs. She longed to sneak into the bedroom one day with the Pledge and a duster, but she knew that something would go wrong. She might press a button by accident or knock over the CDs that went four feet up the walls. Mel looked up at her. 'Sorry,' she whispered. 'Can't you get back to sleep?'

Alison sat on the end of Mel's bed and hugged herself. 'Have you got the day off, then?' Mel nodded. 'Me too. Do you want to go out?'

'Sorry, Ali. I've got to get this finished.' Alison looked at the screen. No notes, no manuscript, just fat black columns bunched together like a city skyline. 'It's called "Manga Man".' Mel disconnected the earphones, pressed a button and leaned back in her chair. The track started with a backbeat, then the melody came in, together with a thin, reedy voice. Alison sat up and smiled. The voice was familiar.

'Hey, is that Daichi?'

'Yeah.'

'What's he saying?'

'I don't know. Some poem he learned at school.' Alison listened. It was beautiful. Unknown syllables, rolling and stretching and stopping suddenly. It sounded so refined compared to the way she and Mel spoke, English with a Croydon twang. The verse repeated, then faded away as great, fat bass sounds filled the room, rattling the CD covers against each other. They danced like lunatics, Alison on the bed, twisting the covers beneath her feet. Below her, Mel bobbed up and down, the unplugged earphones jiggling against her sharp brown collarbones.

'It's brilliant, Mel,' she panted. 'Honestly. Daichi really makes it.'

'Thanks. You should tell him. You working tonight?'

'No, I'm on days.'

'Excellent! Guess what? Daichi has got us on the guest list for DJPX at the Blue Note. He asked if you wanted to come.'

'I bet he did!' Alison was bouncing now like a child, waving her arms around.

'He did, honestly! He likes you.'

'Oh, yeah. I can tell by the way he followed you to work the other morning. Anyway, I can't go. I've got an early start.'

'Throw a sickie. Oh Ali, pleeease! You never go anywhere these days.'

'I do. Think I'll go to Croydon this afternoon. Check on Custard.' The track stopped and Mel's voice was suddenly deafening.

'What for? In case it's got bored and gone for a drive?' She put her earphones down and stomped out to the kitchen. 'You trouble me, girl. You really trouble me!'

'Oh . . . *pooh!*' Alison blew a raspberry at her.

Later, as Alison left the flat, she stopped by Mel's door. She could hear the *tss, tss, tss* of the reconnected earphones. 'You off, then?' said Mel, sliding them down. Alison nodded. 'Do you want me to come with you? I will if you want me to.' She smiled and her eyes said sorry. Alison shook her head. Just before she closed the front door, she heard Mel calling out, 'Take care.'

Alison made the trip to Croydon every few weeks. It was a fiddly one, involving buses and a long walk down a series of side streets. A journey back in time, passing the end of the road where they used to live and ending at a garage door. Autumn leaves had limboed under it. They scuttled across the concrete floor as she entered. She flicked on the light – a long, fluorescent tube with moths caught inside the shade. The window-glass had been replaced by hardboard around which small shoots of ivy were starting to appear. The tarpaulin sheet was covered in dust that shot up to the ceiling as she pulled it aside. Underneath, Custard was the same as ever, though the underside of the doors had long bubbled with a tidemark of rust. Every time she looked, there was a new eruption just below the surface of the paint. The chrome was dull and speckled with brown, no longer smooth to the touch.

She opened the car door and sat behind the wheel. Her feet were nowhere near the pedals. Mel's father was the only one who drove it nowadays, and that was just to take it down the road for an MOT. She pulled the choke out and tried the key in the ignition. It coughed to life after three goes. In the rear-view mirror the yard outside was darkening. She opened the walnut glove compartment and pulled out a cloth. Behind it sat a cassette tape. She didn't touch it. She knew what it was. Her mother had put it there so that it could remain for ever where it belonged. Alison dusted the dashboard and the steering wheel and the passenger seat. A couple of times, she had thought about bringing a vase of flowers and setting them where he used to sit, but they would only go rotten in the dark and stink the car out. She couldn't have that. Custard had a smell that no other car had ever had before or since. It smelt of them. All three of them. Back then.

She knelt in the passenger seat and leaned over to polish the side window and the back seat. The tenth anniversary of his death was coming up, and Alison was toying with the idea of contacting his friends, telling them that the garage would be kept open for the whole day so that they could pay their respects. They might find it a bit macabre, though, considering the way he died. She felt badly that they had missed out. He had been buried in Ireland, near his parents' house. His only memorial in Croydon was a lamp-post. It was the nearest to where the accident had taken place. Halfway down the hill, opposite the newsagent's. Within hours of his death, there were a few bunches of flowers propped up around the base. They were urinated on by dogs, so someone took action and they started to shin upwards, fastened by string and sticky tape. Running ink on florists' cards said goodbye and best wishes. For days people stopped and stared at the skinny carnations in tissue paper bowed and battered by the rain. A lady from their church had looped a rosary around it, making it into a shrine, and one Tuesday, Father Ngobo passed by with a couple of nuns and they stopped and said a few words. Alison spotted them on her way home from school, standing with their hands clamped together in prayer as people ran past them with their shopping swinging at their sides trying to beat the bus to the stop. Alison took another route home. The next time she passed the lamp-post, the flowers had gone. All that remained was the gummy ghost of the Sellotape.

*   *   *

She continued to polish Custard, moving outside now, rubbing the bodywork, noticing the tiny flecks of yellow duster fabric which had snagged in the rusty bits last time around. She pulled them out with her fingernails, then moved over to the windscreen. Angie had wanted to trade it in for a Fiesta, but Alison wouldn't hear of it. It was theirs and nobody could ever love it as much, even though it broke down with increasing regularity. When Alison turned seventeen, Angie presented her with driving lessons and a set of L-plates. She was ecstatic.

But it all went horribly wrong. Not with the driving instructor: she was fine with Mr Bloom in his Nissan, even passed her test first time. It was Custard. Whenever she started the engine, he was there, standing with his hands on the bonnet, smiling in at her. His eyes were telling Alison that she was safe, but she knew differently. Sweat poured over her, dripping from the steering wheel. She couldn't move forward. Not with him there. It was then that she realised she had made a terrible mistake. She shouldn't have kept Custard and watched it rot. She should have buried it alongside him, like they used to do with chieftains and their horses.

She had a Halifax savings account. The Custard account. It was a present from Angie when she sold the house and moved back to Ireland. It came with the ownership documents made out in Alison's name so she could insure it and take it through the MOT and have a few good times of her own, driving along with the wind in her hair. Alison wasn't fooled, not for one minute. It was Angie's way of saying 'get over it'. Alison was over it. She just didn't like driving.

She pulled a bar of chocolate from her jacket pocket and crawled into the back seat, deciding to wait for an hour so that Mel and Daichi would be gone by the time she got home. She had been to clubs with Mel so many times, and always felt like Princess Anne when she walked in. When Mel danced, she smiled as if she had been let into an amazing secret. Her eyes were closed and tiny jewels of perspiration sparkled on her cheeks. In her tracksuit bottoms and crop top, she spun and zigzagged over the floor. Alison saw the way people watched her and danced up close to her so that they could be mistaken for her friends, but Mel was oblivious. She only cared about the music.

Alison liked the music too, in fact, she liked most of the clubs she went to with Mel. She loved dancing when there was plenty of room to move, feeling the beat welling up into her voice box and the floor pounding beneath her feet. But then came the turning point. It came at different times, but it always came. Right in the middle of a favourite song, she would feel as if everybody was watching her, then she'd miss a beat and fall out of step with Mel and the rest of the crowd. She would try to get back, but it was difficult. Her feet didn't want to cooperate. Everyone was taller than her; sporty girls and boys in snow-boarding jackets. She would suddenly feel dwarfed and buffeted by their movements like a Mini being overtaken on both sides by National Express coaches. She usually ended up pressed against a wall, terrified of getting their elbows or their cigarettes in her face.

Alison finished her chocolate. The car windows had steamed up and she wrote 'Hello!' on the glass with her fingertips.

'Damn!' Alison closed the front door behind her. 'Hey, I thought you were going out.'

'I've been ready for half an hour, but bug-a-lugs here has been fiddling about on the computer.' Daichi appeared behind Mel, wearing black turn-up jeans and a polo neck. 'Oh, hi Alison,' he grinned. 'I'm glad we waited. Do you want to come?'

'See!' Mel mouthed to Alison. 'He likes you.' Then she disappeared into her room.

Alison took her coat off. 'Thanks, Daichi, but I'm going to give it a miss.'

'We can wait, if you want to get changed.'

She sat down at the bottom of the staircase, smiling up at him. 'I'm knackered. Couldn't dance if you paid me.'

'Aw, come on. I just sway if I'm tired, you know.' He illustrated, clasping his hands behind his back and staring into space like an extra in light opera, then sat down beside her.

Mel shouted from her bedroom. 'For God's sake! It's not *Come Dancing*. Mind you, that's more your style, isn't it, Ali? Hey, Daichi, can you do the waltz?'

'Shut up, Mel,' said Alison.

Daichi turned to her. 'I learned the waltz when I was little,' he said. 'Treading on my mother's feet. No, not treading. You know when you are a kid and you put your feet on top of your mother's?'

'I did that with my dad when I was a bridesmaid.' They fell silent.

Mel came out of her bedroom, zipping up her jacket. She stood for a moment watching Alison and Daichi leaning against either side of the staircase like bookends. 'Oh, you two are so cute.' Mel put her arms around their necks and kissed them both on the cheek. 'Now, are you coming? Yes or no?' Alison looked at Daichi, then at Mel. She had that matchmaker expression on her face. Alison suddenly wanted to go, but something made her shake her head.

'Have a good time,' she shouted as they headed towards the bus stop. 'I'll tape *EastEnders*.'

'Thanks, Mum.' Mel waved as Alison shut the door.

Chapter Nine

A car was due to take Plum and Blossom to the airport. Plum had been sitting in the hall for half an hour, packed and ready, but Blossom was still in her room, blowing her nail polish dry. At Plum's feet was a small suitcase and the perfectly preserved BOAC airline bag that Shazia had been coveting for months. Plum hadn't been abroad since the time those bags were issued, on a two-week trip to Majorca with a racehorse owner who never did leave his wife.

Blossom's voice came down the stairs before she did. 'Goodbye, Lena dear!' Plum shrugged. Blossom wasn't all that friendly with Lena. She was only shouting so that everyone would look at her. Dressed in a psychedelic trouser suit, Blossom could have been making a guest appearance in *Bewitched*. Plum let Blossom have her Gloria Swanson moment on the staircase. She had gone for a more subdued look: a smart, brown wool dress with a red scarf draped over the collar. Blossom's case had a broken latch and was held tight by a leather belt. She put it next to Plum's and stood over her, waiting for a comment. 'Well?' she said. 'Will I do?'

'Very snazzy, dear, but won't you be rather cold? We're going to Germany, you know. Not Jamaica.'

'Yes,' said Blossom tartly. 'I have been to Germany before, remember?' She had been the sweetheart of countless soldiers at the glum American airbases that were dotted all over Europe in the fifties. Standing high on a stage littered with foaming beer cans, she had twirled her tassels at the gawping mouths below. Plum didn't entertain squaddies. She stayed closer to home, standing as still as a statue, recreating great works of art or months of the year in front of men in suits. Their gawping, she thought, was perhaps a little more refined.

Blossom pulled a book from her handbag, a battered phrase book. The title, *Getting By in German*, was hidden under dog ears of paper. Plum knew that the section marked 'notes' was filled with faded handwriting. She could imagine them all, crowding around an ash-speckled table, scribbling with stubby pencils such classics as, 'If you're ever in Ohio, call me', and a phone number with the area code in brackets. Before Blossom could launch into her story about the man who slept in the next bunk to Elvis, Darren appeared on the landing, holding her fur-collared coat out like a royal robe. Pat said, 'Oh, for heaven's sake!' and the doorbell rang.

When the two of them had finally gone, the place seemed spookily quiet. The rest of the residents were subdued, smarting because they weren't the ones heading for the airport. Shazia tried to cheer things up by plugging in the record player in the lounge and putting on an album of show songs. The older residents sat with their knitting in the strange, high-backed easy chairs that only exist in old people's homes. Those that could hear the music tapped along and occasionally finished off a line for the singers. Ben was sitting by the window playing back-gammon with Lillian the foot juggler. His pipe was giving off the sweet aroma that comes from years of practice. As Yul Brynner sang: '*Shall we dance — one, two, three and . . .*' Lillian chalked up another victory and took Ben's outstretched hand.

Suddenly the music shot up to a level that reverberated against the front of the speaker. Shazia nearly dropped a woman she was helping from a chair and left her hanging onto the arm as she made a dash for the record player. It was Eva, who once did a very successful accordion act. She was well over eighty now, standing right next to the turntable, swaying along with the music. She looked disappointed when Shazia returned it to its usual volume, like a child ordered to clear up her toys. 'For God's sake!' yelled Shazia. 'Loud enough for you, Eva?'

'What, dear?' Alison came in at that moment and put her hand on Eva's shoulder, leaning right into her ear.

'Where's your hearing aid, Eva?'

'Oh.' Eva fingered the back of her earlobe. 'I had it a minute ago.'

Alison beckoned Shazia to turn the record player right down. A few heads appeared around chair backs as the music faded away. With a look of intense concentration on her face, Alison leaned down into a deep bow, her ear brushing against Eva's breasts. 'What the hell are you doing?' said Shazia, but Alison hushed her up. She could hear a faint whining noise and wasn't sure if it was coming from Eva's underwear. Hearing aids were known to slip. Alison straightened up and gave Eva a knowing look. 'Your handbag,' she yelled, pointing to the old black snap-lock bag which was a permanent feature over Eva's wrist. Eva guiltily opened it and fished around inside, pulling out packets of extra-strong mints and tissues before the small pink prawn-shaped piece of plastic appeared. Alison tapped her on the shoulder and smiled as Shazia went to retrieve the old lady from the arm of the chair.

The record finished and the stylus of the old machine crackled as it disconnected from the vinyl and clunked back to its resting place. Alison lifted the record from the turntable, feeling the weight of its age. 'Do you want the other side?' she asked the room. There was a murmur, but Ben's was the only clear voice. 'Certainly not,' he said. 'Find us something a little more civilised, would you, Alison.'

'Like what?' She crouched down to the stack of records. They were old and most of the covers had faded, their plastic coating peeled into yellowing blisters.

'I trust you,' he said, accompanied by the clacka-ta-clacka-ta of the dice in Lillian's cup. Alison didn't trust herself when it came to Ben. He often got a bee in his bonnet over the music they played at Maytime. He knew that the young had a crazy idea that all people over sixty-five were mad for singalongs and war anthems. Vera Lynn wasn't the only singer around in those days, he said. She didn't hold the only key to their fond memories, their days of falling in love. Alison flapped the records forward with her fingertip, pausing between Billie Holiday's *Lady Day* album and Dvořák's *Serenade for Strings*. He liked both of them. She had watched him, once, smiling through the piano solo in 'What A Little Moonlight Can Do', his fingers twitching on the table top as if he were trying to make contact with the ghost of Teddy Wilson, willing it to lay its hands on his and lead him through that smoky little session in the thirties.

She slid her thumb and forefinger in between the softened edges of the cardboard cover and pulled the record out, holding it like a cocktail tray and slowly settling it down on the turntable. Benny Goodman announced the beginning of 'Miss Brown To You', and she looked at Ben. He didn't register at once. He was bent over the board, gazing at the configuration of discs. She sat frozen as if awaiting exam results, thinking that she should have gone for the Dvořák. He turned and winked at her. 'Perfect,' he said, smiling, then turned back to his opponent. 'I've got you now, Lily of Laguna.' Lillian watched as Ben's fingertip looped across the board, and another white disc joined those that were stacked like Scooby-Doo sandwiches on the rim.

It grew dark outside. A deep blue, rain-cloud darkness that sucked the colour out of the wallpaper. A ball of pink wool fell from a sleeping hand and rolled over the carpet, dragging its tail behind it. Alison's limbs were heavy. She was still crouching at the record pile, unable to pull herself up, lulled by the heat that wriggled from the tops of the radiators. Lillian wandered past with the folded backgammon case under her arm. Eddie the cat strolled in and head-butted a couple of chair legs. He spotted the ball of wool and before Alison could stop him, pounced and flipped it into the air, pulling loops from its centre. She prised it from his grip and he gave her a parting swipe that cut a thin, blood-beaded line along her arm. As she stood and sucked it, Ben came up to her. 'In the wars?' he asked, taking her arm.

'It's nothing.' She rubbed the faint O of lipstick from the skin around the cut. Billie Holiday started a song called 'If You Were Mine'. Alison smiled over at the record. Way beneath the tune was the sound of each revolution, like a dropped plate spinning on its rim. Ben still held her hand. If she didn't look back at him, she could believe that the record was new and free from background hisses and pops, and that he was the young Ben with the pencil moustache who still thought he would sound like Teddy Wilson if he practised hard enough.

'Care to dance?' He put his hand around her waist and they started to move. At first her feet were set in clay, but she quickly got the feel of him. The smell of the pipe tobacco was tucked between every stitch in his jacket. His face was so far above hers. She could feel the soft silk of his cravat against her forehead. She closed her eyes, smoothing away the carpet underfoot and replacing it with polished boards. The nets at the window were blackout curtains; the sleeping residents were wallflowers who wished they were dancing with him. He sang along with Billie unselfconsciously with a tremor that gave his age away. The words came down the back of her neck, disturbing the strands of hair tucked over her ears.

Even my heart, even my life, I'd trade it all for you
And think I was lucky, too. If you were mine.

The sixth-form boys she had slow-danced with on occasions knew nothing of such promises. They didn't know how to hold her. Nowadays, her height was a joke, but back then it would have been an asset. Film stars were tiny little things who went on tippy-toes to kiss the leading man. 'Five feet two. Eyes of blue.'

That was her, and Ben was her leading man, but someone had blundered and got the times all wrong. She was dancing with him in God's waiting room, and he was singing to some other girl who wore her hair in pinned rolls and painted stocking seams on the backs of her legs.

Pat came in as the song finished. 'Alison, what do you think you are playing at?' Ben let go of her and they parted, her hair clinging to his jacket.

'She was making an old man very happy,' said Ben, patting her on the head like a child. 'You should pay her double.' Alison didn't know whether to smile or run away screaming. The volume shot up again, waking the wallflowers. Pat spun round and saw Eva, singing along with 'Summertime'.

Alison put her palms to her ears and ran forward. 'She's got her hearing aid in her handbag.'

'Hand grenade?' said Eva with panic in her eyes.

Chapter Ten

———————◆———————

Shazia loved the image of Eva in her surgical stockings, holding the caterers to ransom with a hand grenade. Alison was meeting Mel in the pub that night and Shazia had tagged along, not ready to go home yet. They sat munching crisps, rosy from the log fire and their halves of lager.

'Where's Darren, then?' asked Alison. 'Is he on nights this week?'

'Yeah, Pat changed the chart. She's got it in for me, man.' Shazia licked the remnants of salt and vinegar from her fingertips. 'Just 'cos she's got no life.' She plunged into the packet again, searching out the last few crumbs.

'How do you know?'

'Oh, come on.' Alison thought how young Shazia was. 'You going out with anyone?' she added.

'No, not at the moment.' Alison took an unnecessary gulp from her glass. It was the thought of 'going out' with someone. For as long as she could remember, romance had been like a red dress in a shop window. Lovely to look at and dream about, but put it on and she'd look ridiculous. Once there had been a man, an ex-boyfriend of Mel's she bumped into at a party. Six feet four with a mane of dreadlocks. Not a bit like Cary Grant. She liked him in a way she had never liked anyone before. He was beautiful and smelt of cocoa butter, and she felt hot inside talking to him.

He took her into his bedroom and she let him kiss her. It was wonderful. He wanted to go further and so did she, but then, as he slipped his hand under her T-shirt, she started to panic. It was like freewheeling down a hill. She felt all out of control and didn't know how to put the brakes on. So she bit him on the neck. She never saw him again.

Shazia's mobile phone played a muffled melody in her bag. 'Hi, babe,' she said, tucking it under her chin and lighting a cigarette. 'No, I'm having a drink with Ali . . . What? . . . No, Alison . . . yeah, from work . . . Who did you think I meant? Some bloke my parents are fixing me up with?' Alison was half listening to her. She could still see the mark she left on that guy's neck. A little round railway track. 'Well, that depends how rich he is,' said Shazia. 'How much money you got, then? . . . Ooh, well you should come and have a chat to them . . . No, I mean it . . . All right then, bye.' She threw the phone into her bag and leaned back smugly. 'Sucked in,' she said, winking at Alison.

'You are cruel. Darren runs for cover whenever your father comes in.'

'He's just paranoid, that's all. Have I said anything bad about my parents?' Alison shook her head. 'Well then it's Darren's fault, innit? He just assumes that my family are going to kill any white guy who lays a hand on me. I mean, you've met my dad, haven't you? He's dead laid-back. So's my mum. They don't mind me going out or anything. So long as I don't do nothing stupid.'

'Do they know about Darren?'

'Yeah. They're dying to meet him. That's why Dad looks out for him every time he comes to Maytime.'

'And he's hiding in the shrubbery.'

Mel came in like a bullet, then spun on her sneakers looking for Alison. 'God, sorry,' she said. 'The tills were all out and we had to stay behind.' She flopped down at the table, shoving a plastic bag on the floor.

'Going skiing?' Alison tugged at Mel's dark blue salopettes.

'You've seen them before.' An Oxfam purchase from way back. Padded pants, yet she still looked slim in them. Alison introduced her to Shazia, who said it was her round and went off to the bar.

'What's in the bag?' asked Alison, though she had a pretty good idea. Mel kept things on reserve at the back of the shop all the time, hiding them in the stockroom until she had a space on her credit card that wasn't filled by second-hand electronic equipment. She pulled out a top in swirling lime green and pink. It looked a lot like the fabric of the trouser suit Blossom had been wearing that morning. Mel held it under her chin, smoothing the sleeves along her arms. It looked fabulous against her brown skin. Shazia came back from the bar with her fingers snaggled around three glasses. 'That's gorgeous,' she said as Mel folded the top and put it back in the bag.

'It's for a special occasion.'

'Out with it,' said Alison. Mel pulled her mouth back into a huge smile and pounded her fists on the table.

'Guess who I'm going out with on Saturday?' She looked like she was going to explode.

Now Alison was smiling. 'Daichi,' she said, jumping in her seat. Mel relaxed her fists and made a face at her.

'Of course not. Let it go, Alison. No . . .' She announced the name like an Oscar winner. 'Puxley!'

'Who?'

'DJPX. That's his real name.' Alison deflated. Another poser, probably, who wore black girlfriends like accessories.

'*The* DJPX?' said Shazia, wide-eyed. Apparently everybody in the whole world knew who DJPX was. A bedroom Beethoven from Norwich who was huge in Europe and had all the major names in the dance-music industry baying at his heels for a remix of their tracks. 'I wrote my number on his combats,' she said, proudly. 'I didn't think he'd remember me, but . . .'

'You wrote our number on some bloke's trousers? Anyone could have seen that.'

'Yeah, anyone with their nose in his bottom.'

Their 'date', it turned out, was more of an all-night dash around the country. Puxley had four gigs, starting at ten in Reading and ending up at six in the morning at a rave in Nottingham. But to Mel, this was a million times better than a candlelit dinner and a stroll along the seashore. It was as if she had lived her whole life for it. She and Shazia got on like a house on fire. They sat and listed their current top tens, favourite clubs, favourite DJs. Alison tuned out and toyed with the idea of playing the Trivial Pursuit machine by the bar, or walking back to Maytime so that she could sit with Ben instead. She'd never bite him.

Shazia was so busy becoming Mel's best friend that she forgot the time. 'Oh, God,' she shrieked, leaping up from her chair. 'I'm dead. I'm so dead.'

'Why?' chuckled Alison. 'I thought your parents were really laid-back.'

'It's not them,' she said as she wriggled into her silver anorak. 'It's my granny. She's down from Wolverhampton for the week. I was hiding out here, pretending I was working late so my mum wouldn't hassle me. But now, it's like: "Be afraid. Be very afraid." Jean-Claude Van Damme in a sari.' With that, she swung her bag over her shoulder and ran off, waving back at them.

Mel didn't come back from her date until Sunday afternoon. Alison was watching a Bette Davis film on the telly. Good, dramatic stuff with lots of lying and deceiving and men in suits. She heard the front door go, but before she could say hello, Mel breezed in and turned the telly off. She was still wearing the swirly top, but now it smelt of sweat and cigarettes. She looked wrecked. Her green glitter eyeshadow had folded into lines. 'Hey!' said Alison, reaching for the remote control. 'I was watching that.' Then she realised that they had company.

Puxley sloped in carrying a can of Pepsi. He nodded 'all right' when Mel introduced him, then sat with his legs wide apart and stared out of the window, flicking the ring-pull with his middle finger. He wasn't what Alison had expected. Shorter than Mel and quite cuddly, with a chalky complexion and one gold tooth at the front. He was wearing a large, red T-shirt with a Rizla packet set in plastic on the front and a pair of loose trousers with reflective strips up the sides. There were dark circles under his eyes and his bleached hair was matted.

'So? Did you have a good time?'

'Awesome,' Mel said, yawning. A word she would never use just with Alison. She had seen the symptoms before. Mel starts going out with a guy from the club scene and immediately acts like a fictional character, dealing out one-liners like she had joined the cast of a sitcom. It made Alison ache. She wanted to shake Mel and tell her she was so lucky just to be her. Mel relayed the events of Saturday night. Most of it seemed to involve driving at breakneck speed in Puxley's BMW, which had air-conditioning and a seven-thousand-pound sound system. People had chased them around giving them demo tapes and white-label records. It was all just so exciting.

Puxley yawned and went over to the CD player. He shuffled a few of the discs, turning his nose up at Alison's Nat King Cole and Madonna albums. 'So, Puxley,' Alison said. 'Mel was telling me you do a lot of work in Europe?' He looked out of the window, trying to see his car. A bubble of spit glided over his gold tooth-cap. Alison tried again. 'I hear Iceland is really hot . . . I mean, in the music sense, rather than temperature-wise . . .' She drifted off, feeling ridiculous. Puxley stared at her blankly.

She turned to Mel. 'Have you seen my birthday-card box?' Mel shook her head. 'It's Lillian's birthday today. The nurses are throwing a party for her.'

Puxley perked up. 'Nurses? Can I come?'

'Yeah, if you like. You could DJ.'

'She's taking the piss,' Mel explained. 'She works in an old folks' home. They'll all be on the sweet sherry.'

'Oh, right.' Puxley laughed in Alison's direction, then shuffled over to the sofa and put his hand on Mel's shoulder. 'I'm off. I'll call you.' He didn't lean down to kiss her. Instead, he stood straight and waited for her to pull herself up. Alison turned away until they had finished. She said goodbye, but he ignored her. She heard him belch as the door clicked. He didn't say 'pardon'.

Mel reached for the remote control. There was still an hour of Bette Davis to go. She stretched out and kicked her boots off. 'I'm done in,' she sighed. 'Wake me up for the *Antiques Roadshow*, will you?'

'Your mum rang. She wants to talk to you about Justin's eighteenth?'

'Nightmare!'

Justin was Mel's little brother. Well, he used to be her little brother. He was taller than his father now. Once, he had been interested in things. He had a chemistry set and kept scrapbooks. He even visited an old lady who taught him to play the musical saw. If anybody mentioned it now, he would give them a look that could blister paint. His hair, which used to hang in loose ringlets like Mel's, was shaved down to the bare minimum. His broken-toothed grin was now self-consciously covered by his top lip, and he walked like all boys walked: head down, shoulders hunched, frowning at his feet. He came to stay sometimes when there was something on up in town, looking physically pained if Mel or Alison talked to him.

'You know what he wants for his birthday?' said Mel, her mouth sticky with sleep. 'A snowboard. I mean, how useless is that in Croydon?' She grinned, though, knowing how typical it was of Justin, thinking of him still as Alison did; a kid dancing around the living room to '*Hey, you, the rocksteady crew*', his clumsy fists swiping at the air. She drifted off with her smile. Alison went to her room and got ready for work. Before she left, she pulled a duvet down the hall, draping it over Mel in her smelly shirt.

Chapter Eleven

The doorbell rang. When Darren answered it, he stood with his mouth open taking in the vision that confronted him. Though they had only been gone a week, Plum and Blossom had changed almost beyond recognition. Their puffed-up hairdos had been replaced by modern styling, rollers discarded in favour of scissors and the expert fingers of a German hairdresser. The black and yellow dye had been toned down to silver-grey and salt and pepper. Their make-up took twenty years off them. Pink powder, blue eyeshadow and coral lipstick had been replaced by translucent beige and toffee browns. Blossom's psychedelic pants suit was in a Berlin rubbish bin, together with the wool dress. Both of them were in tailored suits with padded shoulders and matching leather accessories. 'Hello Darren, dear,' they said, brushing past him, smugly aware of how good they looked. The cab driver trailed after them, carrying a set of matching luggage.

Pat stood in the doorway of Plum's room and watched her unpack, looking at each item of clothing as if she were taking an inventory. Her eyebrows shot up when she caught sight of a silky bundle of underwear being squashed into a drawer. The collection of hotel soaps and shower caps that followed it were more in keeping. Pat wanted to ask her all about it, but she knew it would come out wrong and Plum would think she was being interrogated. Down the hall, Darren was having no such problems. He was sitting on Blossom's bed with his feet up on the counterpane, watching her as she held up her new purchases and trimmed off their price tags. The numbers on them were meaningless to him, but they looked expensive. 'So,' he said at last. 'Tell me all about it, then. Did you have a good time?'

Blossom sighed and ran her freshly manicured fingers through her hair. 'Wonderful,' she said. 'They treated us like queens. We stayed in a lovely hotel and they sent cars for us every morning. The girls in the costume department took us shopping for a photo shoot and let us keep all the clothes.' She drifted off, returning in her mind to the luxury of it all.

'Well, you look fabulous. I'd go for you myself if I didn't think Shazia would kill me.' Blossom flounced over to him and kissed him on the head. He took her hand. 'I hope it isn't too much of a comedown, here.'

'This is our home, dear.' She smiled at him graciously, but Darren noticed a fleeting expression on her face. He changed the subject.

'So, did you have to learn lines?'

'A few,' she said cautiously, 'but they're in one ear and out the other.' She mimed the passage of the words. 'You know me, daft as a brush.'

'So when can we see it? Won't they send you a video?'

'I don't think so.'

'But surely . . .'

Blossom snapped her handbag shut and headed for the door. 'Come along,' she said. 'Time for a cup of tea.'

Alison arrived just in time for Lillian's cake. It was being wheeled through from the kitchen on the tea trolley as she came through the front door. The cold air she let in pulled the candle flames horizontal. She went ahead of the procession into the lounge. Things were buzzing in there. Music was playing, and Shirley was swamped by empty glasses. A couple of girls from the day shift were sitting around a table, red-faced with laughter, and at the end of the room, in the window seat, two glamorous women were blowing smoke out of their nostrils and raising their glasses to Lillian. Alison stopped in the doorway, realising who they were. Maizel shunted her with the handle of the tea trolley and the lights went out.

'*Happy Birthday to you,*' they sang, processing through the darkened room. Alison walked towards Plum and Blossom. 'Have a drink, darling,' they hissed between lyrics. 'It's on us tonight.'

'You look fabulous,' mouthed Alison. Plum and Blossom nodded as they sang, clapping their hands, beaming at Lillian, who was struggling to blow the candles out. '*She's eighty-five today!*' sang Shirley. '*Eighty-five today,*' they all joined in. '*She's got the key of the door . . .*' Lillian had hauled herself up from a sitting position and was braced against the arms of her chair, extinguishing the last of the candles. She looked around her. Nobody else had seen the irony of it. When you're eighty-five and live in a residential home, the one thing you do not possess is the key of the door.

When Alison had changed into her uniform, she was approached by Maizel and handed a piece of cake in a folded serviette. 'This is for Ben,' she said. 'He wouldn't come down. Perhaps you can coax him. I think Lillian would like it.' She put her hand on Alison's shoulder.

'Is he all right?'

'Physically, yes.' Alison made her way upstairs.

At first there was no reply when she knocked. She opened the door a crack and peered round. He was sitting by the window with his back to her, looking ahead. As she opened the door, her own shape appeared on the glass, framed in the amber light from the corridor. She saw only the crown of his head above the back of his armchair. 'Well, come in if you're coming,' he said, watching her shape grow as she moved towards him. She sat down in the other chair. A tray was on the coffee table in front of him with an uneaten sandwich on a plate. A cup was half-filled with cold tea, rimmed by the cream risen from the milk. Ben looked drawn. There was no cravat at his neck and his skin bunched loose and sallow around his Adam's apple. 'Are you all right?' asked Alison.

He nodded very slowly, examining the question. 'I suppose you've been sent to drag me downstairs? Well, that's kind of you, dear, but I'd rather stay here all the same. Nothing sinister. I just want to be quiet.'

She set the cake down on the tray. 'From Lillian,' she said.

'I heard the singing. Tell her I'm sorry. Most unsociable of me, I know.'

'OK.' She went to get up, but noticed that the photograph of his wife had been moved from his bedside table and was standing in its frame beside the tray. It had been taken when Vera was a young woman. Her pale straight hair was pinned back over one ear, revealing one round apple cheek. Her mouth was unpainted, just showing the shape of her smile. Her hair hid the other side of her face, falling across one eye. The black and white film had translated her eyes to a pale grey, but Alison imagined them to have been light blue. So different from the women at Maytime. No heavy make-up, no exaggeration, just a pretty girl who looked as if she had been gathering corn on a hot harvest day. It was the only photograph he had of her, so Alison had no idea how she had aged or what they looked like as a couple. Because of Vera's smile, Alison saw Ben behind the camera, a tall handsome man in a white shirt with his tie loose and his sleeves rolled up because of the heat, crouching over his little box Brownie, shading the lens from the sun with his hand.

'It's her anniversary today,' he said, looking up from Vera to Alison. 'Bad timing.'

'Oh, Ben.'

He had come to Maytime the year after Vera passed on. They said he was little more than a ghost. Couldn't cope with the loss. He had stopped eating the food Kenneth gave him, never left the flat above the florist's. Of course, Maytime was delighted to take him on. When he arrived, the other residents were all prepared for a party. The piano was tuned and a stack of his records were pushed to the front of the pile in his honour. Many of them had worked with Ben, and had tales to retell of late-night drinking and railway-carriage poker games. They were disappointed, therefore, when Ben sat in his room day after day. Maizel told Alison that she had never seen a person mourn so, and that Ben must have loved his wife more than most. That was where Alison's feelings for Ben had begun. The moment when she first looked at Vera's photograph and saw that shy little face, and knew that he had turned down all the glamour girls and band singers for her.

But Maytime was a magic place, and the other residents were able to bring him slowly around. They came and sat with him, brought photographs and programmes from bills they'd shared. They asked him to settle arguments over who sang what or who played drums in such and such a band. They pleaded with him to play the piano for them, and applauded loudly. So Ben retreated from the brink and returned to the life of a musician, the life he never really shared with Vera, who had stayed at home with Kenneth. He came to her only in the quiet hours of the night or on special days such as this. He was a visitor to her in death as he was in life. Away on the road with his jolly companions, then back to Vera. Always back to Vera.

'What was she like?'

'She taught piano,' he said. 'To children, you know, in the afternoons. She had a lot of patience.' Alison imagined their house to have been a country cottage with a rambling rose arch by the gateway. She could see Vera in a pastel-pink dress gathering roses from the garden and putting them in a big crystal bowl on top of the piano. She was all alone, waiting for her next pupil, pinning her hair back over her other ear so that she could see the little hands splaying over the octaves as she sat on the stool beside them. And on the mantelpiece, next to the wedding photograph which surely must exist somewhere, there was a letter rack filled to the brim with Ben's news, each envelope with a different postcode, all starting: 'My darling.'

'Did she teach Kenneth too?' The image of Kenneth as a child was difficult.

Ben snorted. 'She tried. God knows she tried, but he never took to it.' Kenneth was a little clearer in her head now. A lumpen boy with tufty hair and the same large spectacles he wore as an adult. He probably didn't make friends easily. He preferred to cultivate his own square of garden or cut and paste pictures from magazines. He hid in the folds of Vera's skirts when visitors dropped by, and sat diligently at the piano every night thumping out 'Carry Me Back To Old Virginny' as she stood and cheered him on.

'I wish I could have spent more time with them,' said Ben. 'We went everywhere by train, so you couldn't just go home after the show. You stayed in digs. Some had their families with them, but Vera had her work and Kenneth had to go to school.'

'I'm sure they understood,' Alison said, putting her hand on his knee. 'It must have made it special when you did come home.' Ben reached for the untouched sandwich. Alison could see Vera and Kenneth all prepared, with the house filled with the smell of baking and Ben on a train somewhere, counting down the familiar landmarks to the station. As Ben munched his sandwich, Alison was standing at the front window with little Kenneth, waiting for his cheery whistle down the lane.

There were different images in Ben's head. He remembered the way Kenneth used to hide when he came home. How he dreaded the journey back to their poky little house in Balham, seeing the strain in Vera's face. She put up with so much; he was amazed, every time he turned the key in the front door, that she was there at all, let alone with a smile on her face. The smile he could look at for ever. She was never prettier than she was on the day he took that photograph. There wasn't a line on her face back then.

Ben finished the sandwich and made a start on the cake. Alison picked up the tray. The photograph of Vera clattered face down on the table. Ben retrieved it. 'Do you know?' he said. 'You're very like Vera. You reminded me of her. Little things . . .'

With wobbly knees, Alison descended the stairs. The music from the lounge met her halfway. Ben's music: 'Million Dollar Baby'. Everything was perfect. Apart from the timing, of course.

Chapter Twelve

Alison was in a good mood. She and Mel had a day off, the fridge was full, the gas fire was alight and the television was on. Alison was preparing toasted teacakes in the kitchen. She scooped an extra surf-wave of raspberry jam from the pot, sensing that Mel deserved a treat. She was down in the dumps because Puxley hadn't called.

'Why don't you call him?' Alison suggested as she brought the tray through. Mel was in a foetal position on the sofa watching a rerun of Quincy.

'He's calling me.' She paused. 'Anyway, his mobile's switched off.'

'Kick him to the kerb, girl!' said Alison in an American accent.

Mel pulled herself into an even tighter ball. 'Shut up, Ali.'

'Sorry! Now, come on, have a cup of tea.'

Alison was wearing that satisfied look she had when she finished the spring cleaning. Mel scowled. 'You'd love it, wouldn't you.'

'What?'

'If he didn't call. You'd love it.'

Alison stared at the screen. It was one of those middle-of-the-night sessions, where Quincy and his sidekick were hunched over an enormous seventies computer, searching for that toxin that would point to the murderer. She hated it when Mel was right. Of course she hoped he wouldn't ring. Puxley was ruining what was left of their friendship. The phone rang. Mel sat up, then sank slowly sideways. It was on the telly. Quincy was calling his girlfriend. She was sitting in his houseboat wearing a negligée, waiting for him with a bottle of champagne in an ice bucket. 'Now I am depressed,' Mel groaned as Quincy said, 'I'm sorry, baby, but you know how it is.' The woman on the TV was all a-flutter, listening to his explanation. She was twirling the telephone wire around her fingers as he spoke. 'That's sick,' said Mel. 'I mean, look at her. She's a babe. What's she doing going out with some old bloke who drives a hearse?'

Alison gestured to the screen with her teacake. 'And he never comes home before about three in the morning.'

'Yeah, and when he does take her out, they go to that bar and sit with all his mates.'

'Well, there's obviously something about him. Maybe he's, you know, a bit of a tiger.' Alison clawed at Mel with her fingernails, tickling her under her arms.

'Alison!' Mel feigned shock at her last remark and slapped her hand. 'Where did you learn to speak like that, my girl? A tiger!' Mel shook her head at a close-up of Quincy wearing one of his snarly expressions. 'A tortoise, more like. He's about a hundred.'

'No he's not. He's probably what, mid-fifties? Sixty?'

'Yeuch.' Mel shuddered. 'Imagine snogging that. It would be all sloppy.'

Alison felt a prickle in her cheeks. 'Some women like older men.'

'I don't know why they don't run off with his assistant. I would.'

'He's a bit like Daichi.'

'Don't start on that again!'

'But he's so nice, Mel.'

'You go out with him. You know you want to.'

'I do not!'

'Might sort you out.'

'What do you mean?'

Mel sat up. 'Look, don't get upset when I say this, but I'm getting worried about you.'

'What's there to worry about? I'm happy.'

'With a small h.'

'It's better than being dumped with a big D.'

There was a hurt silence. 'At least I don't spend half my time sitting in a lock-up garage or drinking with a bunch of geriatrics.'

'They're my friends. Unlike some people.'

Mel put her arm around Alison and said very softly: 'They're your patients, Ali. You look after them. You, I don't know, wipe their bottoms and stuff. That's not friendship.'

'It is to me. Anyway, they're not like that. You've never met them.'

'I don't want to meet them.' Alison shrugged away from her. 'Look, I'm only saying this because I care.'

Alison went to her room. She threw herself onto the bed in that patented way used by all the old movie stars. It was uncomfortable, though. After a while her shoulders started to ache and she sat up. Mel knew nothing. Alison had other friends. There was Darren and Shazia at work, Yvette and Nicola from school. That was six, including Mel and Daichi. *Friends* on TV only had five each. Mel was the one who had lacked friends before Alison came along. She was really gawky at school, and the only one who couldn't dive for the brick in swimming.

Their friendship had started when Alison was a bossy eleven-year-old with a spiky haircut. It was half-term, and she was on her way to Nicola's house. She had decided to cut across the playground and pick up a Twix at the petrol station. It was one of those winter days when the sky had not brightened at all. It was like being in a black and white television programme. As she got near to the park, it started to rain, a fine mist that chilled her face and amplified the smell of dog shit on the pavement. It was an ugly park. Just a square of wasteland by the side of a dual carriageway. The play area was known as Cape Croydon because it was dominated by a huge climbing frame in the shape of a space rocket. The rest of the items were more down to earth. A row of swings on rusted metal chains that turned your hands brown, a tall stainless-steel slide that ended so abruptly that the council had to rubberise the ground around it. Like everything else in the Cape, it was chipped and covered in graffiti.

If the child hadn't screamed, she would never have noticed him. At first, she thought some boys were hiding behind the toilets. It was only when the child screamed for the second time that she looked up. Way up. He was in the nose of the rocket a good twenty feet above her head. Just a little blob of blue against the flaking red paint. Alison put her head and shoulders between two bars and looked up into the centre of the rocket. 'What the hell are you doing up there?' she asked. The hoarse roar of his tears grew louder. She could see his feet curled around the bars. He wasn't wearing shoes, and his mud-caked socks had all but worked themselves off. They hung like two elephant trunks from his toes, leaving his bare heels against the metal. Alison felt her chest tighten. He was so little. His tracksuit bottoms bulged over a nappy and his thin T-shirt flapped in the wind.

She looked at her watch, knowing that if she helped the child, there would be no time to get the Twix. 'Oh, bloody hell!' she said, clunking up the frame in her new Doc Martens. 'OK. I'm coming. Don't let go.' He took her literally, and it was a struggle for her to loosen his fists when she reached out to him. He stayed, braced against the bars, his chest heaving, and studied her with dark brown eyes. She guessed that he was about two years old, a dark-skinned black boy with fluffy eyebrows that curled up as they reached the bridge of his nose, like two cartoon caterpillars. 'What's your name?' she asked, but he just screwed up his face and wailed 'hooo, hooo' like a train whistle, his eyebrows squinching together. 'Are you a spaceman?' Alison looped her arm around his waist. She felt his head twisting *no* against her face, his hair like wet wool on her cheek. Eventually she latched him onto her side. Holding him across the back with one arm, she moved downwards, her muddy shoes slipping on the rungs.

On the ground again, Alison looked all around her. 'Where's Mummy?' she asked, but the boy was silent, his fists wrapped around her hair. 'I'll kill her, whoever she is.' She turned three hundred and sixty degrees, but there was nobody around. A man was walking a dog along the pavement, but he was white and over sixty. She had no idea what to do. The police station was miles away and the child was heavy in her arms and shivering. She undid her anorak and tucked him under it, then moved towards the road. There was a phone box a few hundred yards up and she waddled towards it, trying to think of a song to calm the child. All she could think of was 'Wake Me Up Before You Go-Go.' It seemed to work. She bumped him up and down as she sang 'boom boom' and she felt a breathy laugh somewhere in her collar. Just before the phone box, the little boy sat up in her arms and looked at the house to his left. He let go of her hair with one hand and pointed. 'My, my, my,' he said.

'Your house? Do you live there?' The front gate was unlatched and there was a turtle sandpit just outside the front door. 'Here goes.' Alison rang the bell, bumping the child up in her arms. A shape wiggled against the frosted glass. A dark silhouette. Alison was hopeful. The door swung open. It was Melanie Freeland, the new girl with the braces. For a moment, nobody moved. Mel was frozen, wide-eyed, staring at the child. 'Is he yours?' asked Alison. The little boy twisted towards Mel with his arms stretched out.

When Alison explained how she had found him, Mel slumped in the sofa with her teeth chattering. The little boy was Mel's cousin Ryan. She was babysitting him and had set him up with some toys while she watched *Neighbours* and *Home and Away*. 'I thought he'd gone to sleep,' she kept saying. By then,

Ryan was watching TV, unfazed by the fact that he had managed to open the back door, walk around the side of the house, across four lanes of traffic and up a climbing frame. Alison phoned Nicola and told her she wouldn't be coming over after all. She couldn't leave Mel, who was still being pathetic. 'She'll kill me,' Mel said, looking at a framed photograph of Ryan with his parents.

'I won't tell anyone.'

'Promise?'

'I just said so, didn't I?' By the time Ryan's mother came home, the child was clean and sleepy in his pyjamas and slippers. Alison had washed his socks and they were hanging over the bathroom radiator. Ryan jumped up at the sound of the door key. 'Mummy!' he shouted as Mel's aunt Claudia came in and dropped to one knee. He ran into her arms and she scooped him up. 'Sorry I'm late, Mel,' she said. 'Oh, you are good. You didn't have to get him changed.'

'Alison helped,' said Mel, pulling Alison into the hall.

'Hi,' said Alison. 'Hope you don't mind.'

'Of course not.' Claudia grinned, then blew a raspberry into her son's neck. 'What did you do, eh? Was he good?' The girls nodded.

'Went to park,' said Ryan.

'We took him,' said Alison. 'He was ever so good.'

Later on, Mel and Alison sat on the swings. The rocket was a burnt-out shell in the darkening sky. Claudia had given Mel five pounds, which they used to buy magazines and chips and cans of drink. Mel was the tallest girl in the class. As she swung, her sneakers scooped out two little furrows in the gravel beneath them. Alison's were a good six inches clear, and she had to push them out in front of her to match the wide arcs Mel was drawing in the sky.

'God! Look at your feet!' said Mel suddenly.

'What about my feet?'

'They're really small. Look at mine!' They tried to put their shoes up against each other's. The chains holding their swings clanked against their hinges and swayed erratically. 'Sweet!' said Mel. 'Little hooves.'

'Thanks a lot!' Alison kicked her back. 'Yours are like water-skis.'

Mel laughed and pretended she was skiing, leaning right back as she swung forward, her feet parallel, shooting up into the sky. Higher and higher she went, then she passed her arms outside the chains and mimed being pulled by a rope. Before Alison could say 'careful', Mel tipped up. Her legs cycled through the air as she tried to grip the chains with her elbow. There was a clank, and suddenly Mel was in a heap on the gravel. Alison jumped off so fast she had to take a short run forward. 'God, are you all right?' Mel was nursing a scrape on her forehead.

'Ow! Man, that hurts!'

'You donkey!' Alison crouched beside her. 'What were you doing?'

'Never. Never tell anyone I did that.' She started to laugh. Alison laughed too. Schoolgirl laughter, the kind that can never be found as an adult without a good half-bottle of vodka. A woman walked past with her dog and they laughed even harder, lying back in the gravel and watching the underside of the empty swings swooping over their heads. The following Monday, they moved their desks together.

There was a knocking on the door. Alison ignored it. It got louder. 'Come in,' she said at last. Mel slid around the door frame and stood against the light switch with her arms folded. 'It was the guy in the safari suit,' she mumbled.

'What?'

'Quincy found this stuff in the heating. It got into the apartment through the radiator.'

'Oh.'

'I was pissed off.' Mel tiptoed over and sat on the end of her bed. 'I miss going out with you, having a laugh. What's happened to you, Ali?' Alison sniffed and put her arm out. She needed the closeness of someone. Mel gave her a hug. 'Come on. Let's go for a drink.'

'Where do you want to go?'

'Anywhere. You choose.'

'Anywhere?' said Alison, moving away. She wanted someone else's arms around her, but she didn't know whose.

Chapter Thirteen

'No way!' shouted Mel as they got off at the bus stop. 'Let's go to the pub.'

'Oh, come on. You said I could choose. I really want you to meet everybody.'

'You just spent half the afternoon convincing me that you are not obsessed with this place. You are one sad case.'

Alison marched forward. The lights were all on in Maytime, giving it the look of a Christmas card. Shazia opened the door. 'Forget something?' she asked, then: 'Oh, hi Mel. How are you?' They stood for a while talking about a record Alison had never heard of, then Shazia was called away by a buzzer. Mel crinkled up her nose. 'It smells in here.'

'You can't smell anything.'

'Yes I can. It's vile. It smells like the science lab did that time we left the eyeballs in the bin.' Alison stopped short of showing Mel the refectory, fearing the scent of cabbage and gravy. Instead, she took her to the hall of fame. 'That's Eva,' she said, pointing to a photograph of a small woman with pin curls standing on a giant drum. 'And that's Lillian. You'll meet her later. She's ever so nice.' Mel put her ear to her shoulder to look at Lillian's photograph. 'Wow,' she said. 'Breakdance!' Lillian was standing on her head, literally. Her two hands were out to the side, just skimming the floor. Her hair had fallen down, making two little tunnels either side of her face. A wooden barrel painted with zigzags was balanced on one pointed foot and she was smiling.

Shazia appeared at the end of the corridor, supporting a tiny, wire-haired lady in a pink dressing gown. She was handing Shazia something. 'Take these,' she said. 'No,' Shazia replied, pushing them back into the clawed hand. 'They're your teeth.' Mel seemed frozen, staring at the splatter stain of a long-dropped coffee cup on the skirting board. 'It's worse here than I thought,' she said.

'It's not sho bad, shweetheart,' said Humphrey Bogart. Mel jumped. It was Harry in a felt hat and tweed jacket. 'Sorry love. Did I scare you?' He gripped her hand with his wizened fingers.

'I'm fine,' said Mel, but she looked terrified.

Alison stepped in. 'This is Harry. Harry, this is my friend, Mel. I brought her along.'

'For me? Ah, love, you shouldn't have. My birthday's not for a month yet. Still, waste not, want not . . . Brrrrrum-tsss!' He gave himself a quick flourish on the drums and cymbals and headed for the lounge with Mel's arm linked around his. She twisted her neck around anxiously to make sure that Alison was following. They marched straight past the photograph of Ben without giving it a glance.

The usual crowd were in the bar. Plum and Blossom were sitting together. 'Who's your girlfriend?' they shouted as Harry came in with Mel on his arm.

'Lady Wisteria Plantpot of the Devonshire Plantpots,' he said, bowing and rolling his hat down his arm until it rested in his hand. Alison would have curtsied. Mel just stood there trying to hug the embarrassment out of herself.

'Charmed I'm sure,' tittered Plum as Harry put his hat on her head. Alison introduced Mel to the gang. Ben was sitting with Lillian in the corner. 'This is an honour,' he said, pulling up two extra chairs. His hair looked yellow and there was a shaving cut on his chin, a triangle of blackened blood. Lena Chase marched in and tugged at Mel's jacket. 'Who are you? she asked. 'Have you been to America?' Mel shook her head. 'I have. I've been to Boston and to Chicago and to Boston.'

'Great,' said Mel.

As Harry approached the bar, Shirley-whirly reached for a can of bitter and poured it slowly into a tilted glass. 'What'll you have, love?' Harry asked, prising Mel from Lena's grip. 'I didn't embarrass you, did I?'

'I'll get them.' Mel pulled a purse from her jacket pocket.

'You can't,' said Harry. 'It's like a club here. You've got to be a member. Squattez-vous and I'll bring it over to you.'

'Let me.' Alison pushed past them and put a five-pound note on the bar. 'No need,' said Shirley. 'They're paid for.'

'How come?'

'Mystery donation. A big fat envelope. It was stuck in behind the tonics. Maisie wants to see you about it. She's asked everyone else.'

'You mean Maizel.'

'What did I say?' Only what she had been saying for four years. Alison was tired of correcting her. She picked up their drinks and went over to where Mel was sitting. Eddie the cat had emerged from behind the curtain and was twirling around the legs of her chair. 'You're honoured, dear,' said Lillian. 'Eddie's not one for company.'

'Vicious thing,' added Ben. 'We have more tetanus boosters than hot dinners here.'

'Why Eddie?' Mel scratched him behind his ears and he twirled his head around her hand, pushing his nose up against her fingertips.

'He's grey,' said Ben and Lillian in unison.

'Of course,' said Alison. 'I can't believe I never worked that out.'

'Worked what out?' asked Mel. By way of explanation, Ben told her about 'Monsewer' Eddie Gray and the pillar box, but for the first time Alison could remember, he fumbled and lost everyday words. It made her heart beat in her neck. She wanted to shake him and make him funny again. Alison loved the story. This old comic used to throw his voice into postboxes and convince streets full of people that there was a man stuck inside.

Mel turned to Lillian. 'I saw your picture in the hallway,' she said, stretching her arms out to mimic the unsupported headstand.

Lillian struggled to light a cigarette. 'It was a cheat,' she said. 'I had my arms on a, you know, on blocks. They changed the photograph.' Her lower jaw was pulled stiffly to one side and she was in constant fear of biting her tongue. The result was a slow, chewing motion like a camel.

'Oh.' Mel nodded. 'You can't tell, looking at it.'

'That's not . . .' Lillian could see that Alison's pretty young friend was finding her hard work, so she left it there and Ben took over again. She wanted to say that the trick photograph was her father's idea. It was taken in Huddersfield by an Italian recommended by Walter Niblo. Lillian could see him as if it were yesterday. A dark chap with a funny little moustache, he looked like a Victorian trapeze artist. The studio was at the back of his house and it was as cold as ice in there, even with the lights on. He had a wife and a little girl and they watched while Lillian's father fiddled around with his juggling bricks, stacking them up under her wrists. He was certain that she would do the headstand for real any day. She had been practising it for years. Every morning, no matter where their digs were, they would find a little area of carpet by a wall. She would get her cloth-covered rubber hoop and place it on the floor before squashing her head into it like a halo. All those mornings with the strange noises of strange houses and her father's words of encouragement. Her mother usually joined them and they did a run-through, space permitting, to get their timings right. Of course, they didn't have the barrels and the other props with them. They were at the theatre or packed away for the train. Lillian and her parents mimed it. Her mother sang the music, her voice thin and wobbling. Three of them, propped on their shoulders, their feet passing imaginary objects in time. 'One, two, three, one, two, three, one, two, three.' Lillian could still sing the whole act. She could hear it in her head as she sat in the bar.

Her neck ached. Years spent hunched up into a question mark had paved the way for arthritis. She looked down to the side of the bar. Harry had pulled a chair up to Plum's and Blossom's table, leaving a vacant patch of carpet. Green carpet with a gold fleck. The space was wide enough. The bar would support her back. If she could do it just once she would die happy. She had given up on the idea years ago after she had met her Ray. It just didn't seem important back then, but now, all of a sudden, it was gnawing away at her. Pretty soon, she'd be seeing her parents again. How proud they would be if she could tell them she had done it at last. Of course, it was ridiculous. She was wearing a dress and her left leg was still bandaged from her accident in the bath. If she couldn't balance on her feet any more . . . But she was sure, if she got the line right, she would get that even feeling as she started to raise her hands.

Shirley-whirly was leaning back, scratching her shoulder with the ice tongs; Plum and Harry were singing 'All The Nice Girls Love A Sailor'. It didn't seem as cute as it usually did. Alison's stomach had been macramé for over an hour and it was tiring her out. Ben was trying to include Mel by telling her about all the black performers he had worked with: Hutch, Archie Lewis, Winifred Atwell. He meant well, but it was beginning to sound like 'some of my best friends are . . .' Out of the corner of her eye, Alison saw Lillian get up from her chair, walk a few paces, then go down on all fours. Alison thought she had dropped something by the bar and was just about to offer to help her look for it, when Lillian flung her legs up like a bucking donkey. 'Oh, law!' screamed Shirley as a pair of Dr Scholl heels came level with the bar. By the time Alison got to her, her pleated skirt had fallen over her face. She looked like a handbell.

'Blimey! Is it that time of year already?' said Harry, as Alison tried to coax Lillian back to earth.

'Leave me,' growled Lillian, her jaw loosened by her position.

'Let me.' As her thick-veined hands left the carpet, Shirley leaned over the bar and held her very gently by the heels of her shoes. So gently that Lillian didn't feel her. Slowly, two hands emerged from under the inverted skirt and stretched gracefully out until she was cruciform. Alison stood with her head in her hands. She didn't dare look at Mel, even when Plum and Blossom clapped and Harry whistled 'For She's A Jolly Good Fellow'. She stepped forward and closed her fingers around Lillian's tiny ankle bones, guiding them slowly to the ground.

Lillian was sitting with her back against the bar when Maizel came in. She and Alison helped Lillian to her room. 'Ixnay!' she hissed in Alison's ear. Pig Latin for 'one word and I'll kill you'. They told Maizel that she had come over all peculiar and Alison had sat her on the floor to stop her fainting. Before Alison left her room, Lillian took her wrist and shook it in the air. 'I did it,' she said through her stiffened jaws.

'That's it,' said Alison to herself as she headed back to the lounge. She had certainly picked a fine night to show Mel the wonders of Maytime. Toilet smells, Ben on a race relations kick and a mad old acrobat trying to climb the walls. Although Shirley had closed the bar, the room was still buzzing. Alison could hear thumping. Mel and Ben were sitting side by side on the piano stool. The others were on the stage, too, forming a semicircle around them.

'How does it go, again?' Ben was asking. He was hunched forward on the stool, his hands passing over the keys. Mel started to drum on the woodwork and he followed her, sounding bass keys. It took him a while to get up to speed. Mel added another layer of beats, then picked out a simple melody.

'Sorry, I'm not very good,' she said as her fingers faltered on the keys.

'Did you learn piano at school?' Ben asked.

'No. I taught myself. I've got a little keyboard at home.'

'You're doing very well.'

'Why so fast?' asked Blossom, trying to clap along. 'How can you dance to that? It's like film speeded up. I wouldn't know where I was.'

'It's loud, remember. Louder than you'll ever have heard. You can kind of feel it in your chest. Your body just follows. Look, I'll show you.' She got up and moved around the back of the stool. 'Put your hands down,' she said to Ben. Leaning over so that her hair brushed the tops of his ears, she put her arms over his and patted the rhythm onto his chest. 'That's kind of what it feels like,' she said. 'It's direct contact with the body rather than just the ears. Even deaf people can dance to it.' She moved around the group while Ben carried on, ably assisted by Blossom. 'Come on, Ali,' she called over, but Alison clung to the wall and shook her head. She knew she could never compete. They were all looking at Mel like it was fireworks night.

'It's got bounce,' said Ben. 'Like a bossa nova in double time.'

'Well that's just the basic,' said Mel. 'You've got to put a break in every now and then, just to keep them on their toes. That's what I like about DJing, I suppose, the control.'

'How do you keep playing so fast?' Ben flexed his fingers.

'You don't. It's all in the machine. You just turn the button.'

'Lord,' he said. 'Buddy Rich will be spinning in his grave.'

'Who?' Alison tried to fill her in, but she was interrupted.

'Well, I think it's marvellous,' said Plum. 'Alison, you never told me your friend was such a talented girl. She's wonderful.' She leaned forward and patted Mel's arm. The others nodded.

'She certainly is,' said Ben, all aglow.

'Thanks.' Mel leaned over and kissed him. She was wearing the brand of lipstick that wasn't supposed to come off on anything, but it left a mark on his cheek. Two dark lines. Alison stared at them for ages. Shazia came in and Ben played 'Boogie Woogie Stomp' with Mel hand-jiving beside him.

*　　*　　*

On the way home, they sat on the top deck. Alison rubbed a circle in the window with her sleeve and looked into the upstairs rooms of passing houses. Mel hugged her arm. 'Thanks for taking me.' Alison nodded. 'The old strippers were ace. What a laugh. They were really into the beat. God, I've tried explaining it to Mum and Dad and it's like, whoosh!' She passed one palm over the top of her head. 'They said they'd come to my first big gig. I can just see them largin' it out on the floor, can't you?' They laughed. The image was all too real for Alison. 'No, honestly, mate. They're like us. Well, me. In about fifty years. I wonder if there's a home for retired DJs?'

'What about Ben?' said Alison. 'He's lovely, isn't he?'

Mel nodded. 'Kept looking at my tits though.'

Alison spun around so fast, she knocked her elbow on the seat back. 'No he didn't. He's not like that.'

'He is. Most men are.'

'Well, Ben's not.'

'OK, keep your hair on. I'm not saying he tried to feel me up. He was just, you know, having a look.' He never looked like that at Alison. Never let his gaze stray to the neckline of her uniform when she bent over him with his medicine. But then, there was very little to look at. No enticing orbs of flesh. Mel had worn her V-necked Diesel top. It was very Nell Gwyn. Ben couldn't help it: she was practically shoving them at him, offering them to him as a pair of earmuffs while she was showing him her drumbeats.

'What's his son like? He was telling me about him.'

'Kenneth? Yeah, he's nice.'

'Ben said you got on.' Alison stared out of the window.

As they reached the flat, they could hear the phone ringing. Mel nearly broke the door down to get to it. She knocked Captain Kirk for six. 'Hello? Yes it's me . . . Where have you been all day? Really? . . . Wouldn't you like to know . . . Just out, that's all . . .' As she spoke, Mel playfully stuck two fingers up at Alison, then rested her trainer on the right ear of the toppled cut-out. She looked like she had beaten him in a pro wrestling match. Mel was back in the driving seat.

Chapter Fourteen

It was Justin's eighteenth birthday. He had pleaded with his parents to go away for the weekend, but they were too wise for that. Mel had pulled the same stunt a few years earlier. The house was immaculate when they returned, and nothing seemed to be missing. It was only two weeks later when they found vomit in a wellington boot that the whole thing came to light. The entire street had been kept awake until six in the morning, and poor little Alison Mahoney had spent most of the next day snipping cigarette burns out of the lounge carpet with nail scissors. For this reason they had hired the community centre. Alison and Mel arrived early in Mel's battered Renault Five. People were there already, setting out the trestle tables, and the DJ was plugging in a tube of flashing lights that wound around the speakers. The bar opened and the music began, but there was no sign of Justin. His dad had promised to take him out for a beer first, pretending that it would be a new experience for him. Mel looked at the DJ. Judging by his stripy shirt, he didn't have much drum and bass. She was feeling pleased with herself. While talking with Ben at Maytime, she had hatched a little plan.

Alison helped Mel's mother with the buffet. Martine was a tall, red-haired woman with laughter lines around her eyes. 'You don't have to do this,' she said. 'Go and talk to Mel and those boys.'

'I like helping.'

'You're a funny kid.' Martine gave her a quick cuddle. She smelt of fabric conditioner, which made Alison want to cuddle her back. Though she was Irish and about the same age, she was not at all like Angie. She was always phoning the flat, asking Mel if she was dressing warmly and eating right. It drove Mel up the wall, but Alison thought it was wonderful. When the buffet was ready, they moved to the largest of the tables that ringed the dance-floor. As if drawn by a magnet, Mel wandered up onto the DJ's podium and stared lovingly at the turntables. The DJ stared lovingly at Mel.

Cousin Claudia arrived with her two kids. She had hardly changed from the first day Alison had met her; a smart, pretty woman in a business suit. Her son Ryan was a teenager now, a heavy-set young man with a design cut into his hair and a big sovereign ring on one finger. It was hard to believe that this was the little boy Alison had pulled off that climbing frame. His nine-year-old sister Keisha stood next to him, her arms clamped across her chest. She had chosen her own outfit for the evening, a strange combination of patent ankle boots, wool tights and a short skirt. Her little crop top had ridden up over a soft roll of puppy fat at her waist. She was upset. Her face shone with tears. The mystery was solved when they got to the table. She and Ryan had been fighting in the car and he had managed to break her necklace.

'Can I try?' Alison held out her hand. 'I'm quite good with things like that.'

The necklace was handed over. A ring of silver daisies. One of the links had disappeared down the back of the car seat. Keisha approached nervously and watched as if Alison was performing a life-saving operation. 'Is it your favourite?' asked Alison, using one of her own earrings to open the next link in the chain. Keisha nodded shyly, covering her mouth with podgy, glitter-nailed fingers. 'It's very pretty.' Alison looked up. 'Just like you.'

Keisha drew closer as Alison bit the chain to close the link. 'Dad gave it me,' she said. Her breath smelt like Smarties. Dad, it turned out, had moved out a couple of years previously and now she only saw him for a monthly outing. 'Ryan never comes,' she explained. 'He thinks Dad's stupid.'

'No he doesn't,' said Claudia, sharply. 'Don't go saying things like that.' She leaned over to Ryan, but he didn't respond to her brief caress. He reminded Alison of a nightclub bouncer. It wasn't just his big black tracksuit, it was the expression of barely concealed contempt that he wore. It scared her. It took her back to somewhere she didn't want to go.

'All done!' She handed the necklace back to Keisha, prompting a response from the table that made her blush. Keisha leaned against Alison's shoulder.

'You've got a fan, there,' said Martine.

The queue at the bar was soon five deep. The DJ put on a chart record and a few of the teenage girls sprang from their seats. Keisha bobbed along with the music, swinging her feet under the chair. 'Why don't you dance?' asked Claudia. Keisha leaned forward, eager to join in but afraid of the strangers who were clumped together in one corner of the dance-floor. She grinned at Alison, willing her to ask. The record was by a boy band. Alison couldn't remember their name, but knew it was one of the many she'd seen on *Top of the Pops*, a line of shiny-faced teenagers bouncing together with military precision. Keisha slid out of her seat and went over to her brother, who was slumped in his chair, gazing at the floor between his knees. She tried to take his hand. 'Get lost!' he said. Keisha sloped away from him and stood for a moment with one toe on the brightly lit parquet flooring. Her high, frizzy bunches looked like Mickey Mouse ears. The miniskirt had ridden up over her chubby backside, revealing the stitched gusset of her woollen tights. Alison melted, knowing all too well how Keisha was feeling. 'Go on,' said

Martine, squeezing her shoulder. 'There's a love.' Alison got up and took Keisha's hand. Together, they stepped onto the dance-floor. Keisha broke into a hoppy, shuffly dance routine. 'I do this with my friends,' she explained, her hands crossing then recrossing over her chest. Alison tried to copy her. For once, she didn't care what she looked like.

Justin arrived with his dad and a crowd of young people from the pub. As soon as he got through the door, he regrouped with his friends. Derek strolled confidently across the dance-floor. He was a good-looking man still, like an older version of Marvin Gaye from his *What's Going On?* album sleeve. 'How's Alison, then?' he asked, kissing the side of her forehead.

'Fine, thanks.' She danced up close to him. This was her sort of party. Everybody gathered together telling stories, children darting under tables, nobody being trendy.

'Hello, beautiful.' Derek lifted Keisha up and gave her a big hug. Alison wished she was young enough to be hugged like that. A different record came on, one that Keisha didn't have a routine for. She looked self-conscious, so Alison took both of her hands. Still dancing, Alison watched Derek as he reached the table. With the exception of Ryan, they were all smiling at her. They thought she was being nice, but in reality, Alison was having a wonderful time. She felt far more at home with Keisha than she did at a club with Mel. Keisha's hot little hands gripped hers tightly, jerking them now and again. Alison looked down and saw that round face grinning up at her. Somebody thought she was cool.

'Oh, my God,' said Mel as she danced by with a couple of toddlers. 'Look at us. It's like the end of the bloody Sooty Show!'

'Shut up,' said Alison. 'We're having a great time, aren't we?' She held up one arm to let Keisha spin under it. Just then, she spotted a familiar face. 'What on earth?' There in the doorway was Ben's son Kenneth. He was wearing a pair of shapeless jeans and a purple shirt which didn't go with his hair. With both hands he clasped a bottle of champagne. He was greeted by one of Mel's aunts and there was a short ballet as he bobbed and swapped the bottle from one hand to the other. Did he go to their church? It was a bit of a way from Lewisham. Alison knew she should go over and say hello. She imagined his surprise at seeing her, but then, all at once, she had a feeling. A horrible feeling.

She danced over to Mel. 'Look.' Kenneth was bleached by the white Exit light, pushing a towering vol-au-vent into his mouth. 'Oh, no!' Mel said. 'That's not Kenneth, is it?'

'*You* invited him!'

'That's Ben's son?' Mel looked devastated. 'Is he adopted?'

Alison shook her head. 'Why didn't you just ask me, Mel?'

'It was his dad's idea. He said you were always joining them for drinks and stuff.'

'I was being polite!'

Mel couldn't take her eyes off Kenneth. 'Sorry, Ali.'

'It's all right.' Some of the vol-au-vent had landed on his purple shirt. Alison felt for him, standing there like a lost child, so she waved until she caught his eye.

'Hi Kenneth.' She stopped short of kissing him. 'This is a nice surprise.'

'Thanks for inviting me,' he said, then there was a moment of embarrassment as he realised that she hadn't invited him. 'I was working about five miles from here today, so it wasn't much of a . . .' Alison couldn't concentrate on what he was saying. His face was splattered with reddy-brown freckles. They were all over his collar, too. She reached out and touched his cheek with her index finger. He pulled an unsavoury-looking handkerchief from his trouser pocket. 'Sorry,' he stuttered, mopping his face and blending the spots together. 'Stamens.'

Mel appeared at Alison's side. 'This is Kenneth.' They shook hands.

'Dad's been telling me all about you,' he said, but by then, Mel was bobbing about with Keisha. Alison didn't see Kenneth as the dancing type, so she led him by the arm to the family table. She dreaded their reaction. They were always going on about what a strange girl she was, never having a boyfriend, and now here was Kenneth with his awful hair and his big glasses. They were intercepted by Justin, who had been pulled away from his friends to accept Kenneth's champagne. 'Cheers,' he said, hugging the bottle. 'Excellent . . . Hey, Ali.' He pulled off his snowboarding hat with a flourish. His head was completely bald.

'Look at you!' shrieked Alison. 'Mister Malteser Head!'

'Jesus wept! What have you done?' Martine sprang from her seat and slapped her palm against Justin's scalp.

Justin was enjoying it. 'It was a birthday present. You know Tim and that lot? Yeah, well they did it down the pub. Got soap all over my top.' He pointed to a tidemark on the collar of his Ted Baker shirt.

Martine swung round to her husband. 'Did you know about this, Derek?'

Derek chose not to answer her. He got up and shook Kenneth by the hand. 'Welcome to the nuthouse,' he said. 'Sit down.'

Kenneth was offered wine from a regiment of bottles and accepted, drawing a line with his finger halfway up the glass to indicate his alcohol limit while in charge of the florist's van. Alison looked out onto the dance-floor. Keisha was lost in a sea of bodies, struggling to keep Mel's attention. Alison wanted to rescue her, but she knew she couldn't. She was a grown-up now. She poured herself a glass of wine, right up to the rim. Wine always made her tipsy, but to quote Mel (or rather, to quote Mel quoting Phoebe from *Friends*), 'she just big fat did it anyway'. The family table was loud and happy. Kenneth chatted with Mel's parents, then with Aunt Lizzie about her flower arrangements for the Baptist church. They liked him, and looking at him in the sunny glow of the Chardonnay, Alison could see why. He really listened and was amusing, given the right subject. Away from Ben, he seemed less self-conscious, less clumsy. If only he were a little younger and a lot better-looking.

*　　*　　*

A rap song faded out and the DJ turned on his microphone. 'OK, ladies and gentlemen, boys and girls. As you know this is a very special day . . .' On the other side of the room, Martine and Derek crouched over a trestle table. '. . . It's Justin's eighteenth birthday . . .' There was a big round of applause and some jeering and backslapping from Justin's table. A few relatives started to sing 'Happy Birthday To You,' but the DJ faded up 'Happy Birthday' by Stevie Wonder. He had forgotten that there is a long introduction and first verse before the sing-along chorus. This led to a lot of general swaying and clapping while Justin stood with his shoulders hunched and his head glowing as his parents advanced with a blazing cake. '*Happy Birthday to you,*' sang everyone who was old enough to remember the record. Justin's friends formed a sort of rugby scrum, bouncing together on the beat. Little Keisha danced with Derek, riding on his shoe-tops. Alison drained her wineglass. Feeling suddenly lonely, she looked for Kenneth. He was still at the table, leaning back in his seat, examining the ceiling tiles while Ryan brooded beside him. 'Come on,' she said, taking his hand. 'You have to dance to this.' She leaned away from him at an angle, until he gave in and joined her at the side of the dance-floor. Kenneth danced like an uncle at a wedding reception, kicking his feet up while his wrists drew concentric circles in the air.

Stevie Wonder faded into Lionel Richie and the dance-floor crowd thinned out. Martine caught Justin's arm. 'Come on, Kojak,' she said. 'Come and dance with your old mother.'

'As if!' he said, cramming a huge slice of cake into his mouth.

'Dance with your mother,' said Derek. 'Go on.' Justin looked at him for a moment, then shuffled over to Martine.

'Oh, Derek,' she said. 'Not if he doesn't want to.' She kissed Justin on the chin and let him go back to his friends.

Reluctant to slow-dance, Kenneth and Alison were finding it hard to boogie to a ballad. 'Nice family,' he said, nodding over to where Derek was now dancing with Martine, her head resting on his shoulder. 'You grew up around here, then? Do your parents still live locally?'

She turned to him. 'They're dead,' she said matter-of-factly. 'Car crash. Didn't you know?'

'No.' He stood frozen for a moment, then slowly held his arms out as if to catch a giant ball. 'I'm sorry.'

'It's OK.' Kenneth's arms closed around her like pincers. Where did that come from? she thought. She wanted to correct herself, but the words caught in her throat. She rested her head on Kenneth's chest, feeling his fingertips splaying lightly across her shoulders. Neither of them were very skilled at slow-dancing. Kenneth's kneecaps cracked against hers as they turned clumsy circles, but it was preferable to adult conversation. When the song finished, Kenneth made a move towards the table. 'Kenneth?' she tugged at his sleeve. 'I said something really stupid just then.'

'Oh, yes?'

'HELLO. OOPS. OH, HANG ON . . .' Mel's voice boomed over the PA system. There was a brief electronic whine, then she returned at a lower volume. 'That's better. Um, the DJ is taking a break right now, so here's some sounds for my little brother. Happy Birthday, babe.' The dance-floor filled with whooping teenagers as Mel launched into the stack of records she had brought with her. Mixing between two decks, she somehow managed to create a funky dance version of the old Grange Hill theme tune. Alison forgot all about her dilemma as Mel's quirky music bounced around the room. Kenneth tried to slope away again, but she pulled him back. She wanted him to enjoy himself, just once. For Ben's sake. Keisha and the little kids joined in. They were sleepy and spun dizzily. 'Excellent!' yelled Alison. Mel was on a roll, mixing in little bits of James Brown for her parents, little bits of hip-hop for the boys. Even the DJ joined in, slopping his pint as he danced.

'Oh, it's that record!' shouted Martine as she heard '*Hey, you, the rocksteady crew.*' Justin's friends slapped his bald head then surged forward, punching the air. Alison turned away from Kenneth and joined them, her head spinning, her legs kicking. She didn't care about him any more. She was surrounded by big, lanky boys. Up she jumped, lost in the music, then . . . *crack!* Something caught her fist. Something hard. She tucked her aching hand under her armpit, looking around to see what it was she had hit.

It was Kenneth. He was down on the floor, genuflecting. The stamen-stained tissue was clamped to his face, absorbing the blood that poured from his nose. Alison dropped down beside him. 'Sorry, Kenneth,' she said. 'I'm so sorry.' Before Kenneth could say anything, a herd of aunties in colourful dresses charged in from the surrounding tables. They went to work, getting Kenneth to lean back, then lean forward, giving him soda water, then tonic water. 'I'm all right,' he said, but his was a faint voice crying in the wilderness. Alison stood to the side and hugged herself.

'Nice one, mate,' said a voice in her left ear. It was Mel, flushed with success. 'Let's get out of here.' Alison didn't need much convincing. She said a quick goodbye to the children, then headed for the door.

As they were moving off in Mel's car, Kenneth emerged from the hall. The vol-au-vent stain on his shirt was hidden under a splatter of dried blood. He came over to the passenger window and Alison wound it down. 'Sorry,' he said. 'I just wanted to thank you.'

'What for? Hitting you in the nose?'

'No.' He saw the funny side.

'Hurry up,' tutted Mel. 'It's freezing in here.'

'Right you are,' said Kenneth. 'Nice to meet you, Melanie. I won't kiss you goodbye.' He lifted the bloody handkerchief by way of explanation.

'That's OK.'

'Bye then.' He tapped the roof of the car with his spare hand, then waved. 'Thanks again for the invite.' After months of searching for a common feature, Alison noticed that he had his father's hands.

'I won't kiss you,' repeated Mel. 'Talk about stating the bloody obvious. Yeuch!'

'Don't be mean. It was only a nosebleed.' As they drove back through London, Alison wondered how many nosebleeds Kenneth had suffered. He probably came home from school with one most days. By the look of him, he bruised easily.

Chapter Fifteen

Winter was a strange season at Maytime, full of highs and lows. During the day, it was bleak and the outside world was threatening. The older residents slept away the dark afternoons, cocooned by the central heating. Those who ventured into the garden found little cheer in the barren flower beds and the occasional clumps of potted winter pansies. The younger residents became stir-crazy and played energetic games of whist and poker, bidding with matchsticks. They were all seasoned gamblers, having acquired their skills on laptop card tables in railway carriages and on tour buses.

Alison heard music from the television room. She glanced around the door and found Plum and Blossom in leotards working out to the Angela Lansbury exercise video for over-fifties. Their hair was newly styled, but not by Joy. She wondered how much of their German pocket money was left. It was their lack of money management which had landed them in Maytime to start with. George Jakobi had popped in to give them some advice, but it just seemed to flow over them. As they continued their workout, Alison went looking for Ben, fearing Kenneth may have filled him in on her performance on Saturday night.

As she headed towards the lounge, she spotted Eva sitting in the hallway with her handbag on her lap, waiting for someone to arrive. Someone of her own invention, probably. She sat there most days, straining to hear the tick-tock of the grandfather clock pulling time along like a loaded sack, watching the pattern on the rug changing with the light through the door-glass. The nurses had given up trying to coax her back to her room, so they let her sit there until teatime. Her face lit up when the phone rang. She was keen on answering it, but her absent hearing aid generally resulted in a two-way yelling match. Alison intercepted her. 'Hello, Maytime,' she said. Over a crackling line, a man's voice asked for 'Miss Plum,' but didn't give his name. Alison put the phone down and went back to the television room.

Angela Lansbury was lying on her side raising her legs. Plum jumped up when she heard the message and ran to the phone, dabbing at her cleavage with a pink hand towel. Eva had taken the receiver and Plum had to wrestle it from her before pushing her out of the booth. Alison tried to listen in. This was one of many phone calls for Plum and Blossom since they returned, and whereas before they would broadcast their gossip all over the lower corridor, they now shut the glass door tightly and talked in hushed, detective-fiction tones, cupping their fingers around the mouthpiece.

'They're up to summat, Alison,' said Harry's voice suddenly. 'You mark my words.' He was standing behind her, wearing a fez and a red jacket, which meant that he was about to call the bingo. No wonder he was suspicious. Plum and Blossom used to be his biggest fans, sitting in the front row with their lamé dresses on and coloured marker pens tumbling from their laps to the floor. It must have been quiet in there over the last couple of weeks without Blossom's excited voice yelling out 'Bisto!' before she jogged up to the stage to collect her winnings. Alison followed Harry to the lounge and spotted Ben, working his way through the *Times* crossword. All around him, chairs were placed in lines facing Harry's bingo wheel. Alison helped to hand out the cards and pens and made sure that residents with good hearing were spaced equally so that they could pass the numbers on to those on either side. Darren wove between them, smiling at all the old ladies, then dashed towards the refectory. Soon, Ben's was the only chair facing the wrong way. He looked up at Alison. 'Any good at these?' he asked, gesturing to the puzzle which was all but completed in neat block capitals. She leaned over, trying to look studious as she read the cryptic clues, hoping for a bolt of inspiration. All she could think of was her false confession to Kenneth. She wanted to run up on stage and shout 'My mother's not dead!' But Harry plugged the microphone into his mini-amplifier and started the show with his rallying whistle of 'Swinging Safari'.

'God help us,' said Ben, springing from his chair and heading for the doorway with Alison in tow. As they reached the bottom of the staircase, Plum emerged from the phone booth and ran to the television room. 'I think I'll go out,' said Ben. 'I'd love to have your company, Alison. I'll treat you to a cup of tea and a bun at the patisserie. What do you say?'

'I can't,' she said, toeing the carpet. 'You know I'm working.'

'Work, work, work. A little bit of rebellion would do you good. You're like an explosion waiting to happen, you are. A big bright thing, like a firework.' He traced the pattern of her ascent and the sparks of her glory through the air with his fingers. She glanced at the lounge door, as if she were asking for its approval. From beyond it came Harry's voice: 'All the fours. Forty-four.'

'I'll have to check with Pat. She's been acting funny all day, so she probably won't let me.'

'Tell her my chest is bad and I have asked you to take me out for a little fresh air. Go on, I'll get my coat and meet you down here.'

'OK.' She ran past the bingo crowd, feeling as if she could turn cartwheels down the corridors. She had been asked on a date. How wonderful to sit across a table from him and gaze out of a café window like a couple in an old movie. Darren bowled into her as she darted through the nursing wing. 'She's gone,' he said.

'Who?' She ran after him to the end of the corridor. Bloody

Beryl the budgie woman, she thought. But Darren ran past Beryl's room. 'Eva,' he said. 'Have you seen her?'

'She was in the hall a while ago. Have you checked the ground floor?' Darren nodded. Together, they went through all the possible places she could have hidden herself. Darren and two of the kitchen staff had been circling the building for twenty minutes, checking every nook and cranny. 'She hasn't taken her medicine,' he said, opening his fist and showing her a couple of half-dissolved tablets. 'I found these in her bin.'

'Don't worry. She couldn't have got far.' Alison knocked on Pat's door and popped her head around it. Pat was rummaging in the bottom drawer of her desk. She sat up straight, looking flustered.

'Pat? Oh, there you are. Look, we've got a tiny problem. Eva appears to have gone for a little walk. She's been spitting her tablets in the bin again.'

Pat ran her hands through her micro-fine hair. 'I told that stupid boy to stay with her until she had swallowed them. Well, go on, you'd better go after her. It'll be getting dark soon. Come back here, both of you, the moment you find her. I'll want a word about this.' Alison and Darren headed back to the lounge, checking behind each door. 'How do I know when she's swallowed her tablets,' he moaned, jogging beside her. 'I'm not going to go checking under her tongue. She's not a bloody dog, you know. She tells me she's swallowed them and I take her word for it.'

'OK, OK.' They reached the hallway. Ben was waiting, wearing his dark felt hat. 'Ready?' he said, reaching out to take her arm.

'Change of plan, I'm afraid.'

They agreed to split up. Darren said he would check the garden and the roads behind Maytime, and Alison and Ben headed for the shopping centre. It was a fine cold day and the air smelt sharp and clean. Ben took long, measured breaths. He was enjoying the adventure of it and kept making her laugh, coming up with Sherlock Holmes deductions. 'Think, Watson,' he said in a strangled, upper-class accent. 'Put yourself for a moment inside Eva's mind.' Alison closed her eyes. 'Hmm, it's a bit muddled in here,' she said, seeing Eva's mind as a room filled with ringing telephones and old friends standing in doorways, peppermint wrappers and sheet music. She opened her eyes again. Ben was gazing down at her. He put his hands on her shoulders and for a moment, she thought he was going to kiss her. 'Anything?' She shook her head. A bus swished past. 'Did she have any money on her?'

'Not much. There's usually a couple of fifty-pence pieces rattling around in the bottom of her handbag. Perhaps we should try the sweetshop?'

'Good idea.'

They raced ahead, swaying to avoid pedestrians and puddles, holding tightly to each other's hands. The newsagent's was filled with schoolchildren stocking up with crisps and chocolate. 'Bingo!' said Alison. 'The lady thinks she came in ten minutes ago for a packet of strong mints.' Ben nodded. Strong mints were Eva's props, that was for sure. 'She can't have gone back to Maytime,' Alison continued, 'or we would have seen her, so she must have gone this way.' A row of shops confronted them.

Alison hoped that the lady in the shop was wrong and that Eva was emerging from an airing cupboard at Maytime, leaving them the rest of the afternoon to wander around the shops after an imaginary senile accordionist. They walked on, swaying into each other. He put his hand on her shoulder. Slowly, she lifted her arm, holding the back of his coat, then pushing in until she found his waist. She had to walk faster to keep up with his long legs, to keep herself pressed into him. 'Ben?'

'Mmm?'

'Did Kenneth come over yesterday?'

'No. I had some other visitors yesterday. He's coming tonight. Will you stay on for him?'

'No. I saw him on Saturday.'

Ben stopped. 'Of course. How was Melanie's party?'

'Fine.' He waited for her to say more. 'I was a bit drunk, actually.'

'I say. Were you? Well, well.'

'I never get drunk usually.'

'Don't look so worried, Alison. I think you should get drunk a little more.'

'What?'

'I'll tell you a secret.' He leaned down so that his lips were close to her ear. 'It's good to make a fool of yourself every so often. Get drunk, dye your hair, have a romance with someone you shouldn't.' He paused. 'So long as you're not hurting anyone.' He moved off, leaving her standing there for a moment with the wind cooling her cheeks. She heard his footsteps scraping to a halt. 'Come on, sport.' He had his hand stretched out to her.

They scoured a couple of fashion boutiques and a record shop, but there was no sign of Eva. They had nearly reached the end of the road when they heard a melody, combed thin by the crowds of shoppers. Following it, they found a music shop. The window was cluttered with drum kits and guitars, but the music pouring from the door was not heavy metal. Blasting out at an incredible volume, Eva stood on a podium, her little body dwarfed by a giant electric accordion. All around her, long-haired young men in leather jackets sat frozen to their guitar stools, watching her fingers as they flew across the keys. Her zip-up sheepskin boots hopped from side to side as Khachaturian's *Sabre Dance* spiralled towards its climax. Ben removed his hat and clamped it to his chest while Alison wandered, wide-mouthed, to the front of the podium. Eva spotted them and winked happily, squeezing the massive bass notes out of the box, hearing them properly for the first time in years.

'Sorry about this,' shouted Alison to the shop assistant, who was sitting on the counter, slapping his lap in time with the music. 'She just wandered off.'

The man shook his head. 'She's bloody brilliant!' A skinny guy plugged a Fender into an amplifier and joined in, shaking his head over the strings and matching her nearly note for note. Another joined in on the drums. It seemed as if the whole shop was bouncing along the road with the force of the sound. People were coming in the door, forming a crowd around Eva and the mighty accordion, jumping and clapping and shouting, 'Go on, Grandma!' Alison felt lifted to the rafters. It was like something out of a movie. Eva and Ben were cool and she was their friend.

When Eva finished, the crowd went wild and shouted for more. She blushed and said, 'Well I never,' and took several bows. The shop assistant leaped up onto the podium and helped her remove the accordion. 'Oh, thank you,' she said as they congratulated her.

'Have you ever played professionally?' asked the guitarist. Eva pushed her earlobe forward in an attempt to catch his words.

Ben answered for her. 'For over forty years. Best in the business.' He clasped Eva's shoulder proudly.

'What you doing Friday?' asked the guitarist. 'We've got a gig in Hanwell.' Eva heard him and shook his hand between hers. She, Ben and Alison strode arm in arm back to Maytime.

'Ben?'

'Yes, sport?' A nickname. A term of endearment. She was dear to him.

'What colour, do you think?' He looked at her. 'I'm thinking of changing my hair.'

'Your hair's lovely as it is,' he said, and he put his hand on her head. He stroked once slowly downwards then rested his fingers on either side of her neck, tickling the nape. What about the affair, then? she wanted to ask. Were you talking about us? Me and you, or did you have somebody else in mind for me? She didn't want to think about Kenneth, so she joined in with the song that Eva had started to sing. 'We're off to see the wizard,' they sang, strolling three abreast on a yellow brick road of their own making.

Of course, the wicked witch was there to greet them. As Eva and Ben were tucking into their evening snack, Alison and Darren were standing in Pat's office. 'You think it's all a joke, don't you?' chimed Pat's shallow voice. 'She could have been wandering along the dual carriageway all that time. Who would have been responsible if she had been knocked down? Not you, no.' She slapped herself on the chest with her fists. 'Me, that's who. I'm the one who has to be accountable for everything around here. I'm the one who has to explain things to their families.' While giving lectures, she had a habit of half-closing her eyes as if the script were written on the inner side of her blue-veined lids. Sometimes she rolled her eyeballs back at the same time, hiding them inside her head. Darren pulled faces at her, stopping whenever her pale grey irises rolled back into place. Alison couldn't stop smiling.

Three days later, Plum and Blossom came down the stairs together carrying a small suitcase each. 'We're off,' they announced. 'Just to see a friend on the south coast, and to do some Christmas shopping.' Darren went into a flat spin, forcing them to write down an address and tell him the exact time they were to return. As they fumbled with scraps of paper and whispered to each other he ran to fetch Pat, desperate for her to know that he was doing his job.

'Why didn't you tell me this before?' She tucked the address into her file.

'You didn't ask, dear,' said Plum.

'Don't get smart with me, you two,' she snapped. 'I can't have you wandering off whenever the mood takes you.' A cab beeped outside.

'Oh, get a life, dear,' said Plum as they pushed past her with their bags. 'We're over twenty-one.'

'Although you'd never know it,' added Blossom with a giggle. Darren waved them off. He was sure he heard Plum say something to Blossom as they climbed in. *Have you got your passport?* He decided he must have heard wrong.

Chapter Sixteen

Alison came home to find Mel and Daichi dancing around the kitchen to some funky jazz. 'We're celebrating!' Mel announced, pouring Alison a glass of pink fizz. Daichi was propped up against the work surface. He had no shirt on again, even though it was freezing cold in the flat.

'What?' She put her bicycle lights on the table.

'My debut as a DJ. I've got a gig.' They formed a triangle and jumped up and down. Alison was so pleased for Mel. Pleased that at least somebody's dreams were coming true. Pleased, strangely enough, that Mel wasn't cheating on Puxley as she had first suspected. 'It's just a house party really, but everybody will be there. Puxley, DJ Rap, Doug from the Sprawl club.'

'Christopher Biggins?'

'Shut up, Ali.' Mel laughed. 'I have the boy wonder here to thank for this.' She leaned over and patted Daichi's bottom. He was chopping vegetables.

'Trevor was looking for names,' he said. 'I just put yours in the hat. Puxley seconded me.'

'Trevor?' Alison sat down very quickly.

'Yeah. You know Trevor. It's at his place.' Alison glazed over. 'Oh come on! It was a year ago. Nobody will remember.' She turned to Daichi. 'Alison got absolutely ratted last time we were there.'

'Yeah?' Alison nodded. Thank goodness Mel didn't know what really happened. Trevor was the man who kissed her. The man she ended up biting like she was Dracula. Alison wanted to see him again, but she was scared of how she had felt that night. Feelings that still weren't that far under the surface.

She got up and went over to the cooker. 'Do you want any help, Daichi?'

'No thanks. Ever tried real Japanese cooking?' He went to the fridge and took out a small Tupperware box. He opened it and pulled out a lean piece of raw beef. With a clean, sharp knife she didn't recognise, he started to cut it into paper-thin slices. He was concentrating fiercely. The slivers of meat were fanned out on a plate, twisted and manipulated with the blade of the knife until they formed the shape of a water-lily flower. A spoonful of marinade from the bottom of the box was drizzled over the top. Alison watched the movement of his shoulder muscles under his goose-pimpled skin. She wondered if he was warm or cool to the touch. That's how it had started with Trevor. All she wanted to do was to see if he tasted the same as he smelt – sweet and buttery. She leaned towards Daichi. He smelt like lemons. Maybe it was the marinade. She lifted the lid of one of the pots. 'Mmm. Smells lovely,' she breathed in the steam. 'What is it?'

'Water,' he said.

She returned to the table, flushed with the heat. 'So when's the big night, Mel?'

'Friday. You can bring Kenneth if you like.'

'Who's Kenneth?' asked Daichi. 'Your boyfriend?' His knife stopped in mid-air.

Alison tried to imagine Kenneth at one of Trevor's parties. 'He's a friend,' she said. 'Mel was just being stupid.' She turned to Mel. 'What are you taking? Some drum and bass?'

'No. "Drum and bass" is tired now. We prefer "breakbeat". It covers everything from hip hop to cold cut, you know?'

Alison didn't, but she nodded anyway. 'I'm supposed to be working,' she said. 'It might be too late to change over.' Alison hated the thought of messing up Pat's rota, but she couldn't ignore the big, wide look in Mel's eyes. If this was an old movie, Mel would be Ruby Keeler, working on her tap routines, learning that the big star had hit a banana skin on her way to the dress rehearsal. Alison longed to see Mel's name in lights. She would even brave Trevor and his cocoa-butter neck. 'I'll change shifts,' she said. 'Promise.'

Daichi came to the table with his meat sculpture. 'Only two sets of chopsticks,' he said. Alison said she preferred a fork, but Mel and Daichi insisted. They stared at it for a long time, nobody wanting to ruin the pattern. Alison slowly stretched out her arm, then lowered the chopsticks. She was imagining the ugly bugs' ball of bacteria that was probably going on down there. At Maytime, undercooked meat was treated like a loaded gun. She managed to skewer a piece, but it fell off just before it reached her mouth.

Daichi reached out and took a piece between two impeccably clean fingers. He stretched it towards Mel. 'It's good,' he said. 'I promise.' Mel tilted her head back and opened her mouth. He folded the sliver onto her tongue. *Body of Christ*, said a voice in Alison's head. That didn't help. Not with raw meat on the plate in front of her.

'Don't be scared,' said Daichi. 'It's very fresh.'

'Yummy.' Mel pulled off another petal. 'Go on.' She gave Alison a challenging stare. Daichi ate some himself, then smiled at her. He had a lovely smile and it made her feel better. She grasped the meat again and lifted it to her chin. It smelt like burnt toffee. Still looking at Daichi, she put it in her mouth. They watched every movement of her jaw.

'It's delicious.' She reached out to take another piece.

'See! You've got to try things, Ali,' said Mel with her mouth full.

'I live dangerously.' She popped another sliver into her mouth, feeling deliciously naughty.

'Yeah, right,' said Mel. 'The only person under sixty in London who puts lights on her bicycle.'

Chapter Seventeen

Strange things were afoot at Maytime. Stranger than usual. Plum and Blossom had returned from their little trip to the coast with an extra suitcase each. Both were wearing palazzo pants suits with velvet scarves draped over their shoulders. When Darren asked if they were new, their response was along the lines of, 'Why, this old thing? I've had it for years'. He reported back to Alison. 'I'm worried,' he said, pulling a handful of biscuits from the elevenses tray. 'It's like they're both turning into that Southern woman from *The Golden Girls*. Shazia reckons they're smuggling drugs.'

Alison laughed. There had to be another explanation.

Darren shadowed them for a couple of days. He thought he had cracked it when they sneaked out together and clacked down the road to the bus stop. He got into his car and followed them, but they only went to the library to pick up a set of Linguaphone language tapes. He ended up with a parking ticket and a lecture on how it is never too late to develop new skills. After that, Alison heard no more, because Darren had a couple of days off and she was on nights.

Thursday was usually Zimmer hockey night, but the others weren't in the mood. Alison was wandering along the top corridor at about eleven when she heard a phone ringing behind Blossom's door. A mobile, chiming out 'Rudolph The Red

Nosed Reindeer'. A freebie from the filming, probably. 'Blossom?' she called, but there was no reply. The phone kept ringing. She checked Plum's room, then returned and gingerly opened Blossom's door. It was ghostly in the moonlight; the night breeze through the open window puffed the nets out and filled the air with Chanel No. 5. She flicked on the light. The mobile phone was nestling in the bedcovers, still trilling out its merry tune. She picked it up and pressed the answer button. 'Hello?'

'Hello sexy!' It was a man's voice. A deep, gravelly cockney, like a henchman from an old British comedy. 'How did it go, then?'

His words were like a bucket of water over Alison's head. She couldn't move her mouth for ages. 'Sorry . . . I'm afraid Blossom's out. Can I take a message?' He hung up.

Alison put the phone down. She felt like a snoop, but she had to find out where they were and what they were doing so late at night. On the bedside table, a porcelain pot had replaced a pink plastic denture jar. In the cupboard next to it were perfumes and powders and an expensive-looking tube of cream. She opened it and sniffed, her head reeling in search of an explanation. What on earth did they want with bust-firming cream?

The wardrobe was stuffed with suits, hats, shoes and handbags. She knew that Plum's room would be the same. There was no way they could have made this much doing a commercial. They could have spent the money for the taxman, or kept part of the payment that was set aside for Maytime, but Scatty would never have allowed it. Alison remembered Shazia's comment about illegal activities. That man on the phone could have been a gangster. She could see Blossom as his moll, handing out whisky at card games, stuffing a cut of the winnings into her cleavage. With her stomach fluttering, Alison went to the open window and gazed out. There was a trellis beneath, leading to the garden. She imagined Plum and Blossom in balaclavas, shinning down the drainpipes when the world thought they were in bed, driving fast cars around London and returning at dawn with swag bags over their shoulders. And what about the foreign phone calls? An international racket? Alison couldn't bear the thought of them being arrested and locked away for the rest of their lives. Shutting the window, she sat down at the dressing table and looked at a photograph of Blossom in her former glory. She reached for the tube of bust-firming cream and unbuttoned her dress. It felt freezing against her flesh as she rubbed it in, deciding to try it on one tiny breast and compare the two later. With her head still muddled, she locked the door and headed downstairs.

Laughter was coming from the staff room. Maizel was sitting with Meena, a part-time care assistant. She had just found her TV remote control in her handbag and they were imagining her husband and daughter searching under the sofa cushions. 'Everything OK?' they asked. Alison nodded.

There was a clinking noise from upstairs. Maizel and Meena didn't notice it. Alison looked into the garden. The wall was bare – no pensioners with ropes. A shudder passed up her spine. She went to the bottom of the staircase and listened. It was silent, not even a radio; then there was a noise so faint it could have been a snore. She had climbed that staircase so many times, but this time it felt longer, like it was stretching and twisting up to a tower. It made her feel faint and fuzzy. She stopped short of Ben's door and leaned forward, pressing her hands against it like the sensor on a stethoscope. It was silent. She could hear only her own breath. Then a gasp. It buzzed against her fingers. She turned the door handle and there was Ben and his eiderdown on the floor, together with his radio and a broken teacup.

He was gasping for breath, his mouth wide and his back arched, limbs searching the air. She took his hands and said, 'It's OK, Ben. It's OK.' His emergency button had fallen between his pillow and the bedside table. She pulled it up by the wire and pressed it.

The wait seemed like for ever. He was like a goldfish on a carpet, flapping and flailing. His eyes were fixed on hers, sharp and blue as she raised him to a sitting position. His inhaler was on the floor by the door. She got it and ran her hands down his sweat-dampened back, saying, 'Easy now, easy now.' For the first time, he smelt like an old man. His age was seeping through the disguise he wore. His bones were sharp under his skin, scraping it down from leather to parchment. As she held the inhaler to his mouth, his lips juddered over his teeth, unable to grasp the blue plastic tube. She breathed for him, willing him to find a breath which could take the medicine in, but the puff of white powder billowed in front of him. He bunched her skirt in his hand. Not like this, she thought. Not in an ugly way.

Maizel ran in with the nebuliser and shouted to Meena to call for Shazia's father and an ambulance. She tried, with Alison, to administer the Ventolin. Again it seeped from the sides of his mouth and he lurched forward, coughing. Maizel tried again and again, comforting all the time. The nebuliser was held to his face, pressing against his fragile skin, the soft air inside whirling and clouding. Maizel's skin and her gold rings were warm against Ben's pale neck. Alison held the fabric he had touched on her skirt.

Air was back in his lungs again, squeezing past his tightened chest. It was the only sound in the building. Maizel's red fingernail pulled the strands of hair back from Ben's face. 'Are you all right, Alison?' she asked. Alison nodded, but shook fat tears from her eyes. 'You did very well, didn't she, Ben?' Ben reached out and held Alison's hand. The dampness of his panic was evaporating. Far away, they could hear the cry of the ambulance.

Ben's fingers tightened again and Alison yelped. This was more than a squeeze of affection. She couldn't see him clearly through her tears, but she could hear his breathing getting shallow again. The ambulance was right outside.

'Take him,' said Maizel. Alison wrestled her hand free and held the nebuliser, seeing his blue lips within the plastic mask. He fell against her, his free hand slackening in her lap. Maizel ran out of the door, leaving them entwined. 'Oh, Ben, please,' she whispered. 'Don't.' Who cared what she said now? There was nobody to hear it but Ben. Maizel appeared again at the top of the staircase, accompanied by the paramedics. They were running. They would be in the door any second. She couldn't hear his breathing at all. 'I love you, Ben,' she said, feeling his damp forehead against her neck. Two men were there, holding him, trying to revive him, and Alison was pushed down to the bottom of the bed.

They didn't take Ben with them. Death had left him small, blue and bruised, not handsome and debonair. He was like a big, scary spider that shrivels to the size of a cuff button. Alison pulled a chair up next to his bed and sat down. She wanted to imprint him on her memory, knowing it was her last chance. She found a comb in his bedside drawer and pulled it slowly through his hair, smoothing out the static with her hand. Leaning right over his face, she examined it closely, running her finger along the straight bridge of his nose. There was no way she could have got this close to him before without frightening the life out of him. She wished she could frighten it into him again. She kissed his forehead and his cheek, then buttoned and tidied his pyjamas, arranging the collar just as he liked it. She took his hand and held it between hers for a while. It was warm still, cooling only slightly at the fingertips. His bedclothes were tangled under his knees and it took quite an effort to free them without disturbing his body, but she managed. She didn't cover his face with them. Somebody else would do that later. She turned them down across his chest, then opened them on the side nearest to her.

A car drove past Ben's window, heading for the staff car park. Alison watched its lights slipping over the curtain. She got up and put the chair back. 'Well,' she said. 'Guess this is it.' It was impossible to resist touching him for one last time. She sat on the side of his bed, in the little envelope opening she had made when she turned his sheet back. Slowly, she leaned over until their faces were a millimetre apart. She found herself twisting around and lifting her legs to one side. Just for a few seconds, she thought. Just to know what it's like. She pressed the front of one shoe against the heel of another, working it over her ankle. Before it dropped she heard a noise from the end of the corridor and sat bolt upright. Ben's arm turned on the bedcover with the shifting weight. All at once, Alison felt colder than Ben was ever going to be.

Maizel walked towards her with Shazia's dad in tow. 'Come on, Alison,' she said, taking her arm. She had to pull before Alison moved. Downstairs, Meena made tea and they sat while she fetched the cups from the kitchen. 'He had a long life,' said Maizel, 'and a good one.' Alison sandwiched her hands between her knees to stop them shaking. She knew what the next lines of the speech would be. A little reminder that working with the elderly means dealing with death. She knew all that, and if it had been Eva or Mr Appanowicz it would have been different. Maizel said nothing, and stroked Alison's hair.

Maizel couldn't really give her the full speech. On her mantelpiece at home, between the photographs of her daughter's graduation and her two grandsons in Nottingham, there was a tiny silver frame. Inside, faint and yellowing, was the face of a six-year-old girl. Her name was Pauline and she had been the only child of a Maytime resident. Little Pauline was as frail as a petal, her hair almost white beneath a heavy woollen tam-o'-shanter. She didn't live long after the photograph was taken. She was drowned in a pond formed by a bomb crater where the other children in their lodgings had swum. Her mother had never got over the shock of seeing her lifeless body being fished out by the ironmonger.

Maizel was often called upon to do a clear-out when somebody died. She was skilled at doing it without distress. The old lady had had no family, so it was all very straightforward. Clothes to Oxfam. Rags to be recycled. Likewise all papers, apart from anything official, which went to Pat. Spectacles to Lydia the district nurse for her Vietnamese charity. Trinkets for the stalls at the annual fête. Sheet music in the piano stool. Bottles for the tombola – same old, same old – except for Pauline's photograph. It went into the bin bag, but came out again. Maizel took it home and bought a frame. When her son's friends asked, 'Who's that white kid?' Maizel said: 'That's Pauline. She's just fine there.'

They heard the front door open, then shut again and waited for the sound of footsteps over the tiles in the hall. Nothing came. Meena peered around the lounge door. Plum and Blossom were clinging guiltily to each other as they removed their shoes. 'Evening,' said Plum at last, slapping two black leather gloves into the palm of one hand and taking Blossom by the other. They shimmered past, silent in their stockings, keeping their eyes forward. 'Ben died,' said Meena, her voice thin against the creaking of the stairs. Plum and Blossom came down again slowly. The sandal straps slipped from Blossom's hands and one spun down in front of her. Her make-up dissolved on the spot, fingertips blackening as they caught the mascara. 'Oh, Ben,' she said. Plum leaned on the banister and pulled a neat packet of tissues from her handbag. She tugged one free and flicked her arm out to the side. She felt the tissue leaving her grasp, but fixed her eyes on the door-glass. Beyond the door, way beyond it, was the dark wing of a stage somewhere. Half hidden by the stage manager's booth, a man in a bright light rose from a piano stool and took his applause. Safe in the darkness, Plum was busy checking her fastenings and making sure that the pound notes she had folded into her shoes were not visible (shared dressing rooms were never safe). The man came towards her and smiled. 'All yours,' he said, gesturing to the stage. As he passed, he put his hand on her shoulder, making sure he caught the gossamer fabric of her costume and not her bare flesh. 'He was a lovely man,' she said.

Alison suddenly remembered Kenneth. Somebody had to

phone him. He would be tucked up in his single bed, unaware that he had missed his chance to say goodbye. It made Alison sad, but glad that she had told Ben she loved him. It was important. She wished she could have said it to her father on the day he died. Perhaps Ben would pass it on.

Chapter Eighteen

She awoke in Custard. It was cold. She had come by minicab at two-thirty in the morning. It had cost her £32.50, and she barely had enough to get back. The car rug she found in the boot was covered in little cocoons, as white as cotton wool. She tried to hold one between her fingers, but it crumbled away. The rug was not warm, but it carried the all-important smell that had brought her there. It was a quarter past six. Alison sensed the royal-blue light of morning. The frost had left a pattern on the windows like tiny lace fans. Aching and thirsty, she climbed onto the front seat and sat behind the wheel. The keys were in the ignition and she reached out and touched them, rubbing their plastic coating between her thumb and forefinger.

As the years went by, she had seen her father less often. Sometimes she forced herself, remembering what he looked like in photographs and projecting the image onto the windscreen. Forgetting the accident would be worse than reliving it. She pulled out the choke and started the engine. It took five attempts, then Custard screamed, demanding to be let out of its prison. Still no ghosts. Alison depressed the clutch and put it into reverse. The garage door was open and there was no sound from the yard outside. The yard that led to a side street, then a main street, then on and on as far as she wanted to go. She released the handbrake. 'Come on.' It was like waiting for a shoe to drop.

Slowly, she eased the clutch up. The car shot back a foot, then stalled. The seat belt jolted against her neck and the moment of the accident returned as bright and brutal as a flash frame from a horror movie.

She opened the door. The cold air pinched her cheeks. Outside, the traffic was already rumbling. Lights were coming on in upper windows, shadows crossing the curtain patterns. She locked the car up, then covered it slowly and gently with the tarpaulin. The way Maizel had covered Ben's body the night before. The way the ambulance men had covered her father. Her chest was hollow, scooped out like a pumpkin. She heaved the garage door shut, her hands shaking. The padlock took ages.

Maizel had sent her home the night before, shortly after the doctor left. It was only one in the morning. The flat was dark and freezing. Mel's bed was empty and Alison sat on it for a while, willing her to appear. In the lounge, she put on the *EastEnders* tape, but managed only the credits, scared that Mel might come in and find her. There was nothing much on the television. Highlights of the snooker. She held the phone receiver to her face for a while and listened to the dialling tone. It was too late to call without waking Granny Anne. Angie might not be there. She was probably out with her friends. Her hundreds of new friends.

Alison lay in bed, wide awake, and thought about Ben. About walking up the hill to Maytime with him with his hand caressing the nape of her neck. Dancing to Billie Holiday, the smell of his jacket. 'Come along, sport,' he had said. She closed her eyes and felt his hands, his fingertips. The man in the black and white photograph with the movie-star looks was caressing her, covering her tiny breasts with the palms of his hands. His breath was warm on her neck. She followed the pattern of his hands with her own, feeling her stomach muscles jump and twang. She folded her arms across herself, sensing him, finding the sequence of his vertebrae. Her mouth opened to kiss him, taste his saliva, feel the gentle scratch of his moustache. She let herself go further than she ever had before, because it was Ben. A gift from his passing spirit, the closest she had been to him. Outside, the gutters were overflowing, sending down heavy drops that hit her broad concrete window sill like overripe tomatoes. Splat, splat, splat, in time with his breathing. She started to lean forward, almost sitting. Splat, splat, splat. They slowed down. Then he gasped. The feel of it went right down into her ear canal, the rasp of his breath. The last sound she had heard him make.

She sat up and pulled her knees to her chest, bunching her nightdress between her legs. Her body was damp and shaking. She couldn't stop the tingling inside her, though it shamed her all of a sudden. The faces on her wall were looking at her. Bette Davis all snooty, Cary Grant hiding embarrassment, Jimmy Stewart easily shocked. Ben was no longer young in her mind as they were. She saw him sitting on the bed with the nebuliser pressed to his face. His pyjama top was unbuttoned and his chest muscles were slack, nipples sagging and fluffy with white hair. His stomach was pleated, hiding his navel, turning his torso into a frowning, baggy-eyed cartoon face. She put her hands to her face and cried, then ran to the bathroom because she couldn't bear the smell of her fingers. She showered, listening to the World Service, making sure the bathroom door was shut and the mirrors were all steamed up. After dressing, she picked up the phone again and dialled Angie's number, finger fumbling on the buttons. She put the receiver down before it started to ring, lifted it again and called a minicab.

After leaving the garage, she wandered around the familiar side streets where she had once ridden a small pink bicycle with training wheels, her dad's hand firmly gripping the back of the saddle. She ended up outside their old house. The people who lived there drove a Renault Clio and had satellite television. The dish was under her old bedroom window. It was a strange feeling, standing there and not being able to take a step forward. Her parents had bought the place before it was finished. They had their picture taken standing by the lounge window, in wellington boots, leaning on a yellow cement mixer. She was in the picture too, just a bump, pushing its way through her mother's jacket. It was the mid-seventies and housing estates were rising out of every part of Croydon. Most of them looked like her parents' house: square and detached with red brick up to the first floor, then pebble-dash above. In those days, everybody longed for a new house with central heating and a fitted kitchen. It would be a long time before people got sentimental about decorative ceilings and tiled fireplaces. Their house had a brick fireplace and an electric fire. It never lost the smell of new carpets, the ceilings were Artexed and the walls were covered in coloured hessian that made your eyes go funny if you looked at it for long. If her mother hadn't sold up, they would still have been living there.

The front door opened and a woman emerged in an angora jumper and black boot-cut trousers. She pulled a child after her, who wore a dress down to her ankles. As they approached the Clio, they flashed Alison a couple of hard stares. They could have been watching her for some time, wondering if she was casing the joint. Alison shuffled down the pavement. 'I used to live here,' she said.

'Oh,' said the woman and started the engine. She didn't smile. As they sped away from her, Alison took one last look back at the house. She had no desire to go inside now. Judging by the new owners, it was bound to be all frilly and mock-Victorian with one of those coal-effect fires they had at Maytime, and a stuck-on ceiling rose.

Alison finally called her mother when she got home. It rang for ages. 'Sorry, darling,' said Angie. 'I was up a ladder. Did you see that programme on the telly the other day? Yer woman with the red hair was showing how to make a Gothic pelmet.' Alison had started to shake and it was making her jaw as tight as a rusty hinge. She couldn't talk, even if she had the chance. 'You find some old writing,' said Angie. 'You know, manuscript. They've loads of it in the library and you take a photocopy and then enlarge it. Then you stick the paper onto the wood and paint it with tea. That makes it look the part.' The DIY class went on for a full fifteen minutes. Every so often, Angie said, 'Are you still there? Hello?' and Alison grunted. When Angie finally finished and said 'So how's you?' Alison needed to go to the loo and had to hang up. She felt better, though, just listening to the familiar voice, suddenly understanding how hard it was to share the grief of losing a lover.

Mel came home from work halfway through *The Simpsons*. 'God!' she shouted. 'Bloody Christmas tape going round and round all day. I tell you, if somebody hadn't shot John Lennon already . . .' She pulled the leg of Alison's jeans. 'Tonight's the night. What am I going to wear?'

'I dunno.'

'Come on. Come and help me choose.' Mel stretched out her hand and attempted to pull Alison from the sofa.

'I'm watching this. I'll come in when it's over.'

'But we've got to leave early to set up the gear.'

'I can't go, Mel. Sorry.'

'I bloody knew it!' Mel paused, studying Alison's red-rimmed eyes. 'Are you sick?' She leaned over the sofa and pressed her palm to Alison's forehead. 'You feel all right.'

'Ben died.'

'Oh, God. Oh, Ali.' Mel's warm hand stroked Alison's hair. 'Oh, poor Kenneth. He really loved his dad, didn't he?'

Chapter Nineteen

Maytime was quiet. The nurses squeaked up the corridors. The bar was covered with teacups. All the food was triangular. Meena had brought home-made samosas. They were placed next to the sandwiches in swirling, geometric patterns. Alison stood at the window, waiting for the mourners to return from the crematorium. She had intended to be with them. She was all prepared in her charcoal dress when Kenneth arrived, his van packed with flowers. She had imagined that it would be just the two of them and a few residents, just the nearest and dearest, but the doorbell kept ringing. People she had never seen before filled the hallway. Glamorous women and musicians in faded black suits. Even Scatty Samuels, propped up on either side by Plum and Blossom in immaculate little dresses by Dolce & Gabbana. Three statuesque women joined Kenneth in the funeral director's limousine. He didn't complain. Cars and taxis packed with dark suits and grey heads started off for the service. Alison went and sat in the television room until they were gone. She felt smaller than ever.

The other staff gave her a wide berth. She offered to help them, but they told her to take it easy. She had been given the day off, so she couldn't insist. Instead she sat by herself, pulling the creases out of her dress, watching a woman on the television showing the presenter how to make a special romantic meal by arranging dried flowers around the rim of the plate. Alison imagined a man somewhere looking at his steak and chips, wondering whether he should eat the pot-pourri.

The cars returned. Pat greeted guests at the door, pressing her cool, pink hand into their black leather gloves. Kenneth found Alison right away. He looked quite distinguished, although his shirt was fresh out of its wrapping and still bore the box-shaped creases. 'Where were you?' he asked, stretching out a hand to hers. 'I saved a seat for you.'

'Sorry, Kenneth. I thought it best that I stayed here and helped out. Funerals are for friends and family.'

'But you are a friend.' He had that childish, lost look on his face again. Alison stepped forward to hug him, but he was pulled away by a group of women. They were from the limousine. Two in their fifties, perhaps a little older, and one in her thirties. Alison waited to be introduced, but gave up and went over to the food. While she and Kenneth had been talking, more people had arrived. They were a familiar bunch. Old pros who always turned up for funerals and open days. She imagined that they planned their social diaries around the obituaries.

Two of them were talking to Darren, taking sandwiches from the plate he was holding. A double act in matching blue safari suits and white loafers, their dentures caked with food. 'Oh, yes, we worked with Ben many a time,' they were saying. Another old man was talking to Harry. Alison recognised him as the comedian that Ben had played 'straight man' to for a while. He had been over to visit a couple of times. In their act, Ben had played a piano teacher. During the lesson, the man pulled all sorts of things from inside the upright piano. A table lamp, a potted palm, a bag of washing. At the end of the act, he opened the back of the piano and out came his 'wife' with a tray of tea. She was played by a contortionist.

Harry spotted Alison and called her over. 'Have you met Ben's girlfriend?' he joked as the comedian held out his hand. There was a moment of discomfort. 'Oh, really?' said the comedian, forcing a smile. Harry put him right and they all laughed, but Alison glowed with embarrassment. A macabre bit of wish-fulfilment if ever there was one. 'Nice grub,' said Harry, winking and tucking two samosas, wrapped in a serviette, into his pocket. Alison helped herself to a cup of tea and a chocolate mini-roll. Before she had time to eat it, she was elbowed aside by one of the women who had been talking to Kenneth. 'Hello, darling,' she said to the comedian, pressing his cheek to her perfumed neck. 'What a sad day.' They all nodded.

'Hello Grace,' said Harry. 'Surprised to see you here.'

'Harry, darling!' She swooped forward to kiss him, sending Alison's tea slopping into the saucer. 'Sorry, dear,' said Grace, turning around. 'Didn't see you there.' She handed Alison a serviette from a stack on the table.

'Thanks,' smiled Alison. Both her hands were full, and for a moment she thought she might have to take the serviette in her teeth. In the end, she dropped the mini-roll she was holding into her handbag. 'Did you work with Ben a lot?'

Grace's eyes filled with tears. 'Oh, heck,' said Harry.

'Not really, dear,' Grace croaked. 'I'm just an old friend.' She dabbed at her eyes with the corner of her silk scarf. 'I promised I wouldn't cry. Now look at me.' Across the room, the younger woman turned her head.

'Is she your daughter?' Alison balled the wet serviette in her fist.

'Yes. We thought we'd come and give the old bugger a send-off. Close the book.' Alison felt she was missing something. Harry and the comedian were wincing like they were defusing a bomb. 'The son's a nice man, isn't he?' Grace continued. 'Not a bit like Ben, though. Must take after the wife.' She looked down at Alison's nodding face. 'Not like our Philippa.' Alison's teacup clattered again. The woman was waiting for her to speak, but, as usual, she was stumped. Harry rescued her by offering Grace a sandwich and reminding her that she once had the best legs in the business. In seconds the little threesome was wandering down memory lane, leaving Alison alone with tea dripping off her elbow.

She looked around the room. In between the residents and the musicians in their faded suits were women she hadn't noticed before. A couple were standing by the hall of fame, staring up at Ben's photograph. That face frozen in time that she had animated so many times, imagining those lips forming the shape of her name. Well, these were the women whose names he may have whispered all that time ago. Women who had been in the right place at the right time and had fallen for those charms. Women who forgot he was married, or perhaps he hadn't told them. One every night, waiting at the base of the bandstand or outside the stage door. Lonely housewives with cigarette smoke wafting from between their red, Joan Crawford lips. Chorus girls in empty dressing rooms, their cleavage dusted with powder and their eyelids sparkling. If she had been around back then – Alison Mahoney, a short, mousy half-orphan with bitten nails – would she have stood a chance?

She sat on the sofa, hugging its arm to her chest. 'Are you all right, luvvie?' said a voice from behind her. A woman was sitting on the other end with a plate on her lap. The third one from the limousine. Her voice was refined cockney, like the dolly-birds in *Carry On* films. Alison nodded. The woman held out her hand. 'I saw you with Kenneth,' she said. 'Are you his young lady?'

'Oh, no. I work here.'

'And you came to the funeral. Well, I think that's marvellous. Quite a comfort. You never know, I may end up here if my husband runs off with the family jewels.' It looked like she was wearing the family jewels. She talked about the nurses who had looked after her mother at the end, how devoted they were. Alison wanted to say that she was more than a care worker. She was the one who sat up with him when his chest was bad and brought him hot drinks in the night. His little girl. Only one person knew that. She searched for him among the huddled faces in the room, but he had gone. She made her excuses to the woman and went over to the window. The florist's van was still there. *Forget Me Not.*

She found Kenneth sitting on Ben's bed, which was stripped down to the grey rubber sheet. His suit had risen up at the shoulders. She sat beside him. Far away, the voices were like geese. 'Are you all right?' he asked.

'Fine. What about you?'

'Half the time I don't know what they're talking about. I was at home when all that was going on. Mother preferred it at home.'

'Did she know about the other women?'

'He always came back. She appreciated that.' He turned to her. 'You aren't disappointed, are you? He was fond of you, Alison.' She went to look into his eyes but found herself focusing on the fingerprints on his glasses, lit from behind by the window.

'Your dad was a charmer,' she said. 'I was charmed.'

Duped would have been a better word. She felt stupid. Ben wasn't the man she'd thought he was, the dashing man who loved his wife and missed her so and never loved anyone else. That wasn't the real Ben. Just someone she had got from a Cary Grant movie. And what about Ben's wife? Were there really cut flowers on top of her piano and rose bushes in the garden? Or was she sad and lonely, wondering every minute where he was and who he was with? Did she play her piano with the passion of a woman who knows the meaning of love, or the bitter taste of jealousy? Did she hit those keys, scratch at the ivory with her fingernails as if it were flesh? Alison wanted to cry, but she was too angry. She sat and swung her feet, watching the scuffed toes of her shoes as they bobbed in and out of her vision.

Kenneth said nothing. A better man than his father in many ways, yet he seemed to vanish, slipping away into the paint on the walls until all that remained was his stiff, new clothes. Alison looked at his Adam's apple, sensing the pain there. 'I know,' she said, cupping his cheek in her palm.

He put his own hand over hers. 'Yes, of course,' he whispered. 'Your parents. I can't imagine.'

She took her hand away, flushing, remembering the big fat lie from Justin's party. 'Oh, God,' she said. She was as bad as Ben. Kenneth's arm curled around her shoulder. 'My mother . . .' She tried to tell him, but couldn't bear for him to hate her. She leaned into his shirt, the buttons sharp against her cheek. She let him hold her and believe that he was helping. Around her, Ben's things were tidy. His books were stacked neatly on the shelves in order of height, his post was tucked into a letter-rack, his pipes lined up. Soon they would be bagged and cleared away to make room for a new resident. Kenneth would take some things back to his flat and the rest would be given away, and that would be the end of Ben, apart from a few records in dusty collections. Fading memories of slow dances.

Kenneth's fingertips skimmed a small area of flesh just short of the capped sleeve of her dress. Round and round they went, one of those gestures that wear thin for the recipient long before the other person realises. She longed to squirm out of his grip and scratch her arm furiously, but she didn't want to have to explain herself. Ben's tobacco pouch was tucked into the top of a tissue box on his bedside table. With Kenneth's arm still round her, she leaned over and picked it up: brown, worn leather fastened with a brass buckle. She undid it and smoothed the pleated strap between her fingers. A handful of tobacco nestled inside.

'I told him,' said Kenneth, 'time and time again. That that stuff would be the death of him.' He tried to take the pouch away from her, but she held it tightly.

'It gave him pleasure.' She pressed it to her face, her anger dissolving. The nut-brown shreds bore Ben's rich smell, his bitter aftertaste. She breathed in and her insides lifted, then plunged down as if they were in a car going over a humpback bridge. Deeper and deeper she inhaled, willing herself into the fantasy world she had created for herself and Ben. His arm tightened around her, and she found herself pulling him to her. Her fingers searched Kenneth's coarse hair for a patch of silver softness.

They kissed, tears wet on their cheeks. His stiff shirt collar crackled as she opened it. She thrilled at the buzz of his fingertips, the softness of his lips on her shoulder. Ben's old pearl cuff links traced a line along her thighs like cool liquid. She locked her arms around his neck, holding the tobacco to her face, breathing it in like anaesthetic. She was throbbing inside, wanting to feel the passion that the women downstairs had felt for him. She knew she was capable of it. He seemed to lose interest. 'Go on,' she said impatiently. 'Please. It's OK.' He tugged at the waistband of her tights. Her eyes were squeezed shut so tightly that she saw fireworks.

Movies had been no preparation. Their bodies didn't just slide over each other softly like lotion being rubbed into hands. They stuck, then skidded. Her feet kicked out at the commode chair at the base of the bed as his cold nose tickled her neck. Her bra snapped back as he moved his hand away from her breasts. The tobacco pouch jiggled, sending its contents raining down on her face. Alison arched her head back and laughed, searching out its perfume in the air.

'Nearly there.' A whisper in her ear. The tobacco pouch was empty and she was aware of the unfamiliar scent of Kenneth, the scent that came from deep within him. It was like prawn-flavoured crisps. He pushed into her. Intense pain split her apart. 'No!' she cried, tears running into her ears, but he didn't stop. Suddenly she felt out of control. She shoved against his shoulders. 'Sorry.' The sounds of the building returned. The clanking of the bed; the voices in the room below them. 'Please, Kenneth.'

'Right you are.' He pulled away from her. She felt the bed shudder and looked up at the ceiling, brushing strands of tobacco from her face. Ben was far away, sitting on his tree branch with Vera and a few others. Kenneth was motionless beside her.

Alison sat up so quickly it made her dizzy. She put a hand down to steady herself, but it slipped on something wet and she flew backwards, landing on Kenneth's hip. His buttocks seemed to go on for ever, a marshmallow mountain looming over a grey, rubber river. She peeled herself off him, shuddering, and wiped her hand on the pillowcase. She dressed as quickly as possible. Her clothing was unfamiliar. Her tights snagged against her sticky legs. She stepped into her dress, then sat again, straining to pull up the plastic zip. She couldn't bear to look at Kenneth, all blotchy and squashed against the wall. She didn't know what to say to him. She didn't know him well enough. There was a farting noise as he shuffled himself over the sheet to help her. His clammy fingers traced the line of her spine up to the ends of her hair. 'Thanks,' she said, pushing her feet into her shoes.

'No. Thank *you*.' She turned. He looked even more naked without his glasses. Two red patches either side of his nose marked where they had been. He must have been taught that as a child, how to say thank you and smile and look the person straight in the eye, because even if you have been given something you already have or didn't want in the first place, it's not important. What matters is that the person cared enough to give it to you.

She shut the door behind her and headed for the stairs. The hallway was full of people putting on their hats and coats. George Jakobi had appeared and was holding court by the door of the lounge. Alison gripped the banister, feeling unsteady, keeping her eyes on the stair carpet. She was convinced that they knew what she had been doing. Her shoes were on the right feet and her hair was tidy, but it didn't make any difference. As she opened the front door, she remembered a girl in her year at school who had started her period one day and nobody told her. They just let her walk around the corridors, smiling at everyone, unaware that the back of her summer dress was drenched in bright scarlet blood.

*　　*　　*

Alison had a bath as soon as she got home, soaking away the heat of the packed bus and the sweat that had dried all over her, clinging to every hair on her head. She felt calm and spacey. The water was warm and the flat was empty and her mind was free from everything apart from a thousand bubbles which reflected, in shades of green and lilac, the light through the window frame. A few strands of tobacco swished around the plug hole as the water drained away. She padded into the bedroom, still wrapped in a towel, and searched for her comb. Sitting on the edge of her bed, she opened the little black handbag she had borrowed from Mel. She stared into it, motionless, her hair dripping over her lap.

Just when she thought she'd had the worst day possible. Finding out about Ben. Losing her virginity to a florist from Lewisham on a rubber sheet in the middle of a funeral. After all that, there was yet one more bitter lesson for her to learn.

Never leave a mini-roll in a handbag.

Chapter Twenty

She woke as the blue light of dawn was sitting so low behind the houses it was barely visible. Noises were coming from the direction of the kitchen. Cooking noises, clanging saucepans and the tingle-tingle-tingle of tea being stirred. Frowning with tiredness, Alison reached for her alarm clock. Five-fifteen. Mel must have been out with Puxley, celebrating Friday's success. The deep vibration of a male voice from the kitchen confirmed it. She heard Mel's laughter and turned over, tucking the duvet around her neck. If Mel was all alone, she would have wandered out and had a cup of tea with her, maybe told her about the funeral. She had waited up for her, stirring at every noise, hoping it would be the key in the latch.

When she woke again, the house was quiet. She paused by the door of Mel's bedroom. All she could hear was her own heartbeat. The kitchen was a mess. The worktop was smeared with grease and a line of milk trailed from the sink to the fridge door. Alison opened it and found a saucepan half-filled with solidified mashed potato. There were stalactites of brown fat dangling from the metal rack of the grill pan into the tray. Alison hurled it into the sink. 'Bloody Mel,' she shouted, near to tears.

'You rang?' said a deep Lurch impersonation behind her. Mel's eyes were watery and underlined with last night's mascara.

Alison picked up the chilly saucepan and waved its contents

under Mel's nose. 'It's like cement, that is. Couldn't you have put it in the sink and run some water over it?'

'I didn't want to waste it.'

'You should have put it in a bowl with cling film over the top.'

'I was tried. I'm sorry. No, I'm not sorry, actually. I can leave potato in the fridge if I want. It's my fridge.' Alison turned on the hot tap and squirted the grill pan with washing-up liquid. Mel pushed her out of the way. 'I was going to do it anyway, once I'd had a couple of hours' sleep.'

'You're always *going* to do things.'

'Oh, shut up, Ali.'

Alison sat down hard on the chrome-framed chair. Her body shook awake and a bruising pain started as if she had been sandpapered inside. Wriggling only made it worse, so she drummed the fingers of both hands on the table top. She could hear the rasp of the scrubbing brush over the wire tray. Alison's bottom lip turned down at the sides. Mel put the grill pan on the draining board and Alison watched the lacy suds sliding over it and gathering underneath. She tucked her chin into her neck to stop herself crying, but when Mel turned around and said, 'Satisfied?' the floodgates opened.

Later, Mel and Alison were huddled over the table. 'It's never how you think it will be the first time,' Mel said softly. 'I woke up in a field once, by the side of the M25, and the guy had just buggered off and left me there. At least it was someone you knew.'

'Hardly.' It was impossible to explain what had come over her in Ben's room. It was as if this whole other person had emerged from inside her. This angry, passionate woman. She worried that it was the start of something, that from now on she would regularly find strange men in baggy corduroys and seduce them in furniture showrooms or Photo Me booths.

'Morning,' said a voice from the landing.

'Piss off, will you, Puxley?' said Mel.

'Can I have a cup of tea first?' He wandered over to the kettle and flicked it on. 'Shouldn't you be at work, Mel?'

'I told them I had the runs.'

'Everything all right?' He patted Alison on the shoulder.

'Fine, babe,' said Mel. Puxley shrugged and headed for the front door, leaving the kettle to click off.

'Far from fine,' said Alison coldly.

'Hey, come on. You must have wanted it, Ali. Just a little bit?'

Alison sniffed. 'Do you remember that dishcloth that smelt so horrible we couldn't stop smelling it?'

'Yeah.' They laughed, then Mel said: 'So?'

'It was like that, kind of.'

'Right!' nodded Mel, but she looked confused. 'Poor Kenneth.'

'I'm not saying he smelt like . . .'

'No. Of course not.'

Alison shifted in her seat. 'Was it like that for you the first time? Like, thinking it was horrid, but not being able to stop yourself?'

Mel saw the bleached, blank look on Alison's face. 'Don't worry, mate. It'll be different next time. I promise.'

'If there ever is a next time.'

'Now you're really being silly.'

By eleven-thirty they were down a couple of packets of biscuits and were sprawled out on the sofa watching *Pingu*. Alison was lulled by the *plap-plap* of his little plasticine feet over miles and miles of sparkling winter landscape. She was wrung out, and didn't want to think about anything apart from sliding on her belly towards Pingu's little igloo.

The doorbell rang. 'Who's that?' said Alison.

'Dunno.' Mel got up. 'You stay there.'

Alison stared at the half-open lounge door. A huge bunch of cellophane-wrapped flowers squeaked their way through. 'Oh, God,' she said. Mel plonked them in her lap. They were all vivid blues and pinks, with fuzzy little fronds of peppermint green peeking through here and there.

'Well?' Mel kneeled down beside her and tugged the small envelope from its holder. 'Who are they from, as if I didn't know?' She waved the envelope under Alison's nose. Alison stared at the blue Paisley paper they were wrapped in, then took the envelope and opened it slowly. But there was nothing. It was empty. Mel leaned over and searched between the stems in case the card had fallen out, but Alison knew it wasn't there. She took them to the kitchen and found a vase. She could see Kenneth in his florist's shop, his fingers shaking over the card, looking at a list of all the things he could put on it but realising that none of them were right. He couldn't say thank you or sorry, and certainly not I love you. There were no roses in the arrangement. Nothing that could be misconstrued.

When she returned to the lounge, Mel was imitating Pingu's little trumpety way of speaking. Alison put the flowers on the coffee table. 'Well?' said Mel, her mouth still forming a little O. 'What are you going to do about lover boy?'

'What do you mean?'

'Well, he thinks he's on to something, doesn't he?'

'Not necessarily.' But Mel was wearing her 'oh, come off it' expression. Alison lay back against the arm of the sofa, her stomach sinking. On the way home from the funeral, she had sworn she would never see Kenneth again. She would blot him out of her mind so that one day she might not even be able to recall the colour of his hair. She hadn't considered that he would be feeling anything, that he might be humming romantic songs to himself as he was delivering his arrangements.

'Call him.' Mel held the phone out to her. 'Go on!' Alison took it and tried to remember the number. It was printed on the back of the van, but all she could recall was the last three letters of the number plate. She called Directory Enquiries. The number they gave her was engaged. Every time she pressed the redial button, Alison felt more stressed. Her ribcage seemed to be caught in a vice. 'Press five,' said Mel, but Alison shook her head. The call-back button would mean her losing control over the situation. She paced up and down with the phone in her hand, listening to the slow beep, beep, beep of the engaged signal. It was the smelly dishcloth all over again. On her fifth redial attempt, she threw the phone on the sofa and grabbed her coat from the banister.

Chapter Twenty-One

The journey to Lewisham took nearly two hours. By the time she got there, the head of steam she had worked up in the lounge was all but gone. She knew she wouldn't be able just to walk in, grab him by the scruff of the neck and tell him to leave her alone. Her approach would have to be a little more low-key. Alison spotted the florist's sign in the distance and stood, taking in the sweet breath of a launderette. It was just as she had imagined it. One of those sixties glass-fronted high-street shops with potted cyclamens lined up outside next to galvanised buckets of early, tight-budded daffodils. She looked through the door trying to see Kenneth in between the Interflora stickers on the glass, but there was a woman behind the counter. She was bent over, writing something in a book. Her hair was long, thick and dark and parted in the middle with such accuracy, the top of her head looked like a huge coffee bean. As Alison went in, the woman looked up and smiled at her. She was the one from the photograph that Kenneth had put in his pocket. 'Hello,' she chirruped, putting down her pen and pressing her palms onto the counter. She had really big teeth. They looked as if they were made of plastic and could be removed and popped into her cardigan pocket. 'Hi,' said Alison. 'I'm looking for Kenneth.'

'Oh, yes, I'll just get him for you.' She turned and pushed a door at the back of the room with her shoulder. 'Ken!' she shouted. 'There's a lady here to see you.' She turned back smiling. 'He'll be out in a minute. Are you the bride?'

'What? Oh, no. Just a friend.'

'That's nice.' The woman gave Alison a curious look, pressing her teeth into a well-worn crease in her lower lip.

'Well, a friend of his father's.'

'Really,' she beamed, stretching the word out like elastic. 'Oh, sorry.' Her smile disappeared and she put a hand up to her mouth. 'You must think I'm awful. Oh, I was ever so sorry to hear about his passing. Ken was very upset.' She composed herself and tilted her head to one side.

Alison looked around the shop. The left-hand side was all flowers, ranging from small bunches of carnations and freesias tied with elastic, to giant glass containers of lilies and long-stemmed roses. On the other side, vases, porcelain pots and dried arrangements were lined up on shelves. 'Alison?' Kenneth made her jump. He was wearing his rubber-soled shoes and was only a few inches away from her.

'Hello there.' She couldn't bring herself to call him Ken. He wasn't a Ken, he was every inch a Kenneth. He looked at her face, then at the flowers, then back at her face again. It was as if he were getting it absolutely straight in his mind that Alison was there in his shop.

He reached out his hand. 'This is a surprise.'

'Well, I thought I'd come and see, um, where you work.' She shook him awkwardly by the wrist.

'Long journey?'

'Not too bad.' Neither of them said anything for a while. Alison watched Kenneth's assistant out of the corner of her eye. She was gripping a teddy bear on a length of wire, stabbing it into the oasis of a blue arrangement. 'Sorry,' said Kenneth, breaking her stare. 'Would you like to come through?'

He led her to the door at the back of the shop. In order to get through, the three of them had to squeeze together in the small space behind the counter. 'Keep an eye on the place, will you,

Jan,' said Kenneth to the woman as he navigated her bosom. She looked around the empty shop. 'I'm sure I'll cope,' she said.

They entered a room filled with small Christmas trees in red buckets. The air was cold and crackled with the smell of pine needles and soil. An open door led out to a small courtyard which was also crammed with little lime-tipped pines. As they made their way over to a high table at the back of the room, Alison felt like a giant striding through a forest.

'Thanks for the flowers, Kenneth. They were lovely.' He remained silent. 'The pink daisies were nice. I've never seen those before.'

Kenneth sat on a stool and tucked his knees under the table. 'It wasn't me,' he said quietly, and Alison felt a sudden rush of blood to her face. 'I mean, it was me, but I didn't do them. I don't cover north London. It's not our area.' He didn't look at her. 'You were very kind to me . . . and to Dad, of course.' He pulled a tray of greenery towards him and studied it for a moment. 'Do you mind?' he asked. 'You see, we've got a wedding later on today and I have to do the buttonholes.' Alison said, 'Sure,' and perched next to him. A ring-marked mug was on the table in front of her. It had the name Janet printed on the side with flowers all around it.

Kenneth picked up a small white rose and snapped the stem off just below the head. He snipped a length of silver wire from a bobbin and pushed the end up into the base of the bud. His hands shook as he did the same with a sprig of heather, then twisted the two wires around each other. 'Could you pass me the sage?' He pointed to an old ice-cream tub. She peered inside and took in the scent of Sunday lunch. Reaching in, her fingers found the velvet softness of the leaves. She passed him two little stems.

'You're very clever,' she said as he peeled off the lower leaves and threaded each of the upper ones with wire that looked as fine as a strand of hair.

'Just a matter of knowing how.' He looked up at her. She smiled at him and pulled her chair closer so that she could see how he bent each of the sage leaves to frame the little white rosebud. The skin on his thumbs was ragged and tiny particles of dirt lurked in the cuts.

'Don't put yourself down, Kenneth. You're very talented. I couldn't do that to save my life.'

'I couldn't do what you do. Wouldn't have the patience. You care for them. You're a caring girl.'

She didn't feel very caring. She pulled her coat around her as Kenneth bound the buttonhole with green tape and speared it with a pearl-headed pin. 'There,' he said, and handed it over to her. She turned it around in her fingers.

'Lovely. Brilliant.' She shivered.

'Sorry, are you cold, Alison?' He got up and shut the door. She looked at the way his trousers bagged over his broad backside. He had missed a belt loop and the corduroy had puckered, showing the light blue elasticated waistband of his underpants. She tried to block the memory of his marshmallow buttocks from her mind.

'Kenneth?' Her throat was dry with nerves.

He turned around suddenly. 'Would you like a cup of something? Sorry, I should have asked you before.'

'No, I'm fine.'

'Are you sure? It's no trouble.' He gestured to a kettle at the end of the table. Alison shook her head. 'Sorry,' he said. 'You were going to ask me something.'

'Yes.' She wished he wasn't smiling. 'Is it a big wedding?' She held the buttonhole up.

'Registry office. They're going to the Caribbean, I think, so this is just for the families.'

'That's nice. My cousin got married in the Caribbean. The pictures were lovely.'

'It wouldn't suit me.' He pointed to his red hair. 'Too hot . . . Not that I'm thinking of getting married. Not yet, anyway.' He stared at her for a while, then said: 'Look, Alison . . .'

'What happened at the funeral, Kenneth. It was all a bit, um
. . . I'm not usually like that.'

'Oh, I know that. Neither am I.' They fell silent. 'Alison,' he
said in a half-strangled voice. 'I don't know if you were wanting
to, you know, go out some time. I'd like to. If that's what you
want.'

'Yes. That would be nice, but I'm a bit busy at the moment.
I'm working the next five days. Well, I'm probably going to work
right over Christmas, actually, and you must be so busy, what
with all these trees. Rushed off your feet.'

'It is very busy, yes.' He was fiddling around with another
buttonhole, but it didn't seem to be going as smoothly as the
first. 'But I'll make time. How about Wednesday? Are you on
days or nights?'

Alison thought fast. Kenneth worked days. 'Nights,' she said.

'Good. It's half-day here. I can catch up in the evening.'

'Right then. Wednesday it is.'

They passed through to the shop. The warmth was very
welcome. Janet was placing twelve long-stemmed red roses in a
box and tidying up the red ribbon rosette. 'You were in there a
while. Everything all right?' Those teeth again.

'Just talking,' said Kenneth quickly. 'We were just talking.'

'About your dad?' Janet's nose wrinkled up.

They nodded. 'Bye then,' said Kenneth. He reached out and
shook her hand. His was sticky with sap and scented with sage.
Janet made a cooing sound and returned to her roses as Alison
went out of the door. She ran all the way to the station.

Chapter Twenty-Two

The boxes marked XMAS huddled under the rim of the stage. The Maytime tree stood tall and naked in a bucket of sand, too big for a suburban living room. Pat had given Darren the job of dressing it. It took him all morning to untangle the lights and lay them out in tracks across the stage, tweaking one bulb at a time. He had a captive audience in the chairs below, who nodded and woke to view the progress in stages. The tinsel garlands were broken and tarnished. They lolled on the branches like glamorous caterpillars. Midday, Darren went to Woolworths and returned with several packets of silver threads and draped them extravagantly until just the green tips of the branches were visible, like hands coming through the slits of a cape. The baubles hid the last of the green and Darren stood back, happy with the effect. Harry said it looked like Liberace.

Alison knocked on the office door and opened it automatically. 'Oh, sorry!' she said as she spotted two men sitting across from Pat, and went to close it again. She recognised one of the men, but was surprised when he leaped to his feet and came over to her. 'Hello darling! How's you?' said George Jakobi, shaking her hand firmly and beaming at her with his capped teeth. 'This is one of our angels, Martin,' he said to the other man who was gaunt and middle-aged with a droopy, greying moustache. 'How are you with difficult old women, dear?' George continued, gripping Alison's hand.

'Oh, all right I suppose.' Her head swam with the smell of George's aftershave. The one with the moustache remained crumpled and expressionless in his chair as she exchanged false grins with Pat. 'That's what I like to hear,' said George. He pointed his two index fingers at her like guns and flicked his wrists in a firing motion, winking at her as she closed the door. In the corridor she clutched her chest, checking that she was unhurt. It was her first day back at work and she was in a bit of a daze.

The difficult old woman in question was June Hartley. Even Shazia knew who she was. Although her name topped the bill on posters along the corridors, most people knew her because she had appeared in *Coronation Street* for a while in the mid-eighties. Not a big role, but memorable for her over-the-top performance. She didn't last long. She was killed off in a factory explosion. The last image of that tragic event was of June's character crawling through a smoke-filled office, the flames lighting her perfectly made-up face while all around her was soot. The papers said that her demise was due to contractual problems, but the Maytime residents reckoned it was because she was never much of a team player. News that she might soon be joining them sent many screaming to their rooms.

Back in the fifties, June Hartley was hot property. *Who's Who in Variety 1956* lists her as 'Top female vocalist. Born June Gibbon, 1930, West Hartlepool. First performance West Hartlepool Empire 1946. First London performance March 1948 Metropolitan Edgware Road.' By the time that listing appeared, she could sell out any venue overnight. A big blonde singing sensation in the uncool British corner of the rock 'n' roll world. She appeared in her own TV series in pearl-embroidered dresses. Her hair was as round and pale as a marshmallow, her body buxom to the point of being matronly. The public loved her. As the younger generation jived and twisted, she was seen descending staircases singing her upbeat numbers, lazily snapping her fingers, or leaning over a stove in a heart-shaped pinafore, conducting the band with a spatula. Off-stage, she was never seen without fur coats and six-inch stilettos. Champagne was delivered to her dressing room every night. She went to glamorous clubs, socialised with all the latest criminals and crowned heads and had her vocal cords insured for a million pounds. June Hartley stories were common currency at Maytime. She was a legendary 'cowbag'. Divorced four times with a string of tuxedoed men forever trailing after her carrying hatboxes and toy dogs. She was a show-business legend.

She never believed that she would be pushed off her perch by a bunch of dim little girls with miniskirts and fringes in their eyes. By the late sixties, show business had done with her. As the saying goes, 'she couldn't get arrested'. After drinking herself out of her own house and home, she drank her way through the homes of her friends. There was a well-publicised suicide attempt in the late seventies. She cut her wrists. (Cynics suggested she should have aimed for her throat: someone may have benefited from the insurance.) Until *Coronation Street* came along, June was in the wilderness. Her resurrection as a minor soap character brought her back to the memory of many who had once been fans.

People like Martin who was now cowering in Pat's office. He was not June's son, as Alison had suspected, but a fan who had offered her a home when she was destitute and who now found himself at his wits' end. The poor man had adored her from childhood, when he had gazed at her swaying black and white image, safe in the arms of his mother. Years later, he had sat on the same sofa looking at the same woman. Not on the telly, but in the chair opposite him. His mother was gone, but her idol had been delivered into his care. Martin did everything for June, sure that one day he would get something in return – a little thanks, an occasional pleasantry. It took eleven years before he finally threw in the towel he had used to absorb the insults and mop up the spilt drinks and the gravy from smashed dinner plates. June Hartley was shunted to the front of the Maytime waiting list more for the sake of Martin's sanity than for anything else.

George, ever the agent, knew that it could be a good move. It had been a few years since Maytime had housed a real star, and stars were good for publicity. Handled carefully, her presence could attract some new funding. A concert could be staged with all proceeds going to the foundation. She must still have some admirers in the business who would be willing to give their services for free, other stars from the years of television light entertainment. He sat and gripped his knees, wondering if June could still hold a tune. George was in no doubt that she would be up on stage again before he could say Jack Parnell, but as for her agreeing to move to Maytime, that was going to be very tricky indeed.

Beside him, Martin sat quietly. Pat's weightless voice floated past him. He struggled to concentrate on what she was saying. It was eleven-fifteen. June would be wondering where he was now. He usually brought her up a pot of coffee at half ten. Sometimes she invited him into her room and they listened to a few of her records. In spite of her temper tantrums, Martin knew that she trusted him and had a sort of grudging affection for him. It wasn't easy for her to trust anyone after the world turned its back on her. He was closer to her than anyone, and yet here he was, betraying her, talking to a smarmy agent and a woman who couldn't sing one note of 'Smiles And Tears' if there was a million quid riding on it. He tried not to think about what would happen if they took her in. At the very best, she would never speak to him again. At the worst . . . He pawed at the flesh under his chin, almost feeling her stiletto heel on his windpipe.

He wanted to tell them that he had changed his mind. The house would be empty without her. He was concerned that she might not find the sandwiches and the note he had put on the kitchen table. A hand touched his shoulder. It was George

Jakobi, motioning towards the door to show him the room which had recently become available. An old bandleader had popped his clogs.

Alison was heading for the nursing wing when she heard the front doorbell. Opening it, she was surprised by the appearance of Scatty Samuels. He had removed his undertaker's outfit and replaced it with a mustard blazer and a pair of white slacks that clung to his legs in the breeze. With his beige loafers peering out from beneath them, he looked like two cigarettes sticking out of a packet. He couldn't have come to see Plum and Blossom: they were off on another of their jaunts. 'Good morning, young lady,' he said, doffing his white golf cap and handing it to her. His hair stood out like a halo. 'Mister Jakobi, please.'

'Oh.' Alison helped him across the threshold. 'He's in a meeting at the moment.' Scatty's hand locked around her arm. His fingers were all bent over to one side with arthritis. She wanted to put her palm over them as she did with the residents, but she stopped herself. He was on business.

'Scatty, my friend!' George's voice came booming down the staircase. 'I'll be with you in just a tick. Now Martin.' He shook the sad-looking man, who was standing two steps above him, by both hands. 'Don't you worry about your June. She'll be queen of the castle, here.' Martin nodded and George vaulted down the rest of the stairs to embrace Scatty Samuels. 'Sorry, darlings,' he gasped as if he had just completed the London Marathon. 'I'm all awry this morning.' He pumped the old man's hand vigorously. 'Let's have a cuppa, Scatty.' He turned to Alison. 'Can you do that for us, darling?'

Alison nodded and the two men headed for Pat's office. With George in his salmon-pink bomber jacket and checked trousers, they would have looked more at home in a Miami condominium. Since his comeback, Scatty seemed to be using George Jakobi as a role model. It would be the Teddy-boy haircut next.

Chapter Twenty-Three

The florist's van wove through streets she didn't know. A tin of sugar-dusted travel sweets rattled in the glove compartment. Mel's words were ringing in her head — her offer to be Alison's bridesmaid when she stood in front of the altar with Kenneth, still unable to tell him that she didn't want to go out with him. She could have told him then, as the van swung onto a three-lane carriageway. Kenneth was silent and the van smelt like rain. But it was the beginning of their afternoon together, and if she told him right away, she would have to sit with him for the next few hours knowing that he was hurting.

He wouldn't tell her where they were going. She hoped it wasn't to a hotel. They went through a big stone gateway. 'A garden centre?' she said, glancing at the sign.

'No, that's next door.' They lolloped over speed ramps, passing a great house on the right-hand side. Alison gazed at it through Kenneth's window. Oblong and plain, its flat roof was patrolled by stone lions pointing like hunting dogs. Beyond it, a large glasshouse rose through the trees. A middle-aged couple were walking their dog. They were in matching anoraks and gripped each other with fat, mitten-covered hands. Kenneth would be like that one day, she thought, but not with her. Not if she could help it. They stopped in a huddle of cars to one side of the car park and Kenneth gestured to a small building hidden by trees. 'The butterfly house,' he said. 'I love to come here. It's a bit out of the way, I know.'

Oh, joy, she thought. 'Lovely,' she said.

They made their way up a gravel path. A chilly wind stung Alison's ears. She clamped her hands over them and stood for a moment blinking sudden, frost-induced tears from her eyes. 'Come on.' Kenneth swam into view. He stood with one arm extended towards her. His fuzz of ginger hair was puffed up by the wind. It looked as if his head was on fire. A new, carefree Kenneth waiting to grasp her and run with her through buttercup meadows. She tucked her hands under her armpits and waddled over. He pulled her up next to him. He was wearing old-fashioned driving gloves with poppers at the wrists.

The ticket booth was in the gift shop. As they entered, the young man behind the counter was playing the *William Tell* overture by flicking his fingers against his Adam's apple. They stepped through a wooden door at the back of the shop and felt the hot, moist air rushing up to greet them in their winter jackets. They were in a tropical forest, verdant and steamy, the treetops tickling the mesh far above their heads. Thin, winter sunlight filtered in through opaque glass. Vines and passion flowers curled over trellises, forming arches. Clumps of trees chattered with flightless birds, and all around them, the butterflies zigzagged.

'They're free,' she said. 'I thought they'd be, you know, in a cage or something.'

'Oh, no, that's the beauty of this place. They're all around you, just like they should be.' He rocked on the soles of his shoes, scanning the bushes for activity. 'Isn't it marvellous?'

As Kenneth lunged into the foliage, Alison stood with her arms wrapped around her, pouring with sweat, scared to move in case they came towards her. She had always hated moths, the way they bumbled blindly at walls. The sound of one approaching was enough to send her windmilling and knocking things from shelves. Now she was stuck in a room with a million of them. They were all around her, like paperbacks tossed in the air. 'Kenneth?' she turned her head slowly so as not to attract attention. She wished she had taken his hand earlier. She needed to hold onto something. Against the deep green of a trimmed hedge, one flapping, beige corduroy trouser leg disappeared from view. It grew slowly darker. Behind her, she heard a dull thumping. The sound ricocheted against the leaf-covered walls. The beating of enormous wings. Alison screamed: 'No!' Her head was filled with giant moths that could pick up humans and carry them off to their lair. She covered her eyes, waiting to feel the brittle legs closing around her waist. The smell of her own perspiration belched out of the collar of her jacket. A little girl passed her by. Her tiny desert boots pounded against the dirt floor. A mitten, dangling from one of her coat sleeves, brushed against Alison's leg. Silence returned.

She crept through a passageway of leaves, biting hard on her lower lip. She prayed that they wouldn't mistake her for a little brown tree stump like the ones that jutted out here and there, supporting mouldering fruit on trays. Around each apple, wings clasped together like hands saying grace. Tiny Southern belles in jewel-coloured crinolines. Kenneth was sitting on a bench by the central pond, his hair darkened by the heat. Ducks splashed and huge carp knotted themselves in the water at his feet. The passion flower above him had been fooled by the artificial climate and proudly displayed a couple of blossoms. Cherry-pink octopuses hanging slack in the air. Kenneth was drinking them in. As she watched him, he slowly stretched out a hand as if to touch one of the flowers, even though they were a good four feet above his head. He was playing a childish game with his mind. Alison smiled. She could remember doing the same thing, pretending that she could circle the moon with her thumb and forefinger. For a moment, she forgot about the butterflies and imagined herself and Kenneth as a couple. Yes, he was dull, but he was kind and she would never have to worry about being cheated on. What's more, there would be no nervousness about kissing on a first date. They had already gone way past that. They could just go on in their own quiet way, with Alison tending to their chubby, tufty-haired children as Kenneth sat at the kitchen table making buttonholes. As she walked over to him, Alison felt as if a weight had been lifted from her shoulders.

'Hi,' she sat down next to him. Although they had the bench to themselves, Kenneth slid along as if he were making room for somebody between them.

'I forgot my butterfly book,' he said. 'With all the names in it. I know some of them by heart, of course, but others I get muddled up.' A green velvet beauty skimmed over them. Kenneth sat forward and squinted up at it. Alison ducked.

'Are any of them poisonous?'

'No. They're harmless. Very rare in nature.' He followed one with his eyes for some time, then said: 'Usually the beautiful things are deadly.'

A child walked past them. An orthodox Jewish boy with beautiful eyes. Behind two soft, brown ringlets, he proudly displayed a black and white butterfly on each earlobe. His little brother ran up to him. 'Gimme one,' he whined. 'Go on.' The older boy slowly raised a finger to his earlobe and waited patiently for the butterfly to climb aboard. He then transferred it to the side of his brother's head. It opened its wings and basked for a moment on the close-cropped hair above the little boy's ear, before flying away. He ran back to his invisible parents. His brother followed, stepping carefully so as not to disturb his one remaining earring.

Alison turned to Kenneth. 'Do you know what they were?'

'They're called Hasidic Jews.'

'I meant the butterflies.'

'Oh. No, I'm afraid I don't.'

'Never mind.' She moved a little closer to him, but he squashed himself back against the arm of the bench.

'I could ask someone,' he said. 'If you want to know. I saw a man a while ago up a ladder. He might work here.'

'Yes. Why else would he be up a ladder?' She choked back a giggle. 'He could be really mad on butterflies, I suppose. Bit extreme, though, coming all the way here with such a big ladder.'

The smile had gone from Kenneth's face. 'You're making fun of me, aren't you?' he said.

'No. I was just being stupid, you know.'

'No. I'm sorry, Alison. I shouldn't have brought you here.'

'It's fine here. It's me. I'm just a little nervous.'

'I didn't know what to do. I should have told you in the shop. You see, I thought it might work.' He was shaking, and two misty patches had started to form on the bottom of the lenses of his glasses. He reached out and touched the back of her hand with his fingertips. 'I already have a . . .'

'You're going out with someone?'

'Well, not going out as such, but.'

'You'd like to?' He nodded. Alison's mouth went dry. 'Anyone I know?'

'Jan.'

'Janet? You mean the one with the . . . the one in the shop? Oh.' Kenneth had chosen that woman over her. Alison was less attractive to him than Bugs Bunny. She wanted to die. The sweat from Kenneth's hand was starting to seep down between her fingers. His prawn cocktail sweat. She pulled her hand away, their chubby children fading in her mind.

'You're upset, aren't you?' He was looking up at the passion flower with less passion than before.

'No, no. I'm glad,' she said, trying not to let her anger show. 'I wanted to break it off with you too. I just didn't know how to tell you. So, you see, everything is fine.'

'Alison!'

'What?'

'Don't be like that.'

'Like what?'

'I feel bad enough as it is.'

'I'm fine! Read my lips!' Something brushed against her face. Something light and ticklish. 'Aaargh!' She jumped from the bench, screaming and pawing at her cheek. It was a tendril of hair that had fallen from her ponytail. People peered at her from between gaps in the shrubbery. A butterfly approached and she batted it away with her hand. 'Alison!' scolded Kenneth. 'It's more scared of you than you are of it.'

'Well it must be bloody petrified, then!' She dropped to the floor and pulled her knees up to her chest. 'Get them off me!' she wailed, covering the back of her head with her hands. Kenneth walked over and tried to lift her up by the waist. She let out an ear-splitting scream, then struck out, knocking him to the ground.

The attendant came down the ladder at speed and ran over to them. 'Madam!' he hissed. 'You'll have to carry this on outside.'

Alison threw her arms around the man's waist. 'Get me out of here,' she stammered. There were tears running down her cheeks and mucus streaming from her nose. 'I thought he was a moth.' She pointed to Kenneth who was sitting on the floor, holding a bloody tissue to his face.

'How are you now?' Kenneth brought a cup of tea to her in the car.

'Just take me home, will you.' She couldn't look at him.

'Right you are.' He started the car but sat still for a while, staring out of the windscreen.

'Disaster,' he said. 'I take advantage of you at a funeral, then I cast you aside. I'm not proud, Alison.'

'Forget about the funeral.'

'I shall never forget it.'

'Whatever.' Great. Now Kenneth thought she was in the habit of dropping her knickers in moments of grief. She blew on her tea. 'I was missing your dad. I loved him.' She paused. 'I mean, I was in love with him.' Kenneth turned the engine off. 'It's OK. We didn't do anything. You were the first, in case you hadn't noticed.' She gave him a cold stare. 'I just loved him. And he loved you and your mum and, well, God knows who else.'

'Carrying out his dying wishes, were you?'

'Of course not!' She opened the door. 'I'm getting a bus.'

'No! I'm sorry. I'll take you.' They moved off. Kenneth looked exhausted. Alison imagined the two of them in twenty years time. One of those silent couples at Berni steakhouses, sitting on a banquette, pushing peas around their plates, waiting for the waiter to break their silence. She thought about Ben and all his stories and wondered what he would have made of this.

'Goodbye, Alison,' he said as they got to the station. 'Take care of yourself.'

'You too. Good luck with Jan. She's nice.'

'Should I tell her about this, do you think?'

'No. Let her think she's your one and only.' She slammed the door and watched the knotted blue flower disappear. *Weddings. Funerals. Special Occasions.*

Chapter Twenty-Four

There wasn't half the fuss when the Duchess of Kent came on a visit. George Jakobi was pacing about two hours before June Hartley was due to arrive. Ben's old room was prepared with an enormous basket of flowers from The Smoult Foundation. A photographer was standing by. 'Ladies and gentlemen, girls and boys,' said George from the stage. 'As you may know, we have a new arrival today. The lovely and talented June Hartley.' There was a murmur from the crowd. 'Hip-hip!' said Harry flatly. There was no hooray.

'Oh, come along!' said George, radiant in a lemon V-necked Pringle. 'She's an elderly lady, not a fire-breathing dragon.'

'Wanna bet!' said Harry. The others nodded. George shook his head at them and sat on the front of the stage.

'Friends,' he said. 'Remember how you felt when you first arrived here? A little scared, a little unsure of yourself. Knowing that everybody knew everybody.' The residents nodded like schoolchildren. 'Well, that's how she is right now. It's been a long way down for her, remember that. It's up to you lot now to help her.'

A car horn sounded from outside. Alison went to the door and saw a blue Volvo estate, packed to the roof with boxes. In the front seat, a woman in a lime-green hat leaned over the man in the driver's seat and sounded the horn again. George scrambled past Alison and out onto the driveway, opening his arms in greeting. By the time he reached the passenger door, there was quite a crowd on the front step and Martin the fan had emerged from the driver's side, looking even greyer than before. The passenger door was opened. A hand reached out and took George's. A spiky shoe swung onto the gravel and out she came. Her ankles were puffy, her body was large, but she moved elegantly. 'Heaven help us,' said Plum as June shimmered towards them. Her hand held George's high as if they were about to break into a minuet. Behind her, Martin struggled with two bulging suitcases. 'Hello, everyone. Hello,' she said as she crossed the threshold. The photographer called her name and she posed halfway up the stairs. June's smile was pure Hollywood. A practised, even showing of the teeth combined with a raising of the eyebrows to hide the laughter lines.

Everyone helped with June's boxes. There were some beautiful things, including a heavy, gilded dressing table with five mirrors. Alison and Darren carried it up the stairs, but received no thanks as they eased it into place by the window. Alison couldn't bear to turn her head in the direction of the bed. She was scared that past events would appear in a series of bright flashes. Her and the dead body. Her and the all too alive one. Instead, she looked at Ben's replacement. June was like Gloria Swanson in *Sunset Boulevard*, ordering people about in that magnificent way only big stars are allowed. 'Put that there! Careful! It cost more than you earn in a year!' She even had Darren tugging his forelock. Ben's room was transformed into a boudoir. The striped curtains were now floral. Books were replaced by porcelain shepherdesses. Alison was glad. It made things easier. When June yelled, 'Will someone tell that shit Martin to bring my records,' she was the first to volunteer.

Later, sitting in her room alone, June took in the beige of the walls. They had been washed. In the light from the window she saw the swirling sponge marks and a thin film of sugar soap. All around were little white polka dots of Polyfilla covering the marks of Rawlplugs; evidence of somebody else's pictures. The room smelt of air freshener. As there was no smoking allowed in the bedrooms, she suspected that something else was being hidden. The bed was newly made up with crisp sheets and a Laura Ashley eiderdown, but the frame was chipped, and when she sat on it, there was a plastic-coated crackling from the mattress. She got up and sat in the armchair, panic rising inside her. How could she sleep in that bed? It must have been used again and again. The sweat of other people had soaked through it. She would have to sleep in the chair or let her standards drop yet again. At least Martin had brought her a new mattress. He had used his mother's bed. It's different if it's someone you know.

George knocked on her door. 'June, darling,' he gushed. 'I will have to be off in a mo. I was wondering if you would like to join me for a little glass of shampoo and a mince pie in the bar. I've had it opened up specially so that you can get to know the gang.'

June said that she would be down in two shakes of a lamb's tail. Slowly, she moved over to the dressing table and sat down. Snapping open a large leather vanity case, she reached for her lipstick and the gold powder compact given to her by Frank Sinatra's agent. Lifting her strawberry-blonde hair with a long-tailed comb, she turned and checked herself from all five angles, tapping her double chins with the backs of her fingers.

For the first time in years, she thought about her own mother. She had learned everything she knew from her. How to dress, how to walk, how to despise her father. He was a postman, always telling her she had 'champagne tastes on a beer income'. June's mother made it her life's work to ensure that her daughter had a champagne income.

She had been a typical stage mother. Smothering, domineering. Grown men would run when they saw her standing in the wings with a fox's head on one shoulder and its arse on the other. She didn't care what people thought; she knew that her daughter was talented. They had lived on sardines in order to pay for tap shoes and satin pants. She entered June for contests, cleaned houses to finance French lessons, and never let her out of the house unless she was dolled up like Shirley Temple. Needless to say, June was not the most popular girl in school. She had come home most days with spit on her shoes and ink on her ringlets, but her mother was there with a hanky to wipe her tears and a strong arm to drag her to singing lessons. She told June that all the other children in Hartlepool had head lice and ringworm and wouldn't amount to much.

By the time she was twenty-five, June was a star and she hated her mother more than Hitler. There was no getting away from her. When June came off stage, she was sitting in the dressing room. When she came home, she was halfway down the stairs in her hairnet and curlers. By then, she had left her father and was sharing June's rented apartment in Belsize Park. June went to great lengths to get rid of her. She brought home unsuitable men, stayed at hotels, then announced her engagement to an East End boxer. Marriage was a desperate measure, but it worked. With the money she made from her first album, she bought her mother a lovely little house in Hartlepool. She was finally shot of her.

What she had instead was a mess. Four husbands and a string of affairs with nice, clean chorus boys. She had two abortions. Success was all she knew. She wasn't brave enough to give it up and become like her mother. Sitting in Maytime, she wished that she did have children. Even if they hated her, she would never have ended up in a place like this.

Her mother had had a stroke during the *Coronation Street* years. The day June delivered her to the old people's home, she couldn't wait to get out of the door. It was a lovely place — very refined, but in spite of her 'champagne tastes', her mother was still a postman's wife. She had looked so defeated, sitting on the side of the bed with her handbag on her lap and one side of her face like a landslide. June had wanted to put her arms around her, but she knew that if she did, bang would go her own life. She had run out of the place with tears streaming down her face. June Hartley had been shocked to find out, so late in life, that she had loved her mother every bit as much as she'd hated her.

Now it was her turn to be dumped. George Jakobi had given her a look that spoke of adrenaline. Fight or flight. Three guesses which he would choose. He and Martin would gulp down a mouthful of cheap champagne and they'd be out of that door like two greased pigs, leaving her in this godawful place with more bad turns than the Monaco hills. She looked at herself in the mirror and felt like a five-year-old lost in Woolworths. Still holding her comb, she cried loud, ugly tears.

George had asked Alison to pop up and chivvy her along before Martin lost his nerve and sped off in the Volvo. She paused outside the door, straightening her uniform. June Hartley was the biggest star Alison had ever met. June had been to Hollywood, shared a stage with Sammy Davis Jr., topped the bill at a Royal Variety Performance. Alison wanted to hear all about it. She knocked softly on the door and waited for an answer. None came, so she pushed the door open a crack and peered in. Standing there with her heart in her mouth, Alison heard the big star cry. June didn't seem so scary all of a sudden. She was all wind-blown, shuddering into the powdery sprinkles on her dressing-table top.

'June?' she said as softly as she could, taking pigeon steps over the carpet. 'Are you all right?' There was no reaction from the direction of the dressing table. Alison came closer, trying to see the reflected face. She stood there for what seemed like an age, searching for something to say. 'June,' she said again, reaching out a hand and laying it on the padded shoulder.

The crying stopped and for a moment, June was silent. A pair of watery grey eyes flicked forward to the mirror and focused.

Alison smiled. June's hands dropped to the table top and she spun around. 'How dare you!' she bellowed so loudly that Alison shot back. 'Did I say you could call me June? Did I? It's Miss Hartley to you, young lady, and what do you mean, barging into my room like this? Don't I have the right to privacy here?'

'Sorry,' stuttered Alison. 'I was just wondering if you were all right. I did knock, honestly.'

'I don't believe that!' June rose from the chair and stood like a giant billowing curtain, so bright it made Alison squint. 'You just wanted to gawp at me, didn't you? Well, here I am!' She gestured to her tear-stained face. 'Satisfied? Now piss off!'

Alison backed out rapidly. She realised that she hadn't delivered George's message, but she was too afraid to knock again. Plum was standing at Blossom's door, knocking twice, then twice again. She looked around furtively. 'What on earth?' Alison's crumpled face passed her by. She ran over and put her arms around her.

'I'm just being stupid, that's all.'

'You're not stupid.'

Alison told her about June. 'She's a cow,' said Plum, pulling her into Blossom's room. 'She had me fired once.'

'Who?' asked Blossom as they went in. She was cleaning the keys of a manual typewriter with a ball of Blu-Tack. She was wearing a satin dressing gown and her old glasses. Plum told her what had happened and she left her desk and fetched a tissue. 'You saw her crying, did you?' she asked, gently pulling strands of hair back from Alison's face. 'That's one up on her.'

'I don't want to have one up on her. She looked so sad.'

'I know, love,' said Plum. 'You're a nice girl and you're right. We were talking in the bar the other day and we couldn't find one person who had a good word to say about her. Imagine being like that? At least we've got our friends.'

'She's scared,' added Blossom. 'She's burned all her bridges. All she's ever done is work, drink and take men from their wives.'

'That's all we do, dear,' said Plum. Alison laughed. 'That's right. Put a smile on your face. You've got to stand up for yourself, Alison. The trick with the June Hartleys of this world is to give them a bloody good mouthful. You'll only need to do it once.' She took Alison's hands between her own. 'Will you do that for us, darling?'

'What? Now?'

Plum shook her head. 'We won't always be here to stand up for you.'

'Don't say that.'

Blossom sat the other side of her. 'Don't worry,' she said. 'We're not going to die, dear. We're moving out.'

'What?'

'Boxing Day. Scatty sorted it . . . Oh, dear, we've started her off again.'

It was as if the whole cast of *EastEnders* was to be written off in a plane crash. First Ben, now Plum and Blossom. Without them, June might end up running the place. It would be more like *Dynasty* with her at the helm. Alison thought of all the people who had left *EastEnders*. All her favourites. Most of them had never been heard of again. They were probably on their beam ends now, huddled in bedsits watching their old colleagues on TV still earning a good living.

'We've found a flat in Brighton,' said Blossom. 'We're buying it, not renting it. It's got two double bedrooms and a lovely big lounge and a kitchen so we can cook exactly what we like *and . . .*' she stressed the word with a flick of her wrist, '. . . we can have some little friends round if we want.' Alison had a vision of the two of them in an ornate Wendy house like the one that was built for the Queen and Princess Margaret, with a miniature tea set and little hearts carved in the window shutters.

'I love Brighton, don't you?' added Plum. 'All those young people. Not like the other seaside towns. God's waiting rooms. We've had enough of that here.'

'But how will you afford it? Brighton's not cheap, you know, and mortgages go on for years.'

Plum shuffled forward. 'We signed a contract. Three new adverts. Remember when we went into town? It was the night dear Ben . . . you know . . . Well, we had a meeting at the Ivy with our men from Germany. They pay silly money these days. It will keep us going for a good ten years if we're careful. Scatty was very firm with us. "No more fripperies," he said. "It's about time you learned some horse sense." He's too kind-hearted to be an agent. No wonder he hasn't worked for years.'

'He found us a financial adviser,' said Plum. 'Bill. A widower.' She drifted off for a minute, breaking into a melon-slice smile. Alison guessed it wasn't the money she was thinking of. 'Where was I? Oh, yes. Everything we earn can go in the bank, and when it runs out we can sell the flat and move back.'

'But what if something happened?' What if this Bill was a conman?

'You worry too much, Alison. There are old ladies in Afghanistan living in rubble. It's on the news.' Plum smiled a pitying smile at Alison. A smile that hoped that one day she would understand. She and Blossom had been at Maytime longer than they had been anywhere else, since they left their homes as starry-eyed teenagers. Living there was like being stuck on the same bill for ever. Even if it was at the London Palladium, closing the first half for Judy Garland or doing a double with Gypsy Rose Lee in the second, it was bound to lose something along the way, some of that first-night thrill. It was unnatural just to sit there with nothing to look forward to except puréed food.

All pros had found themselves on stage at one time or another, finishing up their act, as the agent that booked them scarpered out of the back door with the earnings. It was never the end of the world. They'd cadge some money off the resident comedian (never musicians. Tight as cats' arses, the lot of them), or spend a pleasant night with someone in the audience. There was always a way out. Alison didn't understand. Why should she? She wasn't born to it. She would probably be as happy as

Larry with a husband and a couple of kiddies. Plum shuddered. The thought of it gave her the heebie-jeebies. Always had. Blossom was more of a candidate. She would have married one of those men who order your food for you in restaurants. She would have called him Daddy and come out of shop changing rooms asking, 'Do I like this?' She would probably be a widow now in a bungalow with a rockery and a framed oil painting of a King Charles Spaniel on the lounge wall because she couldn't have children. They were both better off as they were. No strings, no stretch marks and a damn fine pair of pins on both of them.

Blossom parted her gown below her waist and swung round to reach a jar of cream from the sideboard. She rubbed a dollop lovingly into her left leg, balancing her heel on the counterpane. 'Look at that,' she said to Alison who had politely turned away. 'A leg like that has no place here.' Alison watched Blossom's fingers as they massaged her calf muscles, then slid all the way down to her ankles. She didn't follow them up again because Blossom's gown was open and she had no knickers on. 'I bet June Hartley can't do this. Not with those legs.'

Alison grinned. 'They are a bit bandy, aren't they?'

'Pleasure bent, darling!' said Plum from behind a compact mirror.

That's what Alison would miss the most. Those put-downs. With a loud exhalation, Blossom stretched out her hands and bent down until her nose touched her right knee. 'I used to be able to hold a glass of champagne over my head,' she said, her voice straining. 'Then kick it out of my hand.' She cast off her gown and stepped into a pair of French knickers. 'Of course I couldn't do that now. Too fond of champagne.'

'Come on, slack Alice,' said Plum. 'Put your Archie Pitts away. I can hear a cork popping at fifty paces.' Alison couldn't help watching as Blossom fastened her brassiere. She made a mental note to buy some of the bust-firming cream. 'Up you get, Alison. Let's go downstairs. Show her you're not afraid.'

'I'll try.'

'And if I catch you calling her Miss Hartley,' said Blossom, poppering herself into a denim and lace catsuit, 'I'll shove the bloody ice bucket over your head!' She picked up a large wicker basket brimming with make-up and they launched into a furious attack on Alison's face, blotting and blushing and painting her lips. Just before they left, Blossom ran to her desk and returned with a little box. Opening it, she pulled out a small bottle of perfume. A dot of liquid from the glass stopper was rubbed onto Alison's neck and another on her wrist. 'Joy,' proclaimed Blossom. 'The most expensive perfume in the world. Make sure she smells it on you.'

Chapter Twenty-Five

'Happy Crimble!' Alison burst into Mel's bedroom with a tea tray stacked with presents. 'Oh, sorry, Puxley, I didn't hear you arrive.'

'You must have died in the night,' said Mel groggily. 'Three-forty-five, he shows up and starts singing.'

'Shut up,' moaned Puxley. 'Trying to sleep, here.'

'*Oh, the weather outside is . . . something,*' sang Mel loudly. Puxley pulled a pillow over his head. 'Now you know how I felt.'

'Frightful,' said Alison.

'You're telling me.'

'*But the fire is so delightful.* Never mind. Do you want your presents?'

'Is a frog's arse watertight?'

It was so cold that she ended up tucked in between Mel and Puxley. He liked the card Alison had written to him, and leaned over and kissed her on the cheek. He had that 'bed' smell that men exude on early tube journeys. Mel smelt of CK One. 'Thanks Ali,' she said, spraying it onto her neck. 'Here you go, stinky.' She sprayed some on Puxley, but it got in his eye.

'You witch!' he said. 'You're not coming to live with me now.'

Alison suddenly felt like she was falling down a hole. Mel smiled reassuringly. 'Wouldn't live with him if you paid me. Go on. Open your pressie.'

Alison unwrapped a trinket box, still feeling unsteady. Inside was a clear perspex ring, filled with glitter and a typewritten word on a tiny strip of pink paper.

'Ange? That's my mum's name.'

'It says angel. Turn it this way, then you can see the L.'

'Oh, yeah. Thanks Mel. It's fab.' She put it on and held her hand out in front of her.

'Very trendy girl,' said Puxley, sinking under the duvet again. There was something about the way he said it. It wasn't nasty. Alison had realised that he wasn't a nasty bloke. Quite the opposite, in fact; he was sweeter than he wanted to admit. No, it was an assumption that she was younger than him. About ten years younger. Very trendy girl. A thirteen-year-old in Miss Selfridge make-up and platform sneakers. 'Oh, well,' she said, trying to sound as grown-up as possible. 'Some of us have to work.'

'Poor baby,' said Mel. 'Mind you, we've got Aunt Lizzie on the organ to look forward to. Whoopee!'

'I've got my mum and Neil Diamond,' groaned Puxley. 'Count yourself lucky, young girl, to be working in an old folks' home.'

Alison did count herself lucky. She had spent two previous Christmases at Maytime and they were the best she could remember since her childhood. It was like being in a huge family and having Granny over, except that there were ten extra grannies and a couple of gandpas thrown in for good measure. It was a day when everyone there was alone and made the best of it. They were the leftovers, and they all joined together to make something comforting. Bubble and squeak.

For the middle Christmas, she had travelled over to her mother's house in Galway. Angie had greeted her at the airport. She was wearing a strange purple knitted beret and a matching floor-length scarf that got caught in the door. She had dyed her hair, too. It was an unreal, reddy-brown like a freshly peeled conker. 'Ali, Ali, Ali!' she had shouted before swooping on her. Alison's face made contact with the rough wool at great speed, forcing it up her nose. The result was that she sneezed non-stop for just under a minute while Angie patted her back and said, 'There, there, darling.' When they pulled themselves apart, Alison's face was scarlet and streaming. 'Oh, angel,' said Angie, the lids of her concerned eyes the same purple as the hat and scarf. 'I'm never going to let you out of my sight again.' They trailed through the car park and stopped by an orange beetle with a daisy sticker on the side. 'The Datsun was no fun,' said Angie by way of explanation.

There were more surprises to come when they got to the cottage. Not Granny Anne, there was nothing surprising about her. She was waiting at the door as they came up the driveway, wearing her old-fashioned floral pinafore. It looked like she had a summer dress on over her Christmas trouser suit. 'Let's look at you,' she said, standing back and folding her arms across her mighty bosom. 'Not a pick on her, is there, Angela? No wonder she hasn't got herself a fella yet. They like a little something to hang on to.'

'Come on, you,' said Angie, pulling Alison away from her grandmother. They headed through the lounge, which was littered with odd items rescued from skips and farm sales. The whole place had been streaked, sponged and dragged since Alison was last there, and every corner and cubby hole was stuffed with milk churns, flat irons and broken violins all with dried flowers and ears of corn sticking out of them. As they approached the kitchen, Angie hung back and put her hands on Alison's shoulders, marching her forward. The walls were lime-green and the worktops were lemon. There was a young man crouched in the corner, installing an old-fashioned solid-fuel oven. He turned around as they came through the door. 'It's lovely.' Alison smiled at him, then followed a line of mango stencils around the wall.

'Not the kitchen, darling.'

When she turned back, she saw that Angie was arm in arm with the cooker man. 'This is Barney,' she beamed, pointing him out with a loving part on his stomach.

'Oh.'

What a holiday! The night before Christmas was spent trying to ignore the faint mooing that came through the thick wall of Angie's bedroom, then the furtive departure of Barney Rubble (hilarious! He had the name painted on the side of his builder's van) just before dawn. Christmas Day wasn't much better. Angie had come bursting into her bedroom at eight with a handmade Christmas stocking and a cup of tea. '*We wish you a merry Christmas*,' she sang as she tore back the curtains, then stretched herself out on the bed beside Alison. Her dressing gown smelt of him. 'Isn't this heaven, darling? A real family Christmas at long last. Just like the ones we used to have with Daddy.'

Alison emptied her stocking slowly. She wanted to throw it in Angie's smiling face. Alison had done some lovely Christmases for them in Croydon. Just the two of them, but they had still been a family. Not to Angie, obviously. Barney had been the missing ingredient. Angie told her how they had fallen in love in a mosaic workshop. Their fingers had touched over the broken blue tiles because they had both chosen a dolphin motif. He was thirty-three but had been running his own business for over ten years. He had a kid. A little girl, but it didn't work out with her mother. He was coming back for sandwiches in the evening. Alison looked at the presents that Angie had stuffed into her stocking, lovely things. Nail files, lip balm, a little book of happy thoughts. She thought they were pathetic. It was always like this with Angie. All year she looked forward to seeing her, but then, as soon as they came face to face, Alison got a knot inside her. It hurt, like holding back tears. She suspected that nothing, short of running off a cliff, would get rid of it.

Her foul mood continued, and she spent most of the morning complaining because the telly didn't pick up BBC 1 and she would miss the *EastEnders* special. When Granny Anne wasn't trying to stuff tarts and scones into Alison's mouth, she was making snide comments about 'yer man with the hair' (Barney had beautiful black curls) and the general moral decline of the household. 'She was at school with his mother,' she whispered to Alison as they sat by the fireplace watching the blackening satsumas that Angie had hung from the boughs of holly on the mantelpiece.

'No, Mammy,' said Angie drily from the kitchen. 'I was at the same school as his mother. Big difference.'

Angie was past caring what they thought. She was all aglow in every sense of the word. The new cooker had a mind of its own. It heated the kitchen to a hundred degrees and gave them a turkey that was black on the outside and pink on the inside. They sat there and stared at it with their paper hats starting to tear around the brims. Alison looked over at the bundles of cinnamon sticks and the white fairy lights on the tree, and wished she was at Maytime with its gummed paper chains and golf balls of Paxo.

Things brightened up when Barney arrived. By then, Alison was tired of being miserable. She made one last attempt, but was brought out of her sulk by Barney's screeching reaction to the remnants of the turkey: '*What* did you put in the stove, woman? Semtex?' They had jam sandwiches. Angie had made Barney a stocking, too, filled with chocolate and Homer Simpson handkerchiefs and a new pair of pliers. He loved it, and made Alison feel sorry for the lukewarm reception she had given hers. He gave Angie a gold necklace hidden in a pot of tiling grout. A drinking game that involved sticking a playing card to your forehead soon put paid to Granny Anne. She was asleep on the sofa by nine, the top set of her teeth sliding down a little with each breath. Barney asked Alison all about her work and she felt herself warming to him. He wasn't a bit like her father, but perhaps that was a good thing. He was nearer her age than Angie's. He liked Marx Brothers films. He had beautiful eyes.

He chased Angie into her bedroom with the pliers and they stayed in there. Alison felt cold all of a sudden, and knew that she had to go to her room and lock the door before they came out again. By the time she heard the thin sound of Granny Anne's rude awakening and the clatter of dishes in the kitchen, she was working out how many Christmases she could spend at Maytime without actually breaking her mother's heart.

Angie phoned just before Alison left for work. 'We've got your present here beside us, but no you. Oh, darling, that bloody job of yours.'

'I know,' said Alison, smiling.

Chapter Twenty-Six

———————◆———————

She arrived at ten, having taken the long way round, cutting through residential areas where children bowled along the pavements on their new bicycles. Windows alternated trees and Hanukkah lights and strips of silver and gold paper with Arabic script. West Indian families snaked towards the churches in smart suits and starched dresses, with grannies taking the lead in shimmering white hats like overblown roses. All around her, cars backed into parking spaces and front doors were flung open in welcome. Alison shouted Merry Christmas at them, knowing it was the one day in the year when strangers looked you straight in the face and smiled.

Maytime was warm, and the bar was filled with visiting relatives. Most had brought an extra gift for the staff. Already, the tins of chocolate biscuits and boxes of Quality Street were piled up in Pat's office. Some residents had been picked up and were being ferried to family homes or friends' houses. The others sat in the lounge. Nat King Cole's Christmas album was on the turntable, loud enough even for Eva to catch the melody.

George Jakobi's secretary had been around earlier to deliver a crate of half-bottles of champagne – one for each resident – as well as a large, luxurious games table. Lillian was sitting at it already, trying to drum up a couple of players, reverently stroking the bright green baize. 'It flips over,' she said to Alison, pulling out two small wooden pegs from the underside and turning the whole top to reveal an inlaid chequerboard flanked by two cribbage blocks. A brass plaque in one corner announced that it had been presented by George Jakobi OBE to his dear friends at Maytime House. 'Typical George,' said Alison. Lillian nodded. Like all the others, she was in evening wear, a floor-length lilac kaftan with gold brocade around the neck and cuffs. A thin layer of pink polish covered her ridged fingernails, and the matching lipstick was starting to bleed into the powdered skin around her mouth. 'You look lovely,' said Alison. Lillian smiled at her crookedly. Her mouth was worse than ever and her hands shook so, she frequently lost cigarettes, burning neat, hard little holes in her nylon skirts.

'Do you play poker?' she asked, gesturing to a pack of Magic Circle playing cards in a perspex box.

'Only rummy, I'm afraid.' Lillian looked disappointed. The games table had come too late for Ben, and now she had to sit at it alone and content herself with patience. She handed Alison two gift-wrapped boxes. 'Take these to my room, would you, dear. My niece came.'

'Don't you want to open them?'

'Not here.' She looked around the room. 'Some of them haven't had a visitor.' Alison tucked the presents under her arm. On her way up the stairs, she collided with Plum and Blossom. They were wearing jumpers with gold appliqué snowflakes. 'Merry Christmas,' they said, and swamped her with perfumed hugs. 'Oh, you are good,' said Plum. 'Coming in here on Christmas Day when you should be at home with your family. We do feel bad, you know.'

'We tell them,' Blossom chimed in. 'We tell them every year that we can look after ourselves for one day. We can cook and make up the beds, but no. They won't let us because it's against the rules. We've never been that bothered about Christmas. It's more for people like you.' Alison hugged them tightly, knowing it was their last day at Maytime. Today they were playful again, determined to make the most of things. Like most of the residents, their Christmases had mostly been spent on the road. People who did pantomime were marooned after the last show on Christmas Eve. No trains to take them to their families. They woke up alone in their digs and either shared a mince pie with the landlord or gathered with other stranded pros for a glass of wine. Harry Jackson told Alison that he spent one Christmas all alone in an attic room. The landlady didn't even serve him some of the turkey she was having downstairs with her family. She brought him sausage and egg, just like she did every day.

So Christmas at Maytime was cheery by comparison. The staff were ceaselessly bright and breezy, eager for the residents to enjoy themselves, thinking of how they would spend the extra few pounds they made. The residents smiled and performed, keen to show the staff that they appreciated them, determined not to let the side down. The free champagne helped. The trolley was a mass of shivering glasses and bottles as it was pushed over the carpet runners into the hall. Lena Chase was at the front of the queue. Shazia attempted to give her just a little in a glass, but she swiped the bottle and trundled off to the conservatory, mumbling to herself.

Ben usually did the accompaniment for the carol concert, but as he was now singing with a different choir, Shirley-whirly's husband Juan had volunteered to pop in for an hour to get things moving. Although there was a perfectly good upright piano dusted and ready for him, he insisted on bringing his multi-level synthesiser. It took ages to set it up and sort out the spaghetti of leads that linked its various keyboards together. While he was busy, Shirley was helping herself from behind the bar, filling her exotic cocktails with maraschino cherries she had been storing away for her own use. When Lillian pointed out that they were past their expiry date, she came over all generous and walked around the room plopping them into champagne glasses.

Right on cue, Father Christmas arrived. George Jakobi had done it once, but this year he was in the Seychelles, so the job had been given to Ernie the handyman. He waddled in, dragging a sack of presents, and sat on the edge of the stage, breathing heavily. Plum and Blossom were going through a yellowed set of sheet music with Juan, preparing their traditional number. After Alison had handed out a few presents, Plum asked for a bit of hush. With a Liberace-style flick of the wrists, Juan played the introduction and Plum and Blossom went into their infamous, highly sexed rendition of Eartha Kitt's 'Santa Baby'. They pouted and parted the white, nylon beard while singing, tickling him under the chin. They kissed his rosy cheeks, then Plum balanced an ankle on his shoulder as if it were an exercise bar. During the second verse, they took turns sitting on his knee and pulling presents from the sack. As usual, the audience loved it, and the Santa squirmed with embarrassment, flushing more with every minute in the heat of the lounge.

Just before the encore, June Hartley came in wearing a dress that was amazing, even by Maytime standards: a cloud of peach chiffon with jet beading down the bodice. It looked as though she had spent the entire morning just getting into it. Though her shoulders were swathed in a matching shawl, its transparency revealed pillows of pink flesh folding over the boned top. She stood in the doorway for some time, waiting to be noticed, her feet in a neat ballet position. 'God help us,' she cried as the song finished, and Plum and Blossom took their bows. 'Father Christmas. I ask you! How old do they bloody think we are around here? Five?' A couple of residents turned round, but it wasn't the reaction she wanted. Shazia came up behind her with the trolley, shouting: 'Beep, Beep! Out the way, June. Have you had your champagne yet?' June gave Shazia a slow, dirty look, taking in the green pixie hat she wore with her uniform, the lipstick circles on her cheeks and the flashing holly wreaths in her ears.

'What kind of champagne is it?'

'Oh, it's real champagne. Not Babycham or anything.' Shazia reached for a small bottle from the tray and handed it proudly to June. June rummaged in her bag for her glasses and looked at the label with disdain.

'Bulgaria?' The word seemed to cause her pain.

'Well, do you want it?'

'If it's all there is.'

Shazia unscrewed the bottle-top, which was shaped like a cork, filled a glass and handed it to June. 'Cheers then,' she said. 'Merry Christmas.'

June raised the glass and took a sip. 'Pooh!' she grimaced. 'It's lukewarm.'

'Put some ice in it, then,' shouted Shazia, who was already surrounded by residents eager for a top-up.

June heard her name being called. It was Alison, squatting next to Santa, or rather Ernie, who had pulled the beard and the wig-hat off and was tucking into a can of lager. Alison had decided to ignore Plum's and Blossom's advice and go for a friendly approach, putting their earlier encounter down to nerves. So far, it had been working. 'June?' she called again. 'Oh, don't you look nice.' June stopped for a moment and returned her feet to the ballet pose. 'It's Hartnell,' she cooed. 'He did all my stage outfits.' There was a look of innocent pleasure in her face that made Alison's heart swell. A teenager at a school dance.

'Well, it's really lovely.' Alison came towards her with a small box covered in cheap wrapping paper. She was wearing a pixie hat, too, and some of Mel's body glitter on her cheeks. She surveyed the beading on the bodice and the jewels that trembled on the puffy skin below June's neck. 'Doesn't she look lovely, Shaz?'

'Yeah, great!' sneered Shazia through a puff of cigarette smoke.

June seemed to have got off on the wrong foot with everyone in the building. Alison knew how it felt to get funny looks from strangers. She wanted June to feel safe with her. 'I've got a present for you,' she said, pressing the box into June's hand. 'Merry Christmas.' It was the best present in the sack. Alison had chosen it herself and wrapped it.

'Hold this.' June shoved her champagne glass in Alison's face, then retrieved her spectacles from her handbag. Stretching her arm out and arching one eyebrow, June made out the wording on the gift tag. TO JUNE HARTLEY. HO, HO, HO! LOVE SANTA. 'Ho, ho, ho,' mocked June. 'Oh, goody. What is it? Roller skates?' She tore at the paper, crushing the gift tag, then threw it into the gas fire. The wrapping caught with a bright blue light then tipped out of the grate, slid over the marble surround and headed for the carpet. 'You're not supposed to put paper in there.' Alison lunged forward, throwing June's warm champagne at it. 'Pat goes mad if you do that.' She gave June a reassuring smile.

June eyed the empty champagne glass, then turned her attention to the bottle of aromatherapy bubble bath in her hand. 'What's this?' she asked, unscrewing the top and sniffing it. 'Wouldn't use it to shampoo a dog.'

Alison felt a strong indigestion-type feeling at the base of her ribcage. 'It's a gift,' she said, and her voice was louder than she expected.

'Well, I'm nobody's poor cow!' The next thing Alison knew, there was a jet of pink liquid coming towards her. She squealed and put her arm across her face. She heard the bottle thumping on the floor and June's chiffon dress rustling back into the hall. When she opened her eyes, she saw a semicircle of faces with open mouths.

'Blimey!' said Shazia.

'I'll kill 'er!' Harry strode forward, rolling up his shirtsleeves. 'She'll be spitting beans by the time I've finished.'

Alison looked at Plum and Blossom. 'Leave this to me, Harry, please,' she said, her voice already trembling.

June was heaving herself up the last few steps, gripping the banister with one hand and cradling three more unopened bottles of champagne in the other. At the top, she turned. 'That wiped the grin off your face, didn't it, Pollyanna?' she said, gesturing to the mark on the front of Alison's uniform. 'What's the matter? Can't take a joke?' She studied Alison's pinched face. 'I suppose it was too much to hope for in a place like this.'

That did it. 'What's wrong with this place?' yelled Alison.

'You tell her, darling!' shouted Plum from the hallway.

June smiled her Hollywood smile. 'There's nothing *wrong* with this place. Of course there's not. It's an absolute godsend to that lot down there, but it's not exactly my league.'

'What makes you think you're so different?'

'You never saw their acts.' (Groans from below.) 'Party tricks! Just the thing for The Palace, Attercliffe. I was at the Palladium for three months at a time, I'll have you know. I owned four Rolls-Royces!' She splayed her fingers at Alison, then rustled down the corridor, leaving a trail of stiletto marks on the carpet.

'No wonder you don't have any money.'

'I heard that, missy. Don't get catty with me.'

Alison took a deep breath and let it out slowly, trying to see things from June's point of view. 'Look. I understand you're angry, and that this is a difficult time for you.'

'You understand nothing.' June flung her door open and yanked Alison in by the elbow. She went to her chest of drawers and pulled out a pile of photographs. 'Look!' she pointed to a series of faces caught in flashlights next to younger versions of herself. 'Do you see who that is, or that?' They were the photographs Alison had been longing to see. Peggy Lee, Danny Kaye, Noël Coward.

Alison paused, studying them. 'No,' she said. 'Sorry. Are they friends of yours?'

'Very. Good. Friends!' June separated each word to drive the message home.

Alison glanced at the pictures again. 'Well, you could always stay with them.'

June's flesh trembled in the soft light. She threw the photographs onto the bed. They slid against each other like playing cards, forming an arc over the coverlet. Alison looked around the room, shocked at her own cruelty. There were photographs everywhere, all of June with her plastic smile. Behind one silver frame a Christmas card crouched, a Dickensian street scene. It was yellow around the edges. Not this year's. June followed Alison's glance. 'He didn't send them on,' she said. 'That shit Martin. They came from all over. America, Australia. His friends are looking at them now, I bet, saying, "Ooh, Martin, you're so popular." Show a little kindness and that's what I get.' Alison raised her eyebrows. 'Oh, that's right. Take his side. He had you all fooled, didn't he? Him with that bloody dead mouse on his face. Made me out to be a right ogre.' June removed her chiffon shawl, then fiddled with the clasp on her gold watch. 'See that?' she said, thrusting her wrist into Alison's face. A silver line like a slug track shone against the mottled skin.

'Yes, we were told.' Alison let her eyes linger on the scar, wondering if June had seen *Sunset Boulevard* and if poor, lonely Martin had written all the Christmas cards himself. Alison thought it was such a sad film. Every time she watched it, she longed for the ending to be different; for the young writer to fall in love with the faded star and make her so happy she forgot about her comeback.

'I'll do it again, you know, if you're not careful,' said June, still waving her wrist under Alison's nose. 'You'll come in here one morning and find me emptied out all over the floor. What would Mr Jakobi say to that? Wouldn't be best pleased, would he? Wouldn't look good in the papers.'

'Please, June.'

'You'd like that, wouldn't you?'

'What I'd like is for you to come downstairs and join in.

They could use a good voice like yours.' Alison held her hand out. 'You never know, you might start enjoying yourself.'

'You might start enjoying yourself,' June sing-songed. 'Oh, *please!* Spare me your amateur psychology, you . . .' She studied Alison for a moment, then spat out the words: '. . . You silly little cunt!'

Alison was taken over by an anger that made her feel as if she was about to throw up her entire stomach. It came too fast for her to stop it. She looked at the clumped mascara on June's eyelashes, the caked foundation on her nose. She wanted to be in a car and to drive it at a hundred miles an hour into a wall. But she was nowhere near a car, and about a foot away from one of the biggest cowbags in variety. 'You bitch!' Alison yelled, and the next thing she knew she was lunging forward.

She came to her senses just in time, stopping just before she reached June's face but not soon enough to miss the shocked expression. June stood her ground. 'Oh, so that's how it is,' she sneered as Alison's hand dropped to her side, her palm hot and prickling. 'Little Miss Holier-than-Thou.'

'I've never.'

'I've heard about this sort of thing. No wonder they all act like the sun shines out of your tight little arse.'

Alison couldn't say any more. June's words were rat-tat-tat-tat-ing against her head, accusing her of God knows what. Nothing more than she was accusing herself of. During her years at Maytime, she had feared the mistake that would end her career. She had gone through a thousand different situations. Wrong medicines, accidental drownings in the bath, chasing runaway wheelchairs down hills, but nothing like this. Not hitting an old lady. She looked down at her new ring. Angel. How ironic. She was possessed by a devil. The happy little Alison she knew was splitting at the seams, pouring out all this anger, and it scared her. Eventually she found the strength from somewhere and stumbled backwards, groping for the door.

By the time she got to the lounge, the carol concert was in full swing. Shazia was moving around the room, waking up those who had nodded off and passing out song sheets. Juan was grinning from behind the keyboard and the room was filled with a lively, swaying rendition of 'We Three Kings'. Shirley was standing at the back glowering at him. 'Bloody show-off!' she mumbled as he launched into a samba version of 'Hark The Herald Angels Sing.' Shazia spotted Alison and ran over to her. 'Are you all right? You look awful. What did she do to you?'

'What did I do to her, more like.'

'You didn't kill her, did you?'

Alison slumped on the sofa. 'No. Not quite.'

'Shame.'

'Shazia!'

'Well, she's such a cow. Look what she did to your uniform.'

'It'll wash.'

Lena Chase stood in front of them. Even though they were sitting, their heads were level with hers. 'I don't like you,' she shouted, pointing at Shazia. 'I don't like you at all. I like Alison. She's nice, is Alison.'

'Please yourself,' said Shazia. 'She's all yours.' She left Alison with a squeeze of her shoulder.

'You're nice, Alison,' said Lena, sitting down beside her. The deep sofa cushion engulfed her and she slid sideways into Alison's arm. Alison could smell the champagne on her breath. It didn't take much with Lena. That little bottle was the equivalent of a magnum to her. The lights on the tree were twinkling and there was music everywhere. Harry was wearing Santa's hat. It was heartbreaking.

Alison slid away from Lena and headed for Pat's office.

Chapter Twenty-Seven

Her panic took on a cottony substance. It was the way she felt sometimes in brightly lit department stores, as if someone had gradually been thinning the air out, so that although she dearly wanted to slaughter everyone queuing at the till or send a shelf full of china crashing to the floor, every scrap of energy had to go on just breathing in. Pat's office door loomed in front of her, plain flat woodchip with a reddy-brown varnish. Pat had been nagging Ernie to oil the hinges, and it appeared that he had finally got around to it because when Alison pushed it, the handle on the other side cracked against the wall.

Pat was leaning against the side panel of the sash window, resting her knee on the top of a radiator and swigging from a small glass bottle. When she heard the door go, she attempted to hide it. She moved so fast that a line of liquid hung in the air before splattering over the window, the radiator and her arm. She lost her footing and slid down the wall. 'Out!' she spluttered. 'Get out!' Alison vaulted back into the corridor. She wanted to run home, but she was trapped in the nursing wing. Pat's room was out of bounds. The emergency exit by the dispensary triggered the fire alarm, which would result in everybody gathering on the front lawn with her. She couldn't go back through the lounge, either. June was probably in there by now. The music floated through. Shirley was doing one of her solos to a calypso beat. Fuzzy with alcohol, she was singing: *Mary's boyfriend Jesus Christ was born on Christmas day.*

Alison turned to Pat's door again. It was only cough linctus, not Scotch, so why the mad reaction? Perhaps there were empty expectorant bottles clinking in the bottom of the filing cabinet and lining the back of the bookshelves. She inched down the corridor, passing the laundry. On the telly, when people resigned, they had it all prepared. There was a neat white envelope containing a letter. If she had one, she could just walk in there and wave it under Pat's nose.

Beryl of Beryl's budgerigars had fallen asleep in front of *Mad Max – Beyond the Thunderdome*. A scene with Tina Turner in her fright wig and a leather bikini flickered on a portable television. Behind it, on a shelf, Beryl's props were lined up. A tiny pram. A little red fire engine and a pole with a bell on the top. Alison tucked her in and stroked her hair. 'Goodbye, Beryl,' she whispered.

'Am I on?' asked Beryl, suddenly alert.

'No.' Alison kept her hand on Beryl's forehead. 'Not yet. Still an hour till lunch.' She let her fingers slide down her cheek. It was as soft as a rose petal. When she first learned to bathe the elderly, she had been amazed by the feel of their skin. For some reason, she had expected it to be all rough and scaly. In reality, it could be as luxurious as the most expensive fabrics sold in Eastern markets. Yes, it was wrinkled, but then those kind of fabrics are always a bugger to iron. She popped in on Mr Appanowicz. He, too, had drifted off after his champagne and didn't hear her. The room next door to him was empty. Its occupant had an electric wheelchair with L-plates on the back. Alison had heard the drone of the motor passing by while she was in with Beryl. All the others in the wing had had somewhere to go.

Feeling calmer, she pressed her ear to the office door. 'Pat?' she called, knocking gently with the backs of her fingers. 'It's Alison.'

'Alison. Yes . . . Well? Are you coming in?'

She kept her hand on the door handle as she entered. Pat was sitting behind her desk. She was one of those people who only put lights on when it is absolutely impossible to see the person next to you. It took a while for Alison's eyes to adjust. She waited for Pat to say something, but in the end it was Alison who broke the silence.

'Are you all right?'

'Yes.'

'I thought maybe you had a cold coming.' Pat stared at her. Alison knew that the cough linctus wasn't to be mentioned. It did make sense of things, though. The sticky rings on the desk, the smell of cherry drops and Pat's permanently pink mouth. It set Alison's teeth on edge just thinking about it.

'How's it going out there?' asked Pat at last. 'Still singing?'

'Shirley's doing a solo.' She noticed that Pat had made a tiny Christmas tree out of the magnetised paper clips. 'That's good. You need a little star for the top.'

Pat got up and looked out of the window. 'I've no time to stand around chatting, Alison.' She couldn't look a person in the face and lie to them. She had all the time in the world. Alison would have been a good person to tell about the cough linctus problem. She trusted her, and in the absence of Expectorants Anonymous or some such organisation, she sorely needed someone to tell.

It hadn't always been the case. When Pat was a teenager, she could have talked the hind legs off a donkey, but she had got out of the habit. A side effect of single-handedly nursing her mother through Alzheimer's. For two years, Pat had mapped her movements from room to room and followed her when she went out. As the condition worsened, their conversations had peeled down and down like the layers of an onion until just a hard nub remained. It made the tittle-tattle of her friends and colleagues sound foreign or indulgent. Eventually, all communication ceased. She glanced at Alison with her pixie cheeks, and thought she didn't know the half of it. Alison laughed when an old lady stood in the middle of luncheon and tap-tapped her toes and sang, 'I'm A Lonely Little Petunia In An Onion Patch'. She would never understand the pressures of her job and the fear that there was nothing else. There was a lot that Pat didn't know about Alison.

'Well?' she said impatiently. 'Haven't you got things to do?'

'I want to resign.'

Pat turned and sat heavily on the side of her desk. 'Whatever for?'

'I nearly hit June Hartley.'

'Nearly?'

'Yes.'

'What stopped you?'

'Nothing. I just stopped, but I was going to. I really wanted to.' Alison buried her head in her hands.

Pat put her arm along Alison's curled spine and rubbed up and down. 'Have you felt like this before?' she asked gently.

Alison sat up. 'No, never.'

'You've never wanted to hit a resident?' Alison shook her head vigorously. 'Well, then, you're a saint.' Alison looked at her in horror. Pat wasn't joking. 'Listen,' she whispered. 'I've wanted to cave a few heads in in my time. Everybody does. It's a frustrating job, but there's a big difference between wanting to do something and actually doing it.'

'Yeah, but I had my hand up, like this.'

'And it scared the life out of you, didn't it? Well, look at you. You'll never forget it. You'll never forgive yourself. And,' she patted Alison's shoulder, 'you'll never do it again. I'd put money on it.' Pat silently remembered how she had locked herself in the shed, scared of lashing out at her mother.

'I can't go back in there.'

'Yes you can. Of course you can. If you feel bad, just come and talk to me. That's what I'm here for, Alison. I do think that you should book yourself a couple of weeks off. I'll need you to help with Plum and Blossom tomorrow, but we'll make that your last day, OK? And no more talk about resigning, you hear?' Alison nodded. 'It would spoil my little plan.'

'What plan?'

'I was hoping to get you some on-site nurse training next year.' She saw Alison's eyes widen and fill with panic. 'Don't think about it now. Go and check on the glee club. And never mind about June Hartley. She's made a life out of being bloody difficult, pardon my French.'

Alison was in a daze. She'd gone in to resign and come out with a promotion. Pat's last sentence stayed in Alison's head as she left the office. *Pardon my French.* Pat had taken on a new persona since she'd said it. She wasn't just Cowpat. She was a woman who came from the kind of family who said 'pardon my French'. Alison could just imagine them all, sitting in a kitchen eating roast lamb at a table with *Family Favourites* on the radio.

When she reached the lounge, Harry was up on the stage doing his Wilson, Keppel and Betty sand dance with Shazia playing the part of Betty. Juan was nurdling something suitably Egyptian on the keyboard. 'Alison!' shouted Harry after his applause died down. 'There you are, love.' Her heart sank for a moment. 'I hear you've got a little message for me from the nursing wing.' It took her a while to cotton on. He had told her about it over a week ago. She fumbled in her pockets, but all she could find was an old travelcard, so she climbed up onto the stage and handed it to him, receiving a little ripple. 'Now,' Harry continued, putting on his spectacles. 'I've been asked to whistle a special tune for one of our oldest residents.' He studied the back of the travelcard. 'I think we should all give her a cheer because it says here she's a hundred and eleven today. How about that.' Everybody cheered, even though they knew what was coming next. Harry looked over to Alison. 'What?' he exclaimed, then made a tromboning movement with his arm, trying to focus on the card. 'Oh, sorry. She's ill today. Oh well, let's give her a song anyway.'

As Harry launched into '*Have Yourself A Merry Little Christmas*' Alison retreated to the back of the crowd. Lena Chase was asleep on the sofa, one of her tiny hands dangling down to the carpet. Plum and Blossom had joined everybody up in a line, linking arms, and they were swaying as one and singing. 'You!' said a sharp voice from the doorway. 'Pollyanna!' June Hartley beckoned her. Alison strolled over, trying to look nonchalant, feeling the glitter frying on her cheeks. June was a little out of focus, and smelt of gin and stale perfume. 'Yes?' said Alison, her heart beating wildly.

'What's your name?'

'Alison.'

'Alison,' June repeated. 'Would you be an angel . . . Alison . . . and get my handbag for me? I appear to have left it over by the stage there.' She pointed to the cordon of swaying bodies as if it was a swamp filled with crocodiles. 'I wouldn't mind with my other bags, but that one was given to me by somebody special.'

'Who?' asked Alison. 'Noël Coward?' She couldn't resist it.

June met her eyes for a second, then said, 'No. My mother. Now, will you get it . . . please?'

'OK.'

Chapter Twenty-Eight

She helped Blossom with her things, folding blouses into an overstuffed case. The scrappy memoirs were bound in cardboard. The typewriter was in its cover. Blossom was sitting on the edge of her desk with an overflowing drawer on her lap, dividing its contents between the waste-paper basket and a cardboard box. 'Oh, goody!' she cried, peering into a crumpled paper bag. 'I forgot I had these.' She offered it to Alison. At the bottom of the bag was a sticky huddle of jelly babies. Alison tweezed one out with her fingers and handed the rest to Blossom, who examined them carefully as if they had their own little personalities. 'You, I think,' she said to a green one before popping it into her mouth. She winked at Alison, pleased with her choice.

Alison couldn't bear the sweet taste. Her mouth was all acid, thinking of Blossom and the big wide world. It was hard to believe that she would survive without someone to get her up in the mornings and keep her chequebook balanced. Alison's one consolation was that she would be with Plum. At least they were staying together. 'Who's picking you up?' she asked.

'A friend.' Blossom craned her neck to see the corner of the driveway from the window. 'A man.'

'He's not moving in with you, is he?'

'God, no,' Blossom laughed. 'Darling,' she said, sliding off the desk and taking her hand. 'Stop worrying. We've got a lovely flat to go to and a couple of charming men to take us there. Have another jelly baby.' Alison took the bag and pulled a biro from her breast pocket. Over the scrunched-up paper she wrote her address and phone number. 'Here,' she said, handing it back to Blossom. 'Just in case you're stuck. Either of you. Also, I can talk to Pat. She might seem like an old dragon, but she's fond of you two.'

'You make me laugh, Alison. I think you'd move in here yourself given half a chance.'

A car horn sounded outside. Blossom sprang up and picked her way through the boxes to the door. Alison put the last of the clothes into the case and pushed it shut. In the front driveway, a hired van pulled up, closely followed by a black BMW. A man in his mid-forties emerged from the van. He was round, and was dressed in faded jeans and a football shirt. He rubbed his hands together and looked up at the façade of the house. 'All right, Terry?' shouted the second man from the car window. Bill, the financial adviser, was a smart Yorkshireman in his sixties. They talked for a while, then the van driver clumped up to the front door.

Plum was sitting on her bed, looking around at the skeleton of her room. She had been at Maytime for five years. She had thought she would be there for ever. She was seventy-one (sixty-eight on her Equity card). Not a sensible time to go launching yourself into the unknown. She clung to the bedstead, looking over at the dressing-table mirror. Her new-found beauty seemed to have slipped from her face. She reached in her handbag for her Dior compact. 'All grown-up now,' she said.

'There she is,' said Terry the cuddly van driver as Blossom cantered down the stairs in jeans and a white shirt. He beamed up at her like a boy who had just got a kite to fly. She stopped before the bottom step, opened her arms wide and toppled into his. She was gripped and squeezed and spun down to ground level. 'Hello precious,' said Terry, kissing her neck. 'How do you feel?'

'A lot better for seeing you.' She thumbed her lipstick from his cheek. 'Where's Bill?' From the corner of her eye, she saw a jumble of faces in the doorway of the lounge.

'He's just parking the car round the back.' Terry didn't get a lot further. Blossom kissed him full on the lips. His grip around her waist slackened and one hand slid down to her bottom. 'Oh, my giddy aunt!' said a muffled voice from the door-jamb. Blossom licked her lips approvingly and tugged him up the stairs. 'Come on,' she said. 'Let's get going.'

'What's all this then?' said Bill as he opened the door of Plum's room. 'I thought you couldn't wait to leave.'

Plum was still looking at herself in the dressing-table mirror. 'What do you think?' she said, cupping her face in her hands and pulling the loose skin back towards her ears. 'A little nip and tuck?' Bill laughed and kissed the top of her head. 'Don't be a lemon,' he said. 'Laughter lines. You don't want to lose them, do you?' He picked up a box from the bottom of her bed and she smiled at him. As he struggled with it out of the door, she took one last look in the mirror. 'Men,' she said, lifting her face again with her fingers. 'What do they know?'

After a lot of toing and froing, the van was loaded with bags and boxes. The doors of the two upstairs rooms were closed, sealing in their emptiness, and the hall was filled with staff and residents. Both Plum and Blossom were in floods of tears, grabbing and kissing their old friends. Alison hovered by the door of the refectory, trying to stop her facial muscles from breaking away in several directions. Across the hall, Pat stood with her arms tightly folded.

'Thanks for the bag.' Shazia hugged Plum. The sixties airline bag was around her neck.

'Bye, bye, Miss Brainbox,' sniffed Plum, holding her tight. 'There's something from Blossom inside.' Shazia held the bag to her chest and peered in as Plum moved on to Darren. Blossom was wrapped around him, practically meeting herself at the back of his skinny body. His limp arms were draped around her waist.

'Oh, sweetheart,' she cooed. 'What are we going to do without you?'

'Keep in touch,' he said. 'I'll come and visit if you like.'

'That would be wonderful, wouldn't it, Plum? Darren says he'll come and see us in our little flat. That will give our gentlemen friends something to worry about.'

'You'd better keep your word,' said Plum. 'You've got our number, haven't you?' Plum handed him a gift-wrapped box. 'This is just for you and your friends.' Darren peeled back a little of the paper and saw that it was a videotape.

'Your advert,' he said. They nodded and kissed his face. 'The first one. We're ever so pleased with it,' said Blossom. 'We know you'll like it. It's rather special.'

They moved on to Pat, and to everyone's surprise, they hugged her too and handed her a present. Blossom turned around and scanned the faces. 'Where's Alison?' Seeing them coming towards her with their arms outstretched was almost too much for Alison. Her face felt like a freshly boiled beetroot. 'I'll really miss you,' she croaked.

'And we'll miss you too, darling. Be happy for us.'

And with that, they were off arm in arm with their beaux. Everybody waved from the front steps. Alison blubbed and hugged her parting gifts to her chest. A bottle of Chanel No. 5 bath essence (*None of your bloody June Hartleys*, said the gift tag), and a huge pink feather boa that smelt of a thousand nightclubs. In her office, Pat unwrapped her present. She was sorry to say goodbye to two of her biggest headaches. Even after what they had said to her: 'You could be quite nice if you tried.' Inside the sunflower-print paper was a cream silk camisole and matching French knickers, so fine that Pat could see her hand through them, and so soft they glided over each other and fell to the floor. The most ridiculous things she had ever been given. Pressing them to her face, she laughed.

In the lounge, June Hartley sat leafing through an old copy of *Hello!* magazine. She didn't know who half the people were. Back in the days of *Picture Post*, stars were stars. Now it seemed you only had to marry a footballer and you were in a royal line-up. Hard work be damned. She pretended not to notice the residents who trickled in from the hall. She hadn't joined the scrum to say goodbye. Plum and Blossom didn't care about her; why should she care about them? What did they look like, playing kissy-face with a couple of hired hands? If those men had been legit, the two old tarts would have had banners made.

Alison left that evening with an end-of-term feeling. As she wheeled her bicycle down the side streets, she turned and looked back at Maytime's imposing chimney pots. She was wearing the pink boa around her neck. The feathers fluttered like cherry blossoms in the wind. 'Smudge!' called a woman from a doorway. 'Smudgey! Smudgey!' Ching, ching, ching went a cat's bell, and round the corner came Eddie with his tail sweeping the air. 'There you are!' said the woman, gripping her knees. 'Ooh! Cold boy!' Eddie sauntered up to her and did his famous stretch, rubbing his face on the door frame. The woman picked him up and went inside. 'You just get fatter and fatter, don't you?' she said as the door closed. Eddie glanced over her shoulder at Alison. She could have sworn he smiled.

Chapter Twenty-Nine

Rosalind Russell sat on the side of Cary Grant's desk, swinging her black sling-backs against the wood. She lit a cigarette with confidence, her head cocked slightly to one side so that the flame didn't scorch the brim of her hat. Cary was on the phone with his back to her, but still the air between them crackled.

Alison felt it. She sat on the arm of the sofa, mimicking Rosalind, holding aloft an imaginary cigarette. The Captain Kirk cut-out was Cary Grant, and any minute now he was going to ask her to sit on his lap. It was New Year's Eve, a time when old movies were shown twenty-four hours a day. Every time she thought about Ben or Kenneth, Alison just pressed the remote control and her monochrome family were there to comfort her. The phone rang, but she let the machine take it. Not because she couldn't bear to miss a moment of the film (she could practically do the script in her sleep). No, she thought it might be Angie, wondering why she hadn't gone running over to Ireland. When she heard who it was, she leaped up and grabbed the receiver. 'Hello, Darren? Everything OK?'

Mel came home from work shortly afterwards. 'Hiya!' she shouted from the hall. 'You excited about tonight?' (Puxley was DJing at an exclusive party near the Elephant and Castle, and he had managed to get Mel, Alison and Daichi on the guest list.)

'Yeah. Darren rang. He and Shazia are popping over later. He says they've got something to show me.'

Mel came into the lounge, weighed down with sale bargains. 'They can't stay long,' she said. 'We've got to get ready.'

Alison looked at the bags. 'Thought you were skint.'

'Before you say a word, Little Miss Sensible . . .' Mel rummaged around in one, pulled out a shoebox and handed it to Alison. 'For you.'

'Oh, Mel!' It was a pair of blue Nike trainers. She jammed her bare feet into them, took them out again to remove the paper wadding, then put them back in again. 'Fantastic! But . . .'

'But nothing. They were so cheap you would not believe it. It's the upside of having such titchy feet. New trainers for a new year.'

'Thanks.' Alison hugged her. 'Thanks for everything. I don't know how you put up with me.'

Mel gathered up her bags. 'A whole new year, Ali,' she said. 'I've got a good feeling . . . You've taken a few steps already.' She proudly eyed the plush new trainers. 'And you've got the night off. And Daichi is coming along . . .' She trailed off to her room, leaving his name hanging in the air. Alison lay back on the sofa cushions for a while and wondered what they were doing at Maytime. Unlike Christmas, it could be bleak there at New Year. The older ones all dropped off in their chairs, waiting for midnight, and the staff had to whizz around the lounge like plate spinners, jiggling one, then another to life as the champagne arrived. This year there would be no Ben, no Plum and no Blossom. Nobody to kiss, just Harry whistling 'Auld Lang Syne' and June Hartley in another dress labelled BBC Costume Dept. Alison felt a pang. She could see June all alone in her room with her old photographs, wanting to go downstairs but needing to be asked. She hoped somebody would make the effort.

* * *

Darren and Shazia had two bags with them. 'Aha!' he bellowed as Alison opened the door. 'We bring gifts of popcorn, beer and . . . hang about.' He pulled something out of his pocket. 'This!'

Alison took it. 'Plum's and Blossom's advert!'

'You got to see it, girls. I watched it with my brother last night.'

'He hasn't let me near it,' said Shazia.

'Oh, that's so sweet, Darren!' Alison took his arm.

Daichi came up the steps behind them. 'Hi, Alison,' he said. 'You look nice.'

'I haven't changed yet.' He handed her a soft package, wrapped in tissue paper. 'For Christmas,' he said.

'Oh. Yours is at Mel's mum's.' She sighed. 'No, it's not. I didn't get you anything. Sorry. I didn't know we were doing presents.'

'It's OK. It's only little.' Alison unwrapped it. It was a blue T-shirt with a 3D plastic cartoon character on it. 'From Tokyo,' he said. 'That's Astro Boy. He flies. See . . .' Daichi turned it slightly so that she could see the effect. He looked like a cartoon character himself with his chunky, hexagonal glasses, his tight orange T-shirt and a pair of enormous trainers under his flared jeans.

'Wow! My God! Thank you!' She slipped it over the top she was wearing and did a twirl for him. It was miles too big for her, more like a minidress. She looked up at him and saw disappointment in his eyes. He wanted it to be perfect. 'It's too big, isn't it?' he said. She assured him that she liked baggy shirts, then stepped forward to kiss him on the cheek. He leaned over and they hugged. 'You're welcome,' he said, and she felt his lips moving against her neck. It panicked her slightly, so she gave him a quick, sisterly squeeze and headed into the lounge, blowing upwards to cool her cheeks. The popcorn was open and Darren was sitting on a bean bag with Shazia on the floor next to him. Alison put the video into the machine. Its label was typewritten in plain black script. '*Die* . . . something or other. Can't pronounce it,' she said as Mel joined Daichi on the sofa.

The opening shot was of a carriage thundering along a country road to the tune of a string quartet. There were close-ups of the horses' hooves pounding and scattering stones and of the man who sat inside the carriage. He was young and handsome with glossy, shoulder-length brown hair. 'There they are!' shouted Shazia, as two names were superimposed over the blond man behind the reins. 'Victoria Plum' and 'Blossom Bailey' shivered in white letters that disappeared into the collar of the driver's shirt. The gardens of a house were seen from above. A tree-lined driveway stretched away as far as the eye could see. It was the view from a window, and the camera pulled back, revealing a lace curtain held to one side by Plum's manicured fingers. The hand released the curtain and Plum was now in full view. She looked more beautiful than ever. Her soft, greying hair was brushed away from her face, blending seamlessly into a long wig that was looped and pinned up at the back of her neck. Her eyes were lined with smoky grey powder and her lips were gently coloured and blotted. She was in a long satin dress with lace around the collar and cuffs. Adorning the neck was a cameo brooch. On a buffed amber oval, a woman's downturned face resembled a younger, porcelain Plum.

With a clip-clopping which could be heard over the music, the carriage came into view, flashing between the green ribbons of the poplar trees. Plum turned from the window and glided towards a polished side table, picking up a silver-framed photograph of a young man in military uniform. His faded face was square, like an American soap star's. She sighed and the camera caught the tremble of her bosom. The music faded out as a doorbell clattered downstairs.

The two men had climbed down from the carriage and were standing in the courtyard with their backs to the camera. The front door swung open and there was Blossom in a maid's uniform. The make-up men had waved their magic wands at her as well. She was gleaming like a fairy godmother. Her body was fluid, unrestrained by corsets. Her blouse was cut low, and a single pearl danced on her cleavage as she welcomed them in. 'Bloody hell! They're gorgeous!' said Mel.

Alison grinned proudly. 'You should have seen them when they were our age.'

'I'm talking about the men, you strange girl. Look and learn.' Mel pointed at the screen. Now in full view, the two men were overwhelming. They had removed their jackets and were tall and tanned in stained and crumpled linen shirts. Their breeches were tight over their pert backsides. They said something in German, and Blossom gestured for them to wait in the hallway. '*Guten tag,*' said a husky voice, and the men turned and looked up. Plum was standing on the mahogany-banistered staircase like Bette Davis. As she descended, the men looked suitably impressed. She was not swayed by their adoring glances, and sent Blossom off to get some coffee with a flick of her wrist. 'Typical Plum,' said Shazia.

The film had already been running for four minutes. There had been no reference to mobile phones, and try as she might, Alison couldn't see how they were going to feature. It was unlikely that one of the visiting men would pull a neat little flip-top contraption from the billows of his shirt, or that Plum would take one from a drawer and dial up her grandson, or whoever the man was in the photograph.

Plum was in the drawing room now with the dark man. As he spoke to her, she fingered cut white roses in a crystal vase. She smelt them and smiled sensuously. He knelt, took her hand and kissed it. She let her fingers glide over his face, and for a moment he looked up with his beautiful brown eyes. Downstairs, Blossom was setting out a tray. The carriage driver handed her the cups. There was much giggling and overacting. The driver was white-blond with blue-eyes, and his face was splattered with mud from the road. Blossom was all smiles and fluttering eyelashes as she took a dripping cloth and handed it to him. He leaned forward and let her wipe away the mud.

* * *

Alison was disappointed with their acting skills. It made her worry even more for their future. She looked around the lounge. Mel was pulling a tangle from one of the ringlets over her brow. She was cross-eyed with it. Her big silver rings flashed pale blue in the TV light. Down on the floor, Darren and Shazia were wrapped around each other like a slack knot. He was grinning, staring up at Alison and Mel. 'So?' he said. 'What do you think of the advert, then?' He laughed again.

Shazia scooped a handful of popcorn. 'Crafty old things,' she said.

Daichi chewed his bottom lip thoughtfully. 'Looks more like a . . .'

'Just what I was thinking,' added Mel, who was now trying to pull her feet into the lotus position. Alison hated moments like this. Moments when the whole world was tuning into one strong wavelength and all she could hear was static. 'What?' she sighed.

'A dirty movie!'

With her face ablaze, Alison turned back to the television, just in time to catch the first contact between Plum and the dark Adonis. He was holding his shirt open, revealing a shiny, fake-looking scar. Plum's spongy fingertips plunged into the cotton and followed the scar down to his nipple. 'Oh, no!' cried Alison as his shirt slithered to the floor and Plum's tongue retraced the tracks of her fingers across his body. The room erupted. Mel screamed and battered her fists against her out-turned knees. Daichi cheered and Shazia buried her head in Darren's chest in a far less erotic way than that which was being demonstrated on screen.

They were paralysed. They watched through laced fingers the loosening of Plum's bodice and her translucent, blue-veined breasts, cupped by the smooth, tanned hands of the Chippendale man. Alison closed her eyes whenever there was a close-up. In the past she had found the sight of Ken and Deirdre kissing in *Coronation Street* to be disturbing. This put them well into the shade. The long shots were bearable. Plum's body, bathed in the pale light from the window, was beautiful, and as soft as a peach beneath an unbuttoned lace camisole. Unlike the circle of friends in the living room, Plum and her young man were having great fun. She had joyfully removed his clothes and was pushing him down onto the silk-covered chaise longue. During the lengthy coupling that ensued, Plum's hand reached up, and at the moment of climax, grabbed at an ornate bell pull.

Ding-a-ling-a-ling! Downstairs, Blossom looked up from what she was doing. Holding a giant natural sponge aloft, she was letting a trail of soap suds trickle down the back of the blond man. He was sitting in a tin bath next to a fire that warmed his freckled skin. As she leaned over to rub his back, he pulled her to him and buried his face in her cleavage. In spite of themselves, they laughed at Blossom's soapy progress out of her clothes and into the tub. 'Ooh, young man!' screeched Mel as blondie emerged from the water, sporting a full erection. (Cut to Blossom mugging delighted surprise to camera.) 'Go Blossom! Go Blossom!' chanted Darren and Shazia, their fists in the air as the suds slopped rhythmically onto the floor tiles. Alison moved her hands to her ears. If anything, the sound was worse than the pictures. That familiar voice contorted. The mooing of Barney and her mother in the bedroom.

When it was over and the carriage was waved down the driveway by flushed and dishevelled Plum and Blossom, a hush came over the room. 'Well,' said Mel, rising from the sofa. 'Thank you for that, Darren. I love to watch old ladies having sex before my dinner.'

Alison said nothing. The sound of Plum and Blossom was still jangling in her ears. This was the final straw. Daichi sat on the arm of the sofa, looking at her. She could feel his look. She wished he'd go away. 'Are you all right?' he asked, reaching out to her.

'Fine.' She batted his arm away and went over to the window where she stood for a while, staring. She was thinking about Scatty Samuels. That pale, confused look on his face the first time he came to see Plum and Blossom. The new clothes he had worn on his last visit. She felt sick, and sweat was sticking her trousers to her legs. Again somebody asked if she was all right, but when she tried to speak, she found she couldn't. She was Scarlett O'Hara, with Mammy tightening those corset strings behind her, pulling at them until they cut into her fingers. She opened the window a crack and pressed her forehead against the glass.

Mel came up to her. 'Come and sit down. Daichi's getting you some water.' Alison let herself be led to the sofa. 'Put your head between your knees.' Mel's fingers curled around the back of Alison's neck, pushing it down.

'I'm fine,' she said, but her voice was lost in the folds of her new T-shirt. The plastic motif smelt like a beach ball.

'She's a bit sensitive,' explained Mel, her fingers still holding Alison's neck. 'About, you know.'

Alison pushed herself back up to a sitting position, slopping the glass of water that Daichi was holding, unhelpfully, over her head. 'I have had sex.' She said it loudly, hoping to shock them. 'And I've seen porn films.' (She hadn't, of course, but her Hollywood fantasies had been taking some alarming turns lately.)

'Of course you have,' said Daichi, and she could tell without looking that he felt stupid for saying it.

Alison got up and paced around the room. She wanted to put her arms around Plum and Blossom and hold them tightly to her. Everybody makes mistakes. She could find somewhere else for them if they couldn't face Maytime again. Somewhere safe and cosy, where they could all be together.

'They're all right, Ali!' Mel was a mind-reader. 'Nobody forced them.' The others nodded.

'How do you know? We didn't ask them, did we? We just let those two guys load all their stuff into a van. I mean, they could have been anybody.'

'They were their boyfriends,' said Shazia. 'They were snogging them.'

Alison's insides churned. She couldn't believe how calm Shazia and Darren were being about this. 'They might have had them on drugs, or something,' she said, thinking of Blossom munching her way through that old packet of jelly babies. There could have been all kinds of things sprinkled on the sweets and she wouldn't have given it a thought. Not until the room started to spin. She had an image of the two of them bound and gagged in their little Wendy house, with the waves crashing outside the window.

Mel was by her side. 'You're being ridiculous.'

Alison gripped her hands. 'We have to find them. They're in trouble. That's why they gave us the video.' Darren snorted. He turned away, but she could tell by the shuddering of his shoulders that he found the whole thing amusing. She turned back to Mel, the one person she could rely on, but she was laughing too.

'OK. Don't worry. We can go down next week if you like.'

Alison screamed. 'Next week!'

The smile fell away from Mel's face. 'You're going now, aren't you?' Alison nodded vigorously. 'Thanks a lot, mate.'

'It'll only take an hour each way. We can be there and back before Puxley goes on.'

'We? If you think I'm driving to Brighton . . . !'

Alison made a pathetic squeaking noise and continued to pace around the room, shooting pleading glances at Mel each time she passed, but Mel was looking the other way. 'I'll go with you,' said Daichi at last, stopping her in her tracks. 'We can get a train.'

'Oh, there's no need to get a train,' snapped Mel. 'Alison can drive you down. Go on, Alison. Why don't you? Get in your car and drive, if they mean so bloody much to you!'

'You have a car?' asked Daichi.

'Well, it's more of a giant ornament, really,' replied Mel.

'What kind of car?' Darren was interested now. 'I didn't know you could drive.'

Mel was on a roll. 'She can drive brilliantly. Go on. Tell him about Custard!' Alison congealed. 'You think I'm being mean, right? This has been going on for years, guys. She won't drive it. She won't sell it. She just sits in it for hours on end. It was *his* car, you see.'

'Whose?' asked Shazia.

Alison slumped into the sofa. 'How could you? Just because I'm worried about my friends. Just because I don't want to go to some club and watch you showing off and going, "oh, look at me everyone, I'm so gorgeous! I've got a famous boyfriend!" You're not the only bloody person in the world, you know! You wait till your dad dies.' Alison stopped, knowing she had gone too far, sickened by the thought of losing Mel. 'Sorry,' she whispered, but sorry wasn't enough. That surging sensation she had had with June Hartley rose inside her again. She grabbed Darren's empty beer bottle off the coffee table and held it up in front of her. 'I'm really sorry!' For a second, she sat still and gathered confidence, then, holding it by the neck, she hit herself over the head with it. It made a light thud. It angered her that she was afraid to hurt herself more, so she did it again, and then again until she could feel her brain trembling like a blancmange inside her skull. Mel made a grab for the bottle and pulled it out of her hand. Alison's frustration drained away. A trickle of beer ran down her arm and she felt stupid. Really stupid.

'My God!' Mel reached out to Alison. She stopped short as if afraid of an electric shock, her fingers trembling over the red patch on Alison's forehead. Alison couldn't remember the last time she had seen Mel this upset. Her lips were quivering. Her eyes looked enormous. She was a Disney character, and Alison had made her cry. 'Why?' she asked, finally touching the hot little bump. The room was silent. This was something they all wanted to hear.

'Don't know.' Alison looked down at the bottle on the floor. 'Can't believe I just did that!' Halfway through, she started laughing. She could see herself from their viewpoint, hunched forward with her eyes squeezed shut, shrinking back each time she took a swing at herself.

'You donkey!' Mel rubbed her head.

At that moment, Puxley breezed in, chucking the keys Mel had given him from hand to hand. 'What's up?' he grinned, keen to share the joke.

'Two of Alison's old ladies made a porn film,' said Daichi earnestly.

Puxley took a moment to absorb the information. 'Classic!'

Chapter Thirty

Mel watched Alison in the car. She was overly jolly, chatting with Puxley and Daichi, leaning forward with her head between the two front seats, trying to convince them that she wasn't bananas. It upset Mel to see her like that. Alison didn't make mistakes. Such things were not allowed. When Mel looked back over the years since the accident, all she could see was Alison doing the right thing. Just before they got to the garage, she leaned over and put her arm around Alison's shoulder. 'You're brilliant,' she said, then let go again.

Alison was desperately trying to think of a way out. Her trip to rescue Plum and Blossom was not just in the bag, it was being treated like some great crusade. Daichi had insisted on driving in spite of several attempts to put him off (he was insured, it turned out, for any vehicle), and Puxley had volunteered to take them to Croydon. She was trapped in her own worst nightmare, forced into Custard by well-meaning friends. All she wanted was to be left alone.

They stumbled into the garage. Mel hugged Puxley as she waited for the light to flicker on. 'We'll stay a bit,' she said.

'Yeah,' added Puxley. 'Might need a push by the look of it.' Alison went to the tarpaulin and pulled it aside. She was embarrassed by the shabbiness of the bodywork. It was a sad wreck of a car, all rust and dust, its jonquil paint faded down to the colour of clotted cream. The others stepped towards it slowly as if greeting an alien craft. 'Hi, Custard,' said Mel. 'Poor you.' She stroked a patch of rust on the boot.

'Triumph Herald!' said Daichi with reverence. 'I don't believe it. You have a Triumph Herald!' He ran his fingers over it like a blind man examining a great sculpture.

'Sorry. It's a bit dirty.' As if they care, she thought, holding the keys tightly, feeling the bite of their little teeth against her palm. It was little more than scrap metal to them. To her dad, it had been solid gold. She could see him clearly in his London Irish rugby shirt and the cheap, supermarket-brand trainers that used to make her cringe. 'Here,' she said, and opened her palm out, but it wasn't Colm, it was Daichi who took them. She felt as if they were attached to her heart by a tiny wire that pulled sharply as they left her grasp.

Puxley sat on Custard's bonnet. 'What a hunk a junk!' he said, leaning back against the windscreen.

'How are you feeling?' Mel pulled Alison's jacket together. 'OK? Look, Daichi has a mobile and so do I, so if anything happens, just call and I'll come. Even if we're in the middle of the set. I'm so proud of you, Ali.'

'Mel. I'm going to Brighton, not up the Himalayas.' She tried to sound airy, like it was something she did every day. She climbed into the passenger seat. Daichi sat beside her and slid his hands over the sporty steering wheel. Right away, she was nervous. What if he stopped halfway and forced her to take the controls? She'd always known that if she drove Custard, something awful would happen. 'That's the lights,' she said, leaning across him. 'Do that if you want to dip them. That's the choke . . . and this is for the windscreen wipers. Oh, and you see this little light here? Well, that's the oil light.'

'I know. My friend has this car.'

'Yes, but you have to keep an eye on them. Especially when they're this old. They eat oil.'

Puxley stepped up to the driver's window. 'She showing you

the ropes, then?' he asked, giving Daichi an admiring look. 'Nice one!'

'This is stupid,' said Alison. 'Why don't you go with them, Daichi? You've been looking forward to tonight for ages. I'll be fine, honestly.' Custard's garage was a perfect place to see in the New Year. She could find Plum and Blossom the next day.

'No.' Daichi struggled to reassure her, gripping her hand. 'I want to go with you. Much better than some club, you know, everybody trying to get excited for midnight. I hate that. This is great. This is an adventure. Exciting.' He was over-egging the pudding, now. 'This will be the best New Year.' He turned the key and to Alison's surprise, it started first time. It must like him, she thought. 'Wey-hey!' yelled Puxley. Mel knocked on the passenger window. 'Now are you sure you're going to be all right?' Alison nodded, winding it down. 'I feel like I've forced you into it. You know what I'm like, Ali. I get this idea into my head and it doesn't matter what anyone else thinks. Like when I made you get that perm.' She leaned in and hugged Alison's neck. Custard started to move backwards. Alison felt like she was leaving her stomach behind with Mel. She closed her eyes and gripped the door handle, fighting the vibration of the engine. Mel and Puxley ran after them as they left the yard, waving with both hands and shouting, 'Happy New Year.' Alison looked back, afraid that she'd never see them again.

'I feel like we just got married,' said Daichi. His hand brushed Alison's knee as he changed gear. She crossed her legs and turned away from him.

They moved into traffic. Someone in front of them threw a cigarette end out of the window, a tiny orange explosion bouncing against the black road. She held her breath as they drove over it, sure that it would make contact with some unnoticed leak from the petrol tank and send Custard up in the air with a blaze of light. The pavements of Croydon were patrolled by groups of young women walking four abreast, and men with no jackets in spite of the cold. One of them could lose their footing and fall into the road, too soon for them to stop. Alison braced her right leg against an imaginary brake pedal. There was a slight give in the floor of the car. The carpet hid a piecrust of rusted metal. If they crashed, her foot would probably end up poking out through the radiator. Custard clipped the kerb. 'Careful!' she screamed.

'Sorry. It's really heavy to drive,' scowled Daichi. 'Like a tank.'

'Dad used to say that.'

'What happened? You don't talk about him, do you?' Her silence answered him.

Once they were out of Croydon, the traffic died down on their side of the road. Opposite them, a necklace of white lights headed into town. Alison tried to imagine all the people inside, dolled up and excited, arguing about who was going to drive home. She wanted to share these thoughts with Daichi, but something stopped her. The fear of sounding like her mother. Angie was forever looking up at planes and wondering out loud where they were going and whether the people on board had packed the right things. Perhaps it was sitting in the front seat that made Alison think like that. She'd be calling him darling next.

They passed through Purley. Alison's grip relaxed on the door handle and she took her foot off the imaginary brake pedal. She listened to the engine. It was the noise little boys make in the playground when they pretend to be cars. An even *brrrr* that rose in pitch as the gears were changed. 'What do you think?' asked Daichi. She was angry at him for talking over it. 'You wanna go on the M23?'

'Don't mind.' She decided to test him. 'You choose.'

'I like the A roads.' He turned to her as he spoke, flicking his eyes back to the road every few seconds.

'A roads will be fine.' Custard liked the chopping and

changing of minor roads. It roared with delight around nippy corners, then purred as the fourth gear was engaged again and it could do a little sprint. She had anticipated every gear change since they left the garage, listening to the engine, waiting for it to make a request. 'Second please, for this hill. Now up to third. Thank you very much.' She could change gears for Daichi if he wanted. She had watched Colm's hands often enough through the gap between the front seats, pulling back, pushing forward. She saw them now. Big, hard-working hands. Large palms and short fingers. Bear's paws.

Angie had forced it into gear. 'Come on! Stupid thing!' She had cursed it, ground the gears down to mush. Alison was surprised it still worked after five years of her jackboot approach. Angie blamed it for what had happened. The only place she had wanted to drive it was to the scrapyard.

They hit big, empty roads. Custard's headlights shot colour into passing trees. Alison slid back in her seat and put her feet up on the dashboard. She felt surprisingly calm. The *Chitty Chitty Bang Bang* song was stuck in her brain. Looking through the top of the window, she saw a million stars. The lights of London scared the little stars away, so they fled to the countryside where there was less likelihood of planes hitting them. Colm's voice, of course. Colm's daft stories. Why had she forgotten them for so long? She wound the window down a crack and let the cold air bathe her face.

'Comfy?' asked Daichi.

'Sorry.' She sat up and put her feet down.

'Do what you like, it's your car.'

'I know . . . but it's like there's someone watching me . . . Do you get that? It's like when I drink Lucozade.' Daichi shot her a crumpled glance. 'They gave it to me when I was sick, like it was some kind of medicine. I know. Stupid.' They used to mark the orange paper on the bottle with felt-tip lines to stop her sneaking it from the larder. When she pointed out to them that Daley Thompson drank it on the telly and he wasn't sick, they said,

'That's different. He's an athlete. He has to keep his strength up. You start hurdling and maybe we can talk.'

Daichi leaned across the gearstick. 'I was only allowed Coca-Cola at weekends,' he whispered. 'Too much sugar.' So he did understand. He got jittery about Coke on a Tuesday, the same way she did about Lucozade when healthy.

Her mind was flooding with memories of her childhood. Not the sad ones that surrounded the accident, not the happiest either, but everyday things she thought she had forgotten for ever. She rubbed her head, wondering whether it was the beer bottle, but it had started before that. Ever since Ben's death, she had been coming apart like a sweater in a comedy sketch, unravelling from the bottom up. The faster Daichi drove, the quicker it was running out, and there wasn't a thing she could do apart from sit there and wait for the last stitch to loosen. She pulled her coat tightly around her and buried her nose in Blossom's pink feather boa.

A twin set of petrol stations appeared on opposite sides of the road. The car was running hot, so they pulled in. As Alison filled the tank, Daichi poured the last of their oil supply into the engine. 'Hungry?' he asked.

'Uh-huh.'

The garage shop was closed. One small dark man sat hunched behind a bullet-proof perspex hatch. Alison knocked gently and he stirred, rubbing his palm down the length of his face. There then followed a strange pantomime as they tried to direct him to the items they needed. 'No. Not that one, the Castrol. To the right. The blue bottle.' It was like operating one of those 'grabber' games at a fairground. While he was heating their food up, Alison noticed that he had been filling in a giant puzzle book. It lay open beside the till, fat with use. The pen that lay across it was attached to the counter with string. He broke her heart, that little man, sitting there all alone with his crosswords, nobody to talk to. She looked over to the other side of the road, visualising an identical man. A woman, maybe. So near, yet so far away. They could wave to each other through binoculars, she thought, or write big marker-pen notes and plaster them against the window. She hoped they would lock up for five minutes and dash to meet each other on the small grass verge that divided the two sides of the dual carriageway, beer cans in hand. Happy New Year!

'Lucozade,' said Daichi, pressing a cold bottle into her hands. 'Live dangerously.' They ate in the car. He had opted for a burger and took enormous mouthfuls, topping them up with swigs of Coke. Alison picked at her apple pie, afraid that the filling would be too hot. In the bay next to them, a man was filling up a new Jaguar. He was an older man in a smart grey suit. His wife sat in the front seat, checking her make-up in the little flip-down mirror on the sun visor. On the way back from the kiosk, he stopped in front of Custard and smiled. 'Nice car!' he said to Daichi, giving him a little wave, then crossed to return to the Jag. Alison wound her window down. 'It's mine,' she said, feeling herself fill up with tears. He gave her the same little wave, then started the engine. She wiped her eyes, feeling ridiculous.

Daichi finished his burger and threw the box into the little dip in front of the gearstick. 'Don't.' Alison took it and walked to a dustbin. When she turned back, Daichi was standing by the passenger door, holding the ignition keys. The multicoloured plastic lights on the forecourt turned the filling station into a strange, Kodachrome island. Custard looked shiny and new; Daichi's clothes were fluorescent, his face was orange; the keys seemed to be made of neon. 'Here,' he said, holding them out to her. 'Your turn.' The road beyond them was silent. The man in the kiosk had dozed off again. 'Go on. Have a try.' She felt as if she was in a road movie and this was the pivotal scene. Any move she made would be followed by a thousand eyes. Hundreds of people sitting out there in the dark, waiting for her to take those keys and drive. 'Will she do it? Come on, Alison!' She imagined the neon key lighting up the dashboard as she put it in the ignition. The radio playing 'Brown Eyed Girl' as she drove off into the blackness, leaving Daichi just standing there. Colm, sitting on top of the Texaco sign, waving her off. 'That's my girl!' Would she stop at Brighton, or just go on driving? A drawing of Custard moving across a globe, leaving a series of little black dots behind it. Past the Hollywood sign. Up the Himalayas. The End.

'No,' she said. 'Please don't make me.' Daichi shrugged and went back to the driver's side.

Chapter Thirty-One

———————◆———————

They finally drew up outside a tall, modern block of flats that was shaded from the sea winds by a row of black-looking trees. The entrance hall was dark. Green marble tiles covered both the floor and the walls. The only lights were over some artificial plants that sat in what looked like a cattle trough along one side of the wall. The larger leaves were plastic and dusty. The ivy was starting to fray. Above them on the wall was a plaque like the ones you find in fish and chip shops, with the names of the residents picked out in removable letters. Plum Bailey. Something off the dessert menu.

When the lift came it was very small. Fat people would have to travel separately. They climbed in and found themselves elbow to elbow, reflected back at each other from three sides by brown mirrored glass. They made an odd couple. He with giant shoes, a bright yellow jacket and green floppy hat, and she in a sensible blue coat with a faded pink feather boa around her neck. She combed her fingers through her hair, which was all stringy from driving with the window down. 'What do I look like?' she mumbled. 'Turning up on New Year's Eve like some mad-woman?' They were probably up there with their boyfriends having wine and nibbles – Blossom presenting a hedgehog of cheese and pineapple chunks on cocktail sticks, Plum leaning up against a drinks cabinet swaying to an old John Coltrane LP. She could imagine their faces when they opened the door. Their false, TV quizmaster smiles. 'To what do we owe this, darling?'

'You're not mad,' said Daichi, squeezing her shoulder. 'You're wonderful.'

'Oh, go away!' She turned from him and covered her eyes, wondering why she had shouted at him. She felt him move out of the lift, but didn't say anything. She was shaking, planning to sink to her knees as soon as the doors shut. They didn't. She peered out. He was sitting glumly on the rim of the plant trough. 'Sorry,' she said. 'I didn't mean you.'

'It's OK.' Still the doors didn't close. They exchanged embarrassed smiles. She pressed the button again, keeping her finger on it this time.

'Please. Come with me. I was just being stupid.' He jumped up and walked towards her. He was only a metre or so away when the lift doors started to close. Alison pushed them open, then the two of them stood side by side for another eternity waiting for them to close again.

When they reached the sixth floor, they were faced with two identical doors. Alison walked up to 6B, but stopped short of knocking. She stood for a moment and composed herself. They could be in there with the cameras and the blazing white lights. Their co-stars might be with them, rehearsing – performing, even. The more she tried to block it out of her mind, the more it was there: Plum, Blossom and the toyboys, rolling around on tiger-skin rugs while Bill and Terry looked on. Her palms were damp. Seeing them on film was bad enough, but in the flesh; the all too pliant flesh.

'You want me to knock?' Daichi's voice made her jump.

'Shh. I'm doing it. All right?' She knocked, then knocked again. There was no answer. She pressed her ear to the door. A radio was playing very faintly. 'Come on!' she said. 'Can you hear the radio?' She pulled Daichi to the door. Rather roughly. 'Listen.'

'Maybe they just left it on.'

'Or maybe they're in there, but they can't get to the door.' She stood on tiptoe and tried to look in through the peephole. All she got was a tiny, wrong-end-of-the-telescope view of their flat, three hundred feet long and two feet wide with dark, boomerang-shaped cabinets clinging to the walls. No movement. Alison slumped against the door. 'I don't believe it. There not even bloody well here! Stupid! Stupid!' She hammered until Daichi stepped in and held her by the wrists.

'It's OK,' he said. 'Calm down.' Her breathing slowed.

'What am I like? It's New Year! Of course they're out. At a club, probably.'

From the other side of the lift, they heard rattling and the snap of bolts being unfastened. Through the door marked 6A a face appeared. An elderly lady, even shorter than Alison, with huge, pink-rimmed glasses that made her look like an owl. 'Who?' she said. Two brass security chains looped under her chin like a necklace.

'Sorry,' said Alison. 'We're looking for Plum and Blossom. They live in there.' She pointed to the door behind them. 'Do you know where they are?'

The old lady retreated into the shadows. There was a murmured conversation, then another face appeared in the door crack. A very old man in a blue blazer with the name of a golf club embroidered on the pocket. 'Yes?' He poked his nose out and looked towards Daichi. Alison knew that look. Mel used to get it from shop assistants all the time. She repeated what she had asked the old lady. 'No,' snapped the man. 'How should I know where they are?' The door slammed in Alison's face, leaving her with the rapid heartbeat she always got when there was conflict.

'Charming,' said Daichi.

She slumped against the wall beside him. 'I hate myself,' she said. 'All the way from Croydon and I didn't even phone first.' She had an impulse to bang her head again, but managed to work through it. They got into the lift.

'I have my phone.' He pulled it out of his trouser pocket. A tiny, silver thing. 'You could call them.' He realised his mistake and went to tuck the phone away again. 'They're not in.'

Alison caught his hand. 'Blossom's got a mobile!' she said gleefully. 'Darren's got the number and he's at work tonight. Oh, I could kiss you.' Daichi smiled, but she was out of the lift again before he could take her up on it.

Plum and Blossom were in an oyster bar in The Lanes. As they approached from the seafront, music came at Alison and Daichi like needles through the cold air. Every pub was filled to bursting, and people were sitting outside restaurants under tall, mushroom-shaped heaters. 'This is great,' said Daichi, as two drag queens clip-clopped past in sequinned dresses. The windows of the oyster bar were streaked with condensation and there was a crowd by the door waiting to be seated.

'Coo-ee!' Blossom waved at them, a vision in purple sequins. 'Over here!' They were pressed into a corner. A cloud of smoke hung above their table, which was overflowing with plates and bottles. As they approached, Bill and Terry stood and pushed their chairs back. They were all smiling at her, their faces red and shiny. The restaurant was suddenly theirs. They had been blown by the breeze and had re-rooted themselves. Alison felt that she was the one that had moved away.

'There she is,' said Blossom, leaning over the table to lock her arms around Alison's neck. 'Are you all right, darling? . . . Only you sounded a bit frantic on the phone.'

'Did I? Oh. This is Daichi.'

'Lovely!' she said, holding his hand. 'Like lychee. I'll remember that. Sit yourself down. The boys will get you a drink.'

'I liked your movie,' Daichi gushed, overwhelmed by the closeness of a woman he had seen screwing in a bathtub just a few hours earlier.

'Oh, did you? That's wonderful. Oh, we like him, Alison. He'll do!'

Alison didn't know what to do with herself. She just stood there, the colour rising up her cheeks, furious with Daichi for bringing up the subject. They were all looking at her, expecting her to say something about the film, and her brain was draining away onto the tiled floor. Plum stepped in. She was wearing a grey, shoulder-padded evening dress. 'Oh. Your tiny hand is frozen,' she said, sending Blossom off into a song. 'Ignore her,' whispered Plum. 'She's pie-eyed. You know Bill and Terry, don't you?' They kissed her, shook hands with Daichi and moved up to let them sit. Alison looked at Plum, then at Blossom. It was so wonderful to see them well and happy, yet somewhere deep inside, she wished that they were in danger. Just a little bit.

Plum studied her closely. 'What brings you here, little one? You didn't come on your bicycle, did you?'

'No. I've got this old car, and . . .' Plum's eyes widened. 'I hadn't taken it out for a while and Daichi really likes cars, so we went for a drive. We were supposed to be going to this club tonight with Mel. Anyway, we were on the road and I said let's just keep going.'

'Quite an adventure,' said Plum, but Alison sensed that she saw right through her.

'We went to your flat,' said Daichi.

'Did you?' Blossom's necklace clanged against a coffee cup as she leaned over to him. 'Oh, what a shame.'

'It looked nice.'

'It's all boxes still, but the boys are giving us a hand.' She slid hers onto Terry's knee, and he put his over it. 'Done in no time,' he said, winking. He had an East End accent. Alison imagined him selling china sets in a market.

Blossom gazed around the restaurant. 'Better than dirty old London, isn't it? I mean, look at this place. Fabulous shops. So many wonderful people, all doing their own thing. Nobody poking their noses in.'

*　　*　　*

Plum sat back in her chair. Brighton had been her idea. She had spent long summers there in tat revues, back when summers *were* long and Max Miller owned half the town. She was always being told off for tan lines. The costumes she wore were little more than chain-linked milk-bottle tops under tall feather headdresses. The young man she was seeing knew a little cove where they wouldn't be overlooked, so they went there in the afternoons with a few friends to bask naked on the rocks. Oh, the feel of the sun all over her body, the glow of it through her closed eyelids! The young man had a movie camera. (Her first starring role.) The picture was all over the place at first, whipping from rock pools to her feet, then up her leg, then stopping short. He got the hang of it, though. She emerged from the waves, a bronzed siren smiling into the lens, lips and nails like scattered geranium petals, her nipples ruby clusters among glistening diamonds. She had kept one small roll of the eight-millimetre when they parted. Could just about make herself out if she held it up to the light and squinted. The old film stock had a glow to it that made her body look drenched in syrup, but it was the sharp cold of the water she remembered, the sweet pain she had felt when her head went under. The most alive feeling in the world. She had longed for that tingle while she was at Maytime, but the taps never ran cold enough and open windows were scorned.

Now the cold sea and the salty air were hers again. She had been swimming every morning since they moved, though the temperature outside was just above freezing. Blossom thought she was mad to be setting off first thing with a towel draped over the shoulder of her padded overcoat, but Plum was not alone. She had spotted a group of diehards, trudging down the beach in dark, Eastern European-looking costumes, heads squeezed into tight-fitting caps. A troupe of semi-naked Max Walls with feet sharpened to arrowheads by bunions, striding purposefully into the grey water. Plum toyed with the idea of joining them. She'd need a new costume first. Hers was much too colourful, and the only cap she possessed was fuchsia and shimmered with rubber daisies. No, she thought. Sod them. Up her end of the beach there were young men in wetsuits pulling surfboards over the pebbles with their strong arms.

A waiter came towards them, skirting tables in a practised, swivel-hipped way. Plum threw a sideways glance at his tight little bottom as he unloaded their drinks. When he left, she leaned over to Alison and whispered, 'You just want to sink your teeth in, don't you?' Alison cast her eyes down. A St Moritz cigarette had been stubbed out in an oyster shell. 'You're shocked.' Alison knew she wasn't talking about the waiter's bottom.

'I thought it was going to be an advert,' she said, still gazing at the cigarette.

'Oh, dear. I'm sorry we lied, but you know what they're like at Maytime.' Alison nodded. 'We did want you to know, though. That's why we gave Darren the video.' She tweaked Alison's chin. 'Oh, come on. It wasn't that bad, was it?'

'No. Not if I didn't know you. It was just a shock, you know, like watching my granny or something.'

'Bet your granny never made them when she was your age.' Plum chuckled. 'Back then, we did them in the back of night-clubs during the day. Terrible smell of gravy. Or worse, up in someone's bedsit. It's a different world now, Alison. The men are handsome. The money's good. They have sets and costumes.'

'Left over from a television show,' said Blossom. 'That was lucky wasn't it? They're letting me wear black leather for the next one.' That grabbed the attention of all three men at their table, and a couple at the adjoining one.

Plum prickled and tried to distract them. 'We weren't sure who would want to watch two old birds like us,' she said, running her fingers through her hair. 'But apparently we're all the rage. They collect our old stag films. Classics, they call them.' Alison smiled. How ironic, she thought. All these years dreaming

about movie stars, and she'd had them all along. The Jane
Russell and Marilyn Monroe of porn.

'How did they find you?' asked Daichi, who looked about to
jump into Blossom's cleavage.

'Good detective work, I suppose,' said Plum. 'A lot of the
Soho gang are dead now, or unsightly. Some got married and
went all Michael Dennison and Dulcie Gray, you know, down
the golf club with their husbands, acting like butter wouldn't
melt.' As Plum and Blossom talked, Alison devoted her attention
to their all-of-a-sudden boyfriends. Bill, the financial adviser, was
as elegant as Plum. A steely-grey well-built man with a good
haircut, a smart suit and a face that looked like it had been
polished. He and Plum weren't all over each other, but they
looked every so often, and their eyes softened. Terry was a
hugger, a squeezer, a cupper of faces in his big hands. He just
about exploded whenever Blossom touched him or made a
suggestive comment. He was so much younger than her (but
then, she seemed a lot younger), and was a sound engineer with
many years of experience capturing the 'ooh, ahhs' of the porn
world. His suit was awful. A shiny, *Miami Vice* number that
seemed to be wearing him, but it didn't bother Blossom. She
dreamed of leather. He dreamed of women in leather.

Blossom was telling Daichi about her co-star in the film. 'He
and his partner Alexander have this humungous flat. You could
land a plane in it.' Alison was nodding along with her when
suddenly it hit her. Danger. Real danger at last.

'He's gay!' She blurted it out. Half the restaurant stopped
what they were doing.

'Yes, he's gay!' said Plum, mocking her outrage. 'Surely,
Alison . . .'

'No. I didn't mean it like that. It's just. Well . . .' She
dropped her voice to a whisper. 'Did he use a condom? I didn't
see one. Not that I looked that closely, but . . .' Plum and
Blossom were laughing at her. 'It's not funny!'

'We wore them,' they spluttered. 'Condoms for women. Did

you ever hear of such things?' Alison shook her head. 'Well, we certainly hadn't, and the director comes out with this . . . thing.'

'He gives it to me,' said Plum, nice and loud.

'Yes, he gives it to her.' They were falling over each other to tell the story. 'And she opens it up and . . .'

'And it was like a windsock! I thought, heavens! What have we let ourselves in for? We just stared at it for ages. Stared and stared.' People at the next table were doing the same. Two middle-aged couples. Their eyebrows couldn't have been any higher on their foreheads.

'Then the make-up girl told us that you put them up your, you know . . .'

'Oh, she did laugh. Made us feel like rank amateurs.'

'Instead of Rank starlets!' Everybody laughed at this, even Daichi. Alison had a good mind to ask him, then and there, what a Rank starlet was. Show him up in front of his new pin-ups.

'Come on,' said Bill, taking his credit card back from the waiter. 'We'd better get moving or we'll miss the festivities.' He took Plum by the hand and led the way to the door. Daichi and Terry were either side of Blossom, holding her up. 'Bye! Happy New Year,' she shouted at the other tables. Only the men responded. Alison was left to follow on with her hands in her pockets.

Chapter Thirty-Two

———————◆———————

Down on the seafront, the wind was so cold it made their heads clang. In spite of this, there were people everywhere. Bars had their doors open and couples had emerged with drinks in hands and camped down on the pebbles. There was an old-fashioned merry-go-round that turned and churned out waltzes and polkas. It gave off a glow that stretched right across the beach. Plum and Blossom stood for a while, entwined with their men, looking at the sea. Daichi reached out to Alison, but she kept her hands firmly in her pockets. He had to make do with linking his arm through hers like an ice skater. The lower half of the beach had been munched away by months of high tides and dropped off steeply. Beyond it, on the twinkling pier, the roller coaster looked as if it was made from matchsticks. 'Aren't we lucky, eh?' said Bill.

They found a space in the shelter of a giant wooden groyne. Terry produced a travel rug and they set out a champagne picnic. 'Strawberries.' Plum pulled two large punnets from a basket. 'Good old Marks and Spencer's!' She sat down on the rug next to Bill, wrapping her coat around her. They looked like a scene from an Italian movie. A few yards away, a young couple were huddled together. She was in a long ethnic skirt and he wore a pointy knitted hat with fringed tassels over his ears.

'Only four glasses, I'm afraid,' said Bill. 'But we can share, can't we, poppet?' Blossom put a strawberry in her glass of champagne and held it up to the lights from the pier. A fairy-lit roller-coaster car swooped into the bubbles. She took another from the punnet and threw it over to the hippie couple. The girl caught it. Her boyfriend was rolling a cigarette. 'Cheers,' he said as Blossom lobbed another strawberry their way. Terry handed one to Alison. She checked it for bugs, then bit in. It was still warm from sitting under the restaurant table. A little bite of summer.

'Dunk it,' said Plum. Alison watched her take a large strawberry by its collar and plunge it into her champagne glass. She pulled it out slowly and, tilting her head back, lowered it onto her tongue. With a slow, circling movement, she licked the fizzy drops off the tip, then sank her teeth in. 'Mmm . . .' She added a little more champagne, then swallowed it all down gracefully. 'Beats digestive biscuits any day.' She winked at Alison. 'Your go.' Alison shook her head, but Plum was insistent.

By the end of her second glass, Alison was getting a little more daring with the strawberry-licking. Her head was delight-fully fuzzy and she was warm all over. The feather boa fluttered under her chin. It had seen more life than she had in all her twenty-three years. It carried the scent of old perfume and cigarettes. The plumes had been stiffened by greasepaint and sweat, and both ends were dark from being trailed over the dusty floorboards of dance-halls. Alison detached one large flamingo-coloured feather, pressed it to her lips and blew. It rose gracefully on its warm, champagne-scented current, then did one final shimmy just for her.

'You should get Blossom to give you a lesson,' said Plum drily. 'She was the Paganini of those things.'

'What's that?' Blossom had her head in Terry's lap in a way that made Alison's heart leap for a moment. 'Oh, the feathers,' she said, rising blearily. 'That's the last of them, I'm afraid. Had them in all colours.'

'I love it.' Alison slid it around her wrist. 'Thank you.'

'What did you do with them?' asked Daichi.

She tittered. 'Oh. You know.' He acted like he didn't.

'Please don't encourage her,' whispered Alison, but it was too late. Blossom put down her champagne glass, which by now was garlanded with lipstick marks. She stood, bracing herself against the wooden wall, then beckoned to Alison. 'My lovely assistant,' she said as the boa was handed over. Plum and Terry clapped as Alison crept back to her side of the rug. Blossom kicked off her shoes, singing along with the merry-go-round, and started to bump and grind. She was unsteady on her feet, stumbling over clacking stones. Other people turned to her and pointed. Alison buried her head in her hands. It was like watching Granny Anne dancing on a table. What if Blossom went all the way and took her clothes off? Alison took a gamble that it was too cold for that, and looked over at her. In Blossom's hands, the feather boa had become a wild animal. It passed slickly between her breasts, then spiralled through the air. Loosened by alcohol, Blossom's sequinned body moved like liquid. She arched her back and caressed the air with the grace of a flamenco dancer. Alison smiled in spite of herself. For a finale, Blossom turned her back on them, skimmed the boa under her bottom, then flipped it up, quick as a whistle, and sent it flying through the air like a python shot out of a cannon. It landed over Alison's shoulder to rapturous applause. 'Come on!' Blossom beckoned to her. 'You have a go.' The others applauded and encouraged her, but she stayed seated.

'No thanks.' All she could think of was *The Generation Game*. Ordinary folk looking foolish, trying to ice cakes and dance like Cossacks. 'Think I'll leave it to the expert.'

'Shame.' Blossom turned her attention to the hippies. They passed her a ragged-looking cigarette. 'Lovely,' she sighed, taking a big drag on it and melting back into the wooden wall. She handed it to Daichi and to Alison's surprise, he dived right in. Its sweet smell wafted over the beach. Alison looked around for a police presence. She felt better when Bill turned it down. 'No thank you!' he said, indignantly.

'No?' Plum mocked him. 'Oh, well. As my dad used to say . . .' She took a toke, held it for a moment, then exhaled. 'We'll all be a long time dead.' She looked up at the stars and raised the joint as if making a toast.

Alison looked up too and wondered about Plum's dad, what kind of a man he was. If she kept looking up, maybe the joint would just pass her by. Avoidance. Her usual tactic. Better not to go up a tower if there was a chance that she might fall off.

'I don't suppose . . .' Plum draped her arm over Alison's shoulder. The joint glowed like a caveman's torch. Its scent was heady and exotic. 'Live a little.' That's what Ben had said. Alison took it, but lost confidence again before it got to her lips. Deep inside she wanted to try it, just like deep inside she wanted to jump off high towers. 'You don't have to,' said Bill. 'Just because two crazy old birds . . .'

'Sorry.' Alison tried to hand it back to Plum, but she was having a mock fight with Bill.

Blossom crawled over to her. 'It's going out. Take a puff or hand it over.'

Alison held it out to her. 'Sorry. I'm just not . . .' She glanced at Plum and Bill. 'Wish I was.'

Blossom reached out and stroked Alison's hair. 'You don't just become a crazy old bird, you know. You have to work at it.' Alison thought of Pat and of Granny Anne, who had worn the same hairstyle for over thirty years. With a beating heart, she took the joint again and put it to her lips.

The merry-go-round started up again, loaded with revellers. The next thing Alison knew, Blossom and Terry were waltzing clumsily on the uneven surface of the beach. 'Come on.' Bill stood and held his hand out to Alison. It was such a big hand. Slowly, she stood, a little weak at the knees, and let him put his arm around her waist. He smelt like clean sheets. Alison looked up at him but found it hard to focus. He told her how happy he was with Plum, and how his late wife never had the heating on because she kept antiques. Daichi and Plum loomed into view. He had taken his hat off and strands of his silky black hair were dancing over the lenses of his glasses. 'Hi!' said Alison, dipping back suddenly to talk to him. She thought she was Ginger Rogers. Blood went rushing to her head and she lost her balance. Bill nearly dropped her. Plum said, 'All change,' and suddenly, Alison was dancing with Daichi. He felt different, so slight. It made her giggle.

'You're out of it!' he said, delighted. She couldn't reply because her mouth was suddenly full of cotton wool. All around them, people were chanting. 'Ten. Nine. Eight.' She couldn't think why. 'Seven. Six. Five.' She joined in. She knew the next bit. 'Four. Three. Two. One.' The whole world exploded. All the stars chose that very moment to break apart and sprinkle themselves across the sky. People were kissing her. It was lovely, feeling their lips against her face, like being tucked in. Daichi led her up the stairs and helped her onto the back of a golden horse. The orchestra played 'Let Me Call You Sweetheart,' and off they went on a race, just like in Mary Poppins, holding onto big sticks of candy. Alison leaned back in the saddle. Up above her head there were light-bulbs and mirrors and there she was looking down, all red in the face. Up, down, up, down, gallopy, gallopy, gallop. There were people by the side of the racetrack. Thousands of them, cheering, all wishing that they were the ones on the horses. *Wave to Daddy.* She looked for him. Couldn't remember what he was wearing. The faces were going too fast. They were smearing like wet paint. She started to feel sick. Scared, too. Leaning forward, she wrapped her arms around the horse's neck. Stop, she whispered into his ear, but still the world went round and round. 'Stop!' she yelled. Someone had sent all this magic down to test her.

'Alison.' Daichi was there. 'We've stopped.'

She swam slowly to the surface and grabbed his hand. Her stomach was still horse-riding, but she knew where she was. The beach. Midnight. The firework display was still going on. Upturned faces all around them like mushrooms in a field.

'How was it?' asked Plum and Bill.

'Great!' said Daichi. 'Alison's dizzy.'

Plum's cool hand brushed her cheek and she closed her eyes for a while. 'Happy New Year, little one.' Plum bent over and kissed her.

'You shouldn't have let her at that joint,' whispered Bill.

'Oh, she'll be fine. You'll see.'

Terry and Blossom were kissing. It was a real kiss. Alison noticed the difference. Their lips brushed and brushed again before playfully exploring necks and earlobes. Watching them made her feel sad and empty. New Year had been blown out of all proportion by Hollywood. Perfect people going to perfect parties, finding perfect romance. The real world was full of amateurs wanting to do the same, but not knowing how.

'Alison?' Daichi leaned into her. His hand slid over her shoulder. 'Happy New Year,' he said. He kissed her on the cheek. She was numb with cold. All she felt was a faint prickle. She turned to him, ready to wish him a Happy New Year, but his lips got in the way. They were warm like tea from a Thermos on firework night. She turned away from him and looked at the pier. 'I've never been on a roller coaster,' she said. Daichi didn't respond. She could sense his disappointment. 'It's not you,' she added, holding onto the sleeve of his jacket. 'I'm sort of getting over someone.'

'Mel didn't say.'

'Mel doesn't know everything.'

She got up and went to where Blossom was sitting with the young couple. 'Aah,' Blossom cooed. 'This is Alison and that's her boyfriend, Daichi.'

'He's not my boyfriend,' said Alison, shaking hands.

'Well he jolly well should be!' boomed Blossom. 'He's a nosh.'

'You can have him if you want, Bloss.'

Blossom took a puff of a huge joint. 'He's a bit young for me, darling.'

'A bit young?' Alison laughed. 'That's rich!'

'Now, now!' Blossom didn't like that. 'What about you and Ben Castle, mmm?'

Alison's mouth hung open. She looked at Blossom, then at Plum. The beach was stretching out of shape. 'We're not as daft as we look, darling,' Plum said. 'We could see it. Sure as eggs.'

They knew all along. Everybody must have known. Her secret love was no secret, and Doris Day was wrong. She didn't want to tell the golden daffodils. She wanted to bury it under them. She felt herself falling away, crashing down and down, as if through tree branches or mouldy floorboards. Where would she stop? The earth's core? She hoped so. She hoped it would burn her up in a puff of smoke. 'Nothing happened,' she said, desperately.

'Oh.' Blossom sounded disappointed. 'That would be a first. You know what he was like.' She and Plum exchanged knowing smiles.

'Who's this?' asked Terry.

'Oh, you know. Ben. That old flame of mine at Maytime.' Terry nodded.

'You and Ben?' Alison shook all over. 'At Maytime?' She could see him in the tin bath from the film.

'God, no!' Blossom looked revolted by the thought. 'Donkeys' years ago. Nineteen fifty-five.'

Alison let out a hoot. 'Brilliant,' she said, shaking her head. 'Nineteen fifty-five.' The year her father was born. How humiliating.

*　　*　　*

247

Blossom smiled at her. That's the way kids saw the fifties these days, she thought. All milk shakes and Elvis Presley. In reality it was beige-coloured coffee, a shortage of dress fabric and Alma Cogan, who couldn't tell a waltz from a tango. It was the March, and Blossom was in Cardiff with a continental revue. Back then she was called Fifi. She and her friend Renée did a double as Parisian models. It wasn't much of a bill. A Mexican table-tennis champion, two comics called Gin and It, a knife-thrower and Ben Castle's band. He was the first person she saw after she had hauled her trunk up from the station on the Monday morning for band call. He was knee-deep in sheet music as he was earning extra by playing the intermission. He looked up at her and she was sunk, then and there. She went over on her heel twice between the wings and the piano. He budged up on the stool and let her sit next to him. 'Dream Of Olwen', neatly copied onto a concertina of brownish manuscript, stretched out before them. 'I wanted to do Gershwin,' he said, sadly. 'But they shouted me down. Still . . .' He paused, then turned and flashed her that smile. 'What have you got for me?'

'What do you have in mind?' she asked, twirling a curl around her finger, giving him what magazines described as 'the come-on'.

'Your band parts, of course.' She blushed. That was her big mistake, giving herself away so soon. She was only twenty-five. Still wet behind the ears. If she had waited, kept him dangling, maybe things would have been different. As it was, they barely made it through rehearsal. Did it on a busted piano in the props room. (She had a ridge across her calves all night.) Renée had organised their digs. An attic room with a funny little balcony outside where someone had once kept pigeons. Blossom slipped her a few bob each night to bunk up with the knife-thrower's assistant and to cause a diversion so she could spirit him upstairs. He gave her a little gold Eiffel Tower for her charm bracelet. 'Nearest I'll ever get,' she said, but he put his arms around her and told her to look out of the window at the grey rooftops and pretend they were in Montmartre. When they said goodbye at the end of the run, he told her he would think of her every day. He gave her a signed photograph in a leather frame: *We'll always have Paris.* She kept it on her dressing table, smearing the glass with lipstick at night.

The charm wore off. Literally. Within a month the gold had chipped away in patches. A shabby little thing. 'You too,' said a girl who did an act with a snake. She was looking at his photograph all misty-eyed. 'Paris,' she said, picking it up. 'You lucky sod, we had Dewsbury!' Blossom threw it in the bin. He should have written *That's your lot.*

She didn't see him again until Maytime, but it only took one glance at the back of his neck and she was there in that tiny attic with the blue colour-washed walls and the pigeons peering in at them like fat little businessmen. He didn't recognise her at first, then she caught him looking up at her hall of fame photograph. She passed him, and whistled a few bars of 'I Love Paris' for good measure. He smiled and shrugged his shoulders, and she knew that Paris was all they would ever have.

As Blossom told the story, Plum looked at Alison. She was sitting so still, watching the bubbles that clung to the underside of the strawberry in her glass, slowly disintegrating somewhere inside. Plum wished they had never mentioned Ben. She hadn't realised how deeply this little girl had felt about him, or them for that matter. The look on her face when she burst into the restaurant would stay with Plum for ever. She and Blossom had seen her nearly every day, year in, year out, yet they knew next to nothing about her. It was a bad habit formed by a lifetime of one-week friendships, of sharing dressing rooms and lipsticks, of promising to keep in touch but never doing so. She broke free from Bill's arms and shuffled across the blanket. Kneeling over, she held Alison as closely as she could without upsetting the champagne glass. 'He was a musician, darling,' she said. 'It's in the handbook. Find a girl for the week. Free digs, free laundry and a bit of the other.'

'He did his own shirts,' said Blossom proudly. 'He wasn't a bad old stick.'

Daichi, who had remained thoughtful and silent throughout, looked up. 'How old is this guy, anyway?' he asked.

'Oh, he's dead now,' answered Blossom. 'Bless him.' Daichi stared at Alison. She knew he had put two and two together. *This* was the person she was getting over? Some old guy from the nursing home? She could see herself as if in a dream. A young girl trying to climb into bed with a dead body. They must have laughed their heads off at Maytime. Not just Plum and Blossom, but all of them. Darren, Shazia, even Beryl the budgie woman for all she knew.

Blossom came up behind her. 'Oh, dear. Me and my big mouth. I should never have told you. Can you forgive me? Can you, darling?' Her breath was a sickly mixture of champagne and marijuana. 'We wouldn't hurt you for the world.' Why were they being so nice to her? Alison wanted them to slap her and tell her that she was sick in the head. Anything but sympathy. It's the last thing a person needs when they have just humiliated themselves. 'Leave me alone, all of you!' she yelled, and rose to her feet. One more second and she was going to hit Blossom, lay her out over the pebbles. She stomped up to Daichi, fire raging inside her. 'Give me the keys!' She beckoned them from him, snapping her fingertips to her palm.

'I'll come with you.'

'No you won't.' She turned her face away from him. 'Just give them to me.' She had a good mind to tell him about Kenneth, too.

Custard's keys jangled from the pocket of his jacket. She leaned over and swiped them from him. 'Thank you!' She was going to get into that car and drive it straight off the nearest cliff.

She stormed up the beach, imagining them all standing around her dead body. She stopped at the top of the steps, tempted for a moment to wave goodbye.

She didn't. 'Sod them!' she said. 'Sod the lot of them!'

Chapter Thirty-Three

She ran to the road, dodging a tribe of drunken rollerbladers who were spread out like a moving fence across the walkway. Custard was lost in a line of cars, nose-to-tail, hugging the pavement. Alison passed Range Rovers and Toyotas, searching for her little patch of yellow. Finally she spotted one pointy fin squatting down against the kerb. The key was in her hand, right side up, ready for insertion. Her throat was throbbing, each breath like a mouthful of acid, and she couldn't get her fingers to work. The door opened at last and she hurled herself in. Clunk. She locked it.

Was this Custard? She looked around, checking that she hadn't climbed into somebody else's yellow Herald. The smell had gone. Their smell had been replaced by the burger Daichi had eaten at the filling station. She pressed her nose into the dashboard, then the passenger-seat cover, searching it out. She spotted Daichi as she shooshed the seat forward. He was some way back, leaning over and gripping his side. A stitch in time, she thought. Matter-of-factly she adjusted the rear-view mirror, pulled out the choke and turned the key in the ignition. Custard started. For a minute, she pumped the gas pedal and watched the needle shoot around the rev counter. Raring to go.

But she couldn't go because there were other cars pressing in on her. She would have to un-park it. Her bravery slipped away as she inched the car forward, trying to remember which way to turn the wheel. She needed Mr Bloom, her driving instructor, who called her Sterling whenever she went over thirty. There was a knock on the passenger window. Daichi's face loomed flat and concerned against the glass. She would rather have driven over the top of every car on the seafront than ask him what to do, so she put Custard in reverse and tugged the wheel around as far as it would go. Easing gently off the clutch, she let it glide back. 'Check your mirror, Alison,' said Mr Bloom in her head. She did so, then slammed on the brakes. The car bonnet behind her had vanished completely, she was that close to it. She tried to move forward, but Custard wouldn't budge. She pumped the accelerator, but there was nothing. Not a sound. Panic rose inside her. She imagined that the car had somehow become attached to the one behind. Even if she did manage to move off, she would have to drag a huge green Lotus all the way to the cliff-top.

Then it struck her. She had stalled. Quickly, she turned the key, praying Daichi wouldn't have noticed her mistake. Custard came to life again. She snapped the indicator on and glided out onto the road, grinning. That showed him. She was absolutely fine. It was just like riding a bike.

The tarmac rolled under her, parked cars flashed by on her left and in the distance, oncoming headlights grew larger. She felt alive. Every sense on overdrive. The engine was deafening and the windows were rattling, but she was not going to take her eyes off the road ahead for anyone. She put her foot down and the noise of the engine got louder. It hadn't made this noise when Daichi was driving. He had broken it. She glanced at the dashboard. The rev counter was off the dial. Mr Bloom helped out again: 'And into second, Alison.' She tugged at the gearstick, but it was solid, stuck in first, nothing would budge it. 'Stupid bloody car!' She had heard stories of gearboxes that just fell out onto the road. 'Clutch!' she said, and pressed down with her left foot.

Brake! Wrong pedal. Custard jolted along the road, not sure

which foot to obey. She felt as if she was on a mechanical bucking bronco machine. Her fingers whitened around the wheel as the windows rattled. She would stay on if it killed her. There was a flash of bright white light. The driver of the car behind her hammered on his horn. She closed her eyes and put her head on the steering wheel, bracing herself, waiting for its headlights to come through Custard's back seat. In doing so, she finally hit the clutch and the car stalled. The other car screamed past her right ear.

Although Custard had stopped, the window was still rattling. Alison looked over. It was Daichi, all red in the face. He must have been running alongside her all the time. She saw the winged statue by the bandstand and realised that she had only gone a few hundred yards. Her anger surged back. 'Piss off!' she hissed, but she knew she'd never get rid of him. Grumpily, she leaned across and released the door lock. He folded himself into the passenger seat and sat panting with his forehead against the dashboard.

'I'm sorry!' he said. *He* was sorry? 'Are you OK?'

'Fine.' Now she'd have to kill him, too.

'Wanna start the car?' His hand went to the keys. 'Is it in neutral?' How should I know, she wanted to say. She checked the gearstick. 'OK. Start the engine,' he said. You do it! she thought, but by the time she had finished thinking it, the engine was rattling away. 'First gear. Great. Now indicate, check your mirror. Well done, Alison. I knew you could do it.' She swallowed hard. Patronising git. He'd be smiling the other side of his face soon. Custard moved off, passed through second, then up to third gear. 'Wonderful!' he said, but she didn't think so. Any chimp could drive.

Custard was doing fine. It purred when she touched it, stopped the moment her foot pressed the brake. Alison wasn't doing as well. Every time she saw a big blank wall on the left-hand side, she wanted to turn the wheel and drive into it at high speed, but she kept losing her nerve. Custard seemed to be in control, carrying her along, a helpless passenger. 'Take a left,' said Daichi. 'Let's get off the main road.' The wheel turned and her hands slid back to the correct position. Ten to two. She scanned the dark coastline, realising that there were no cliffs. They came upon a small boating lake which had frozen over. A huddle of boys were daring each other onto the ice. One stood a couple of feet in from the edge, hunched over, his arms wheeling comically like a duckling. Alison looked at the lake, wondering how deep the water was. How long before she and Daichi would be shapes moving under the ice, but once again, Custard wouldn't co-operate. The lake gave way to a bleak industrial estate. 'Back down to third for this corner, Alison,' said Daichi. She thought about opening his door and pushing him out, but he had his seat belt on. They snaked past square grey buildings and empty car parks. Custard's headlights cast tall cone shapes over the road, finding the mesh of a chicken-wire fence and beyond that, mounds of grey concrete tubes that looked like huge judges' wigs.

'Wanna stop?' he asked. Ahead was a dead end. A heavy chain-link fence. Too big to crash through like the Dukes of Hazzard. She had a vision of Custard being twanged backwards along the road, so she slowed down. To their left, she noticed two circles of light. Something parked at the top of the beach. Custard bounced up a small kerb. 'Where are you going?' asked Daichi as she pulled up onto a bank of shingle.

'You wanted to stop, didn't you?' She pulled the handbrake up smartly.

'Yeah, I need to.' He opened the door, letting in a wall of cold air. 'Won't be long.' He turned, and just before he shut the door again, he said in a trembling voice: 'Well done. You're a good driver.'

He walked away, hunched against the cold, passing the other vehicle, which turned out to be an ice-cream van. Alison stretched out her hand, touching the patch of window she could see him through, wishing she could explain. She looked around.

This beach was bleak and uncared-for. It smelt of tar and rotting fish. Clumps of litter, caught in the glow of the street lights, marked the top of a steep rocky slope. So steep that she could barely make out the waves below as they slithered uphill, then glumly retreated. It was like the edge of the world. On the horizon a few fireworks still spluttered. Cheap ones, like green tennis balls tossed in the air.

Alison sat straight and gripped the steering wheel. It was time to take control. All the order had gone from her life lately, all the comfortable things she had clung to: her mother, her virginity, her daydream romance, even her unblemished record at work. There was nothing left now, except for an Alison she hardly recognised. A mad, angry person who bit men on the neck and slapped old ladies (and other things she couldn't bear to think about). What was worse, she knew that Angie and Mel would welcome this strange little character. Alison shuddered. She could see their triumphant faces, saying, 'I told you there was nothing to be scared of'. She'd rather see them staring into her open grave. They didn't understand. It wasn't Custard that had scared her. It wasn't driving. It was moving forward.

She turned on the ignition, slid the car into first and released the handbrake. She was getting good at this. Her foot stabbed at the accelerator pedal, pressing it down as far as it could go. The engine soared and over she went. For a second, she was falling through air. The slope was much steeper than she had thought. A small cliff. Her stomach sailed up through her ribcage, then bang! The car hit the pebbles below with such force, her mouth clanged shut and her head crashed into the steering wheel. Over the dark beach, she saw the waves like beaten egg whites. She kept her foot on the gas, closing her eyes, waiting for the water to seep in through the underside of the door and swirl around her feet. Slowly, slowly it would come, creeping up her body, combing her hair out, filling her mouth until the last mushroom-shaped bubbles floated to the surface.

Through the engine's roar, she heard a sound that visited her only in nightmares. The pounding of palms on Custard's bonnet. Her heart gave a crack like a squash ball. Was her life flashing before her? She opened her eyes to a slit, afraid to look. Daichi was staring in at her with wild eyes. She put her foot on the brake pedal, but the car had stopped moving. 'What are you doing?' he bellowed, tugging at the door handle. 'The wheels are stuck.' Ignoring him, she put Custard into reverse. The engine screamed and the undercarriage was pummelled by displaced stones. Bang, bang, bang they went. 'You'll wreck the engine!' he yelled. Custard gave up with a resigned shudder. She heard the waves again.

'Damn!' said Alison. 'Damn! Fuck! Shit!' She hit the steering wheel with all her might, then the dashboard, then the ceiling which was soft and tent-like. 'Can't fucking do anything!' She slammed against the side window, hitting her funny bone. Daichi had backed away. He was making lame movements with his arms, pleading for her to stop. Laughing and crying at the same time, Alison yanked the door open. The sea wind blew it shut again with a force that made her ears pop. Suddenly panicked, she shoved against it and sprang out onto the beach.

She bent over and picked up the biggest stone she could find, then threw it against the car. It left a dent in the driver's door. She picked up another, then another, showering Custard with them. They hit home with a series of clangs. Daichi grabbed her arm, but she pulled away from him. Taking another stone, she smashed the windscreen into a million pieces. 'Brilliant,' she shouted, moving round to the headlights. Her arm and her shoulder ached, but she didn't care. Suddenly everything made sense. 'Bastard!' she yelled, hitting the bonnet with her fists. 'Stupid fucking bastard with your stupid fucking car!'

She stopped. Her breathing was heavy and ragged. She stared at Custard, her eyes adjusting to the darkness. It was dented all over, the shattered windscreen-glass like uncut diamonds on the seat covers. 'Shit,' she said, choking back a laugh. She stepped forward and ran her fingers over one of the dents, feeling empty but happy. Leaning against the driver's door, she picked at a bubble of rust. It crackled, crumbled like pastry. Brown, flaky metal appeared underneath. She wished she could do the same to the whole car, peel off all its yellow paint like last week's nail polish.

'I was in love with this teacher all the way through high school,' said Daichi in a faltering voice.

What on earth was he talking about? Alison carried on with her paint-peeling, crouching down to attack a patch on the bottom of the door. Her finger was right through it when she realised. He was trying to tell her that he, too, had loved someone older. 'It's not the same,' she sighed. 'This has nothing to do with Ben.' She opened the door and brushed the shattered glass off the seat. It disappeared silently into the pebbles.

'What is it, then?' he asked, inching towards her. 'Is it me?'

'Course not.' She rubbed her grazed palms together, then turned to him. 'You know when you fall over in the street,' she said. 'I mean, really fall on your face and your friends are there and you're dead embarrassed? . . . And then someone comes up to you. Some poor sod, and they try and help you up and ask if you're all right and stuff.' Daichi nodded. 'You just want to kill them, don't you? You're, like, "I'm fine! OK? Just fuck off!" ' She laughed. It was the most she had sworn in her whole life. 'You must think I'm a right cow.'

He gingerly took one of her hands and blew on it, cooling the grazes. 'What shall we do now?' he asked. 'It's nearly two. Maybe there's a hotel open.' He was shivering. His fingertips trembled against hers.

'What about Custard?'

'It can sleep here.'

She stiffened. 'We can't just leave it.' Daichi let go of her hand.

First they had to try to lift it out of the crater it had formed.

It was agony. Their freezing fingers got trapped under the bonnet. They sank in the stones, but the car stayed where it was. 'Don't you know anything about engines?' asked Alison. 'I thought you were good with things like that.'

'Not cars. I could fix the speakers for you.'

'Thanks a lot.' Daichi pushed it from the back while Alison pressed against the open driver's door, holding the steering wheel with her left hand. 'It's moving!' she said. The rusty door was creaking and opening a lot further than usual. Daichi was stretched out diagonally like a tent peg, his legs scrambling over the beach. When the car moved forward, he ended up on his knees. 'Keep going,' she shouted, turning the wheel. 'Go on! Push!' He shoved his shoulder against one of the tail fins. His glasses were askew. She tried the ignition, but nothing happened, so she returned to the door.

'Alison,' he puffed. 'Please.'

'We're nearly there.'

'No, we're not. We'll never get it up that hill. Not even with the engine running.'

'Yes we will.' She braced herself against the door frame again, but the car didn't shift an inch.

She pushed and pushed until her face was wet with the effort.

'Please!' he said again. The passion in his voice stopped her. 'It will roll back and crush me.'

Alison looked up at the wall of pebbles in front of her, then sat on the front seat, her head in her hands. 'Just go, will you,' she whispered. 'I'll do it.'

'Maybe the ice-cream man can help us.'

'What is it with you?' she snapped. 'I've been totally horrible and you just stand there like a lemon . . .' Daichi fell silent. All at once, the waves were deafening. 'They used to argue in here,' she said at last, stroking the seat cover. 'Mum told me. So I wouldn't hear them.'

'Is that why you threw the rocks?'

'Don't know.' She sat back in the driver's seat, staring up at the dim line of orange street lights from the industrial estate. Far above them, a plane hung like a jewelled crucifix in the sky. 'I don't know what I'm doing,' she said. 'I think I've come to the end of something.'

Chapter Thirty-Four

The ice-cream van was parked by a street lamp. It was a rounded cartoon vehicle in pink and powder blue. Above the driver's cab, there was a giant plastic Ninety-nine like an Olympic torch. The headlights were off and the driver's seat was empty, but they noticed a faint glow coming through the sticker-covered serving hatch. Daichi stepped up to the passenger door and knocked. A gruff male voice said, 'Fuck off! No fucking ice cream!' Daichi turned to Alison. She was sitting on a fence post, shivering. He knocked again. The door swung open, catching him in the face. A heavy-set man in his mid-forties glowered down. 'This had better be good,' he said through a cigarette. There was someone in there with him. Daichi could see the glowing tip of a second cigarette.

'Our car is stuck.'

'So?'

'And my friend is not very well.' The ice-cream man looked as if he was about to give a very bad acting performance. 'We wouldn't ask, but the tide's coming in.'

A woman's face appeared behind his shoulder. 'Gary!' she said. 'Go and help him.'

'Shut up,' said Gary.

'We can pay you.' Daichi searched for his wallet.

'Oh, go on, Gary. A bit of Christmas spirit,' said the woman.

'That was last week.' But he took his jacket sleeve and wiped a hole in the misted windscreen. After a moment he turned to Daichi and said: 'What the fuck is it doing down there?'

'The brake slipped,' said Alison from the fence post. 'It does that sometimes.'

'Go on.' The woman prodded Gary from behind. He sighed and pulled himself out of his seat.

'It's fucking freezing out here,' he said, slamming the door behind him.

'Sorry.' Daichi led him down the beach.

The door swung open again and the woman put her head out. 'Hello,' she shouted at Alison. 'Come in and warm up.'

'I'm fine.' Alison pulled her coat sleeves down over her fists.

'You don't look it.'

Alison got up. 'I should go and help.'

'Don't be so daft,' said the woman. 'They'll call if they need us.' Alison watched Daichi and Gary sliding down the steep bank of stones. She could hear Gary swearing. He scared her. Reluctantly, she climbed into the van.

'Don't you mind him,' said the woman. 'Mr Softee!' She pointed to an ice-cream logo on the windscreen and laughed. She was about forty with a perm that was growing out, small blue eyes and a funny little turned-up nose. Beneath her leather jacket, she was wearing a black party frock with little blobs of silver glitter over it. Alison introduced herself. The woman's name was Tina (she pronounced it Tee-ner). 'Happy New Year!' she said. 'Want a drink?' She pointed to a couple of beer cans bound together with clear plastic. There were four vacant holes where other cans had been.

'No thanks,' said Alison, her jaw still set against the cold.

Tina lit a cigarette. 'Beer,' she sniffed. 'On New Year's Eve. Bloody typical, that is.' Alison managed a flat smile and a nod. 'Thought we were going to a hotel. He says pack your overnight things. I said to my mum, this'll be a first.' Alison wasn't listening. Tina's strong West Country accent seemed somehow out of context with the red streaks in her hair. The black tights she wore had seen better days. They were snagged, giving the impression that someone had drawn a series of ballpoint-pen lines around her calves. The diamanté bows on the backs of her shoes had caused further damage. She said: 'I'm waiting for him in town because he can't come over to mine because, well, it's a long story but anyway, I'm waiting for him, all dressed up, and round the corner comes the bloody van. Said it needed a run. He's had it parked up all winter, and anyway it's part of the surprise.' Her voice had a sing-song quality that made Alison want to sleep. 'I said to him, you're cheap, you are, and I bet you'll be wanting a bit of how's your father later on, and he did and all, look.' She gestured into the back of the van. There was a continental quilt spread out on the narrow strip of floor and a couple of tea-lights in ashtrays on the sliding tops of the freezer cabinets. 'Honestly! Men!' She looked to Alison for agreement. 'How about a cup of tea?'

'Have you got tea, then?'

'Oh, yes. Everything but ice cream, but that's the last thing you need by the look of you. 'Scuse I.' Tina nudged past Alison and trampled the quilt. She plugged in a tiny travel kettle and pulled a mug out of a cupboard above her head. The driver's door swung open and Gary appeared, looking madder than ever. He had a big square head. 'Get my torch, will you. It's in the wafer box.'

'What's the magic word?' said Tina, but she didn't wait for it.

Daichi stood behind Gary. 'Are you all right?' he asked Alison.

'OK.' She couldn't look at either of them.

'Car's fucked,' said Gary as Tina handed the torch over, then he slammed the door again.

'Grumpy bugger,' Tina said under her breath as she watched their progress down the beach. Her contempt for Gary was paper-thin. She accepted his bad behaviour and his cheapness with resignation. She knew he had a wife somewhere. She pushed aside one of the ashtrays and sat on the freezer top, kicking the heels of her shoes against the side. 'What's his name?' she asked. 'Your fella?'

'Daichi.'

'Ooh,' she cooed. 'That's unusual. Nice-looking.' Alison pressed the backs of her fingers against her cheeks. 'Tell me to shut up if you want,' said Tina. 'But I saw you out the window.' She waited for Alison to say something. 'Have a row, did you?'

'No . . . Not really.'

'Trying it on, was he? I know what they're like when they've had a few beers.'

'I lost my temper,' said Alison, rather louder than she expected. 'It's all my fault. Completely all my fault. It had nothing to do with him. He was just there, that's all.' She stopped. She didn't want to cry.

'I know, love,' said Tina in a motherly tone. 'You think you want something and then when it comes to it, you don't and they won't understand that no means no, then you end up feeling all guilty. Story of my life, that.'

'No,' said Alison, but Tina was off on her own track. She came over with a mug of tea in her hand. 'Do you take sugar?' she asked.

'No thanks.'

'Oh . . . You'd better not stir it, then.' She sat behind the steering wheel. 'You got it right,' she said, pretending to steer. 'If you want a bloke to take notice, go for his car. Wish I'd thought of it.'

'It's my car.' Tina gave her a funny inquisitive look like one of the chimps in *Planet of the Apes*. 'My dad's car.'

'Oh.' Tina nodded sagely. 'Doesn't approve, does he? Of the boyfriend?' She looked out at Custard. 'Won't be best pleased when he sees that. I remember when I had my first little prang.'

'He's dead.'

'Oh, God!' Tina made a grab for Alison's shoulder, squeezed, then retreated. 'Oh, well then. That makes sense of it. I mean, it's mourning, Deborah.' She was calling her Deborah. Alison couldn't be bothered to correct her. 'You do odd things when you're mourning. I went to Dagenham after my dad died. Stayed overnight in a Travel Lodge. Don't know why. You're angry with him for leaving you, that's what it is. It's normal, that. Feeling angry when somebody dies. Taking it out on someone else . . . or something.' Alison suspected that Tina watched a fair amount of daytime television. 'When did it happen?'

'Ten years ago.'

'Oh.' Tina nodded, but it was obvious she was disappointed. She couldn't go on with her 'time heals all wounds' speech. She just took a drag on her cigarette, then said: 'You never really get over it, I suppose. Was it cancer?' Alison shook her head. Tina continued. 'My dad had cancer. Had to use one of those machines to talk at the end. It was awful. My little boy kept laughing at him. He didn't understand, bless him. Dad loved to see him laugh. Kept pretending to be a dalek.' Tina's lower lip began to wobble.

'You've got a little boy, then?' Alison grabbed at it like a life-raft.

'Yeah,' sniffed Tina. She pointed to the lapel of her jacket. Pinned to it was a plastic brooch. A chimney pot ridged with snow. Below it, a red bead dangled from a length of cotton. Tina pulled it. 'Bee-bo!' she said. A flat plastic Santa sprang from the top of the chimney, its hinged arms outstretched.

'Cute,' said Alison.

'He gave it me for Christmas. Chased after me tonight with it.' She tweaked the thread a couple more times. 'He loves his mum . . . You wait, my mum keeps saying. You wait till he's a teenager. He'll be a right tough little nut. She never liked his father . . . Oh, well. I'll cross that bridge when I come to it.'

Just then, Alison located where her anger had come from. Long ago and far away. An unpleasant thirteen-year-old girl with spiky hair. 'I hated him,' she said.

'Who? Your boyfriend?'

'He's not my boyfriend!' she shouted. 'Don't you listen?'

Tina was shocked. 'Well, I don't know. You don't say much.'

'My dad. I hated my dad.' The words rang around Alison's head.

'Oh, so did I. Nearly left home when I was fourteen. He wouldn't let me go to a Sweet concert. Don't suppose you remember them. "Wigwam Bam"? No? Had their posters all over my wall. He said they were a bunch of, you know, what with their long hair. I was going with my mate Mandy, had my ticket and everything, and he ripped it up into tiny little pieces. I called him an effing B. and my mum was crying. Oh, I could have killed him.'

'I did,' said Alison.

That shut her up.

Colm Mahoney was an embarrassment, a big fat blob, a dorsal-head (Alison's favourite expression at the time). As he came out of the house that morning, she sank down in the back of the car and shoved her feet between the two front seats, kicking her heels against the handbrake. Angie was late, so he was jangling his keys by the front door to chivvy her along. Alison closed her eyes. The rain was intense, great big drops that peppered the car roof like a shower of bullets.

'Jesus!' Angie slammed the passenger door shut. 'Bloody monsoon going on. Get your feet off there!' She grabbed the toe of Alison's shoe and shoved it back. 'And put your belt on.'

'Sor-ree!' Alison slid around and stretched her legs out across the back seat, looping the seat belt over her shoulder. The smell of sandwich spread wafted from her school bag. She hated sandwich spread. Like eating sick.

'Now what's he doing?' Angie moved her head from side to side like a parrot on a perch. Colm was circling the car, checking the lights and the wing mirrors. He had already done it once when he let Alison in. She longed for the day when he actually found something. A slashed tyre or a snapped-off aerial. It could be arranged.

Colm climbed in. 'Jeez! Some rain!' He put the key in the ignition, then groped behind him, searching for Alison's leg to squeeze. His thing, that was. She shrank back in the seat. He couldn't get out of it that easily. He had forgotten to pick up her *Smash Hits* magazine the night before. Everybody at school would have their copy, especially as there was a pull-out of Bros that week. Gorgeous Matt and Luke in their studded leather jackets, making fists at the camera.

They dropped Angie off at work. She kissed Colm on the cheek, then turned back to Alison. 'I'll have a word with you later, madam.' She held her *Woman's Own* over her head to protect her from the rain (he had remembered to buy that, all right).

They weren't far from school. Kids in grey uniforms were dodging puddles, laughing. Alison said, 'Just drop me at the top of the road, will you, Dad?'

'In this weather?'

'Yes.' But he ignored her. For months she had been begging to take the bus. Everybody else took the bus. There was a boy at the bus stop. They sailed past him most mornings, standing with his sports bag over his shoulders like a turtle shell. If that wasn't bad enough, she had to roll up in this bright yellow banger like one of the Beverly Hillbillies. *And* they were late most mornings, which put them in full view of the assembly hall.

Her face was exhausted from scowling. They passed the turning to school. They were quite a way past it when Alison realised. She looked forward, but couldn't see her father's face in the rear-view mirror, just his shoulder and the back of his ear over the seat. He was wearing his blue windcheater jacket over his suit. They sat for a while at traffic lights and Colm tapped the wheel and hummed one of his annoying 'pom, pom, pom' tunes. She knew that he was going to the newsagent's. He was a weak man. He couldn't bear to see her angry. She should have told him she was being ridiculous and that he should take her straight to school, but she wanted that magazine. It was hers by right.

He pulled over on the hill, opposite the newsagent's. The rain was coursing down the gutters. He looked behind him, opened the door and was out in the road before he could catch her eye through the window. Alison felt something in her stomach. A movement, like going over a humpback bridge. She saw Colm turn. He was gliding back up the hill very slowly. A train pulling out of a station. Then she realised. Custard was slipping down. She sat up, scrambling forward, trying to reach the handbrake, straining against her seat belt, pushing the car further forward. Custard got faster. Down like a roller coaster, then he was there. It must have been for only a second, but time had slowed down like a film, flickering until each frame was a single image. He appeared at the front of the car, standing still as she flailed about trying to release herself. He should have just let it hit the car in front, but that wouldn't do. Nothing that would hurt his precious Custard. He held his arms out in front of him, ready to catch it. He looked so solid, like he could stop a lorry if he put his mind to it. She felt his hands on the bonnet. His knees against the headlamp. He took the pressure. The car stopped and she slumped back in her seat again.

He spoke to her. She could see his lips moving, but couldn't work it out. Rain was dripping off his face. 'What?' she mouthed, annoyed that he was mumbling. Then he slipped over. It was funny. She laughed. His arms flew up into the air, his head jolted back and he disappeared from view. God, he was so embarrassing. Fuckin' Baloo the Bear! Thank God her mates were in school already. Then the car started to slip again. Leaning forward, she finally got to the handbrake and pulled on it. Instead of stopping in its tracks, the car floated up and then down.

All at once, there were people everywhere. They came running out of shops, skidding off the backs of buses. Alison's embarrassment grew. Now everybody knew how clumsy he was.

Hands overlapped on the bonnet, forcing her back up the hill. They shouted for her to let go. Suddenly she knew he was underneath her, squashed flat and this wasn't a cartoon.

Tina's hands were clamped to her face, pulling her mouth into an oblong. When Alison finished, she lunged across the front seat. 'Oh, no,' she said. 'Oh, you poor little mite.' She pawed at Alison, desperate to hug her, but she was batted away. It was hot in the van. Stiflingly so. An ice cream would have been very welcome. 'You don't like it when people are nice, do you?' said Tina, settling back in her seat. 'You're like I am, Deborah. A giver, not a taker.' Alison gazed out at the fences of the industrial estate. When Angie left for Ireland, she cried and said, 'You're the love of my life, Alison. Not Daddy, not Granny.' She went on and on until it sounded like bragging. Alison just stood there, gritting her teeth, unable to accept it.

'What do you do?' asked Tina. 'What job?'

'I work in a nursing home.'

'There you are, you see.' Tina nodded. 'Ah. Your dad would have been proud, wouldn't he? What about your mum?'

'She manages a bookshop.'

'No, I mean . . .' Tina studied Alison carefully. 'There's no one like your mum, I say. Specially when you're upset.'

Alison shifted uncomfortably. 'She's in Ireland.'

'That's nice. Brothers and sisters?' Alison shook her head. Tina pulled a large, mock-leather handbag from behind the seat and took out a mobile phone. 'Give your mum a ring. Go on. My treat. Say Happy New Year.'

'At this time?'

'That's all right. She's your mum. Go on.' Tina waved the phone under her nose. It was big and clumsy like a walkie-talkie. Alison protested, but Tina wouldn't give up.

*　　*　　*

Barney answered. 'Yeah?' he said, groggily.

'Oh, God. I woke you up.'

'Ali!' He sounded pleased. 'Hey, hey! Happy New Year. Still out partying, eh? Well, spare a thought for us old folks.'

Angie took the phone. 'Hello,' she said. 'Are you all right?'

'Fine. Sorry it's so late.'

'Not at all.' She paused. 'Are you sure you're all right, love? Where are you?' The reception was very bad.

'Brighton,' yelled Alison.

'Where are you staying? Do you want me to call you back?' Her voice faded. 'Barney, get a pen, will you?'

Down the beach, a section of Custard's battered body flashed through the beam of Gary's torch. 'Oh, God!' said Alison. 'Mum, I smashed the car up. I mean, I really smashed it up.'

'Jesus! What happened? You're not hurt, are you?'

'No, but Custard's all smashed up and the tide is coming in and the windscreen's broken into about a million pieces . . .'

'Don't you worry,' Tina spoke over her. 'Gary will have it running in no time, you'll see.'

'. . . I drove it and I thought you'd be really pleased, but then I got all angry . . .' Alison started to cry.

'Darling,' Angie said. 'It's only a thing. Do you want me to come over?'

'You don't understand,' wailed Alison. 'Plum and Blossom made a porn movie and . . .'

'Do you want me to come over? I can be there by tomorrow.'

'It's OK. I'm fine, honestly. I'll be with you in a couple of days . . . Anyway, I'd better go. I'm on a mobile.'

'Have you got someone looking after you?'

'Yes, they're being really nice.' She turned to Tina. 'It's late, Mum. I'll call you tomorrow. Promise.' She slid her thumb over to the 'end' button.

'Love you.' This time, Alison believed her. She wanted to say something back, but was crying too much.

Now there was no stopping Tina. 'Come on,' she said,

clamping Alison to her bosom. 'Let it all out.' She followed it up with a selection of similar phrases, then slid into hairdresser's banter. 'You going over to Ireland, then? Ah. That's nice. They Irish then, your parents? Mmm. That's where you get that temper, I suppose.' Alison felt a jacket button pressing into her forehead. 'Be nice to see your mum, won't it? . . . Is your dad over there? His grave?' Alison nodded. Custard's engine started up in the distance. 'That's nice,' said Tina, brushing away Alison's tears. 'Near his family. What he would have wanted, eh?'

Such a stupid phrase, thought Alison. Relatives always said it at Maytime. 'We're taking him home to Cleethorpes,' they'd say, cradling the urn, ignoring the fact that the dearly departed hadn't set foot in Cleethorpes for fifty years and would have thrown up at the thought of sitting on a mantelpiece, watching his boring sister and her husband poring over double-glazing catalogues.

Colm Mahoney was a contrary man. It was impossible to guess what he had wanted at any given time, except maybe to have lived longer.

Chapter Thirty-Five

Dawn took a long time coming, but it brought a warmer wind. Alison and Daichi were cocooned in the quilt from the ice-cream van with Custard's car rug around their legs. As Daichi slept on her shoulder, Alison searched the horizon for a thin line of yellow. There was an advert on the TV when she was a kid. A woman was parked on a cliff-top, crying, and for a moment, you thought she was going to end it all. She had a small immersion heater with her and a mug (which was handy!) so, instead of killing herself, she made a cup of coffee and watched the sun come up. Alison had liked the music at the time. Now it was the hopefulness of it she clung to; the idea of starting again. It wouldn't be much of a sunrise, that was for sure. The sky was overstuffed with soggy-looking clouds. Coffee was out of the question, too. Alison had no mug, no heater and, as from six-forty-five, no car.

Custard was underwater. Only a corner of its yellow roof was visible now as the waves withdrew from the beach. It looked like nothing more than a Formica-topped table beneath the swirling foam. Daichi and Gary had tried their best to get it up the beach. All four of them had pushed, but the incline was too great and the stones kept coming down on it. In the end, they had left it as far up as it could go, but it was way below the line of seaweed that marked the level of high tide. Gary had promised to call out a tow truck when he got home, but nothing arrived, so they were forced to sit and watch. To begin with, Alison had been filled with despair. She had paced over the beach, imagining herself with superhuman powers, carrying Custard to safety, but as the sea fizzed up over the tyres, she grew calm. She felt herself letting go. The waves poured through the broken windscreen, pulling Custard into the sea with a groaning that Alison tried not to interpret as human.

'Gee,' Daichi said, wiping his mouth with the back of his hand. 'What time is it?'

'Ten to eight.'

He rubbed his eyes and pulled away from her, letting a gulp of cold air into the quilt. 'Did you sleep?'

'No.' It would have been like sleeping through the death of a loved one. Daichi yawned and stretched. Alison was tempted to apologise to him again, but she was tired of saying sorry. She felt under the car rug. Her shoes and her trouser legs were damp. (A last-minute dash to rescue the cassette tape from the glove compartment.) His were wet, too. (A mistaken belief that she was going to run straight into the sea.)

'It was a cool car,' he said. 'Pity you never got to drive it.'

'I did!' Daichi shrugged out of the quilt and stood, stamping his feet to wake them up. She worried that her tone of voice had taken him back to the events of the night before. 'Do you think I'm crazy?' she asked.

'Of course not.' He headed for the water's edge. 'Shall we go and get some breakfast?'

'Yeah, if you like.'

'We could go to Plum's and Blossom's,' he said eagerly. 'Warm up.'

'They'll still be in bed.' Alison scrambled out of the car rug and joined him. She tried to catch his eye, but he was watching Custard's dim silhouette. A smile played around the edges of his mouth. 'Do you think Blossom is sexy?' she asked.

Daichi sighed. 'She's old enough to be my grandmother!'

'OK, OK. I'm not asking you to go to bed with her. I just, you know . . .' She made a funny face at him, trying to break his mood. 'Did you see that top she had on last night? Looked like she had her knees up there.' Daichi laughed and shoved her playfully. Alison shoved him back, delighted that she had said something funny. 'She's probably filling up the old tin bath as we speak.'

He screwed up his face. 'Yeuch! Man, I'd run a mile.' Alison linked her arm through his. How right he was. If Ben had reached out one day, tried to touch her breasts, what would she have done? With a final groan, Custard rolled down below the waves. When she had gone for the cassette tape, Alison had released the handbrake and put it in neutral. They began walking, kicking cans and plastic bottles out of their way. 'Daichi? You know I said earlier that you were standing there like a lemon?'

'Not really.'

'Oh. Well, I just didn't want you to think I was being racist or anything. You know, lemon, yellow.' He shook his head. 'It was just an expression my mum used to use. "Don't stand there like a lemon".'

'So what do you want to do, then?' he asked.

'I don't know. What do you want to do?'

'No, you choose.'

Alison had a vision of them standing there all day. 'Let's find a café, then . . .' She squinted out along the beach. Way beyond a battalion of groynes, she could see the tiny white oblongs of seafront hotels. The pier was lost in the morning mist. A faint pencil line, partially erased. ' . . . I don't know. Maybe we could go on the roller coaster.'

There was a *beep-beep* from the road. A green mini drew up where the ice-cream van had been and three people got out. One of them was Tina. She waved over at them. A big brown dog shot out of the car and set off across the beach. Close on its heels was a young boy, but not as young as Alison had imagined. He was seven or eight in a huge new Kappa jacket. His dark hair was

shaved at the back, making him look like a mini-medieval monk.
'Bonnie!' he shouted, holding up a punctured football.

The third person was a woman in her late sixties, wearing a
long mac and a see-through plastic rain hood. She ambled after
the boy, but stopped where the beach fell away and watched him,
flinching each time he ran towards the waves. Tina wobbled over
to them and pulled a packet of cigarettes from her jacket pocket.
She had no make-up on. The red streaks in her hair made her
face look pale and pinched. 'Thought I'd check up on you,' she
said. 'See if you were still here.'

'You can't have got much sleep.' Alison checked her watch.

'Oh, I'm used to it. He was up with the lark, playing his new
video game. Anyway, the dog needed a walk.' Tina's son threw a
stone into the water. The dog dived into the ripple it made, then
scampered around, trying to find it. Eventually, she admitted
defeat and stared sadly up at the boy. 'No tow truck, then?' Tina
gazed hopefully out to sea. 'Bastard. Bet he fell asleep as soon as
he got home.' She looked as if she was going to cry. 'Oh, your
poor little car. I knew I should have phoned them.'

'It's all right,' said Alison in a comforting voice. 'Honestly.
We tried a few numbers on Daichi's mobile, but all we got was
answerphones.'

'Hope you're insured,' said the older woman. She was
carrying a handbag in that needless way they all did at Maytime.

Tina said: 'This is my mum.' Alison introduced herself before
Tina could come out with the wrong name.

'Sorry to hear about your father,' she said, gripping Alison's
hand. 'Oh. It was dreadful.'

'Mum!'

'Oh,' she shrugged. 'Well, you shouldn't have told me if I'm
not supposed to know.'

'Told you what?' asked Daichi.

Alison squeezed his hand. 'I'll tell you later. Promise.'

Bonnie ran past with seaweed in her mouth. Tina called to
the boy. 'Marcus, come and say hello.' He approached cautiously,

pulling down on his jacket pockets. Tina tried to touch his hair, but he twisted away from her. 'Well?' she said. 'Take your hands out of your pockets, then.' He did so with a sigh. 'Just like his dad.' She gripped his shoulder. 'Right bag of nerves.' Marcus mumbled hello to Alison, but it was Daichi who interested him. He squinted up at him with embarrassed pleasure. Daichi responded by picking up a piece of driftwood and throwing it for Bonnie.

'Excellent,' said Marcus as it drew an enormous arc over the beach. He looked back at Daichi, wanting him to join in. 'Go on,' said Alison, letting go of his hand. He and Marcus set off in pursuit of Bonnie, scattering stones behind them.

'Bloody dog,' said Tina. 'Got a bean can stuck on her snout last week. The vet got it off in the end. That cost a pretty penny, didn't it, Mum?' Her mother tutted and looked glassily down at the waves. She reminded Alison of her own grandmother. That aura of self-pity. 'Still . . .' sighed Tina as the boys launched the stick again. 'Our Marcus likes your friend, doesn't he? That's nice. Not enough men around him.' Tina waved at her little boy. Her mother tutted again.

The sun broke through just before they left the beach. Shafts of light that dried the pebbles and made them look like muesli. Tina had promised them a fried breakfast and a lift into town. All that remained was how to fit them in the car. 'You go in the front, Mum,' said Tina, though her mother was already there, handbag on lap. 'And the rest of you will just have to budge up in the back.'

'Just a minute,' said Alison. She handed Bonnie's lead to Daichi and headed down the beach for the last time. She waved to him, liking the fact that he found her unpredictable. At the water's edge, she took the rescued cassette out of her pocket. The case was damaged. The hinged part fell away and landed at her feet. Carefully, she took the cassette and pulled loops of thin black tape from it. They caught the sea wind and flew into the air. *Moondance* stretched right across the beach. She knew why

Angie had left England. She had done it for both of them, so that Alison could end up exactly where she was now. Angie was no longer Colm's brown-eyed girl, the one who went slipping and sliding all along the waterfall with him and Van the Man. She had a new song now.

Alison hummed to herself as the tape spooled away. *Hey, where did we go? The days when the rains came?* Her idea had been to throw the whole lot into the sea, but she had a vision of gulls with their feet tied together in an eternal three-legged race, so she gathered it all up and put it in her pocket until she could find a bin. With a final goodbye, she tossed away the paper sleeve notes. Smiling to herself, she headed back up the beach, pulling the feather boa tight around her neck.

It was a squash. Alison shared the back seat with Daichi, Marcus and the dog, which insisted on standing on their laps. 'Aw, Bonnie,' giggled Marcus as her wet tail swiped him in the face. When the car moved off, she shifted, digging her paws into their leg tops and panting a misty patch onto the side window. Alison looked back at the sea. It was rolling in as if nothing had happened.

'I'm sorry about Custard,' said Daichi.

'It's OK,' said Alison. 'At least I know where I left it.'

Marcus reached into her pocket and pulled out part of the tape. 'What's that?' he asked.

'Just an old song.'

'You're crazy,' he said.